Man of Many Wars

"There are two wars for you, Judah," Ada said to me in Baltimore. "There is the one out there, and there is the one here in your heart." I shall never forget this.

And yet I cannot escape the knowledge that I am as split asunder within myself as the North is from the South. How can one man be drawn to women as completely different as Varinia Davis and Ada Isaacs? One is the bohemian who entertains yelping soldiers every night, and the other is the sedate first lady of the Confederacy.

As I compose these remembrances by dimming lamplight in my office, I hear footsteps down the hall . . .

for Pearl

JUDAH
Allan Appel

LEISURE BOOKS ● NEW YORK CITY

A LEISURE BOOK

Published by

Nordon Publications, Inc.
Two Park Avenue
New York, N.Y. 10016

Even if I had health, and desired ever so so much to help you in your work, I have no materials available for the purpose of your biography.

I have never kept a diary, or retained a copy of a letter written by me. No letters addressed to me by others will be found among my papers when I die.

With perhaps the exception of Mrs. Jefferson Davis, no one has many letters of mine.

For I have read so many American biographies which reflected only the passions and prejudices of their writers, that I do not want to leave behind me letters and documents to be used in such a work about myself.

Judah Phillip Benjamin, 1883

Foreword

In this novel I have depicted real as well as invented people. The historical characters, such as Jefferson Davis, Varinia Davis, and Judah P. Benjamin, are based largely upon the real people, whose names they bear. However, not all the actions I have attributed to these characters actually occurred, although they could have.

A. Appel
Los Angeles, August, 1976

JUDAH

EDITOR'S PREFACE

In 1976 the diaries, letters, and original papers of Judah Phillip Benjamin were discovered by me in a small bookshop on the avenue Huysman in Paris, not far from the house where Benjamin died on May 6, 1884.

I was in the bookshop simply as a tourist, not in my official capacity as an editor for a large American publishing concern. The day was hot, I had an hour to dispose of, so I went inside the bookshop, which, like all such Parisian establishments, featured a little clerk in a beret, fallen asleep on his stool by the door, and a rotating fan which modestly cooled the cluttered space.

The clerk did not awaken when I walked in, and, as I was not intent on buying anything, I did not see any point in disturbing the man's sleep. I quietly walked the two narrow aisles, perusing one volume, looking over the cover of another, but I found nothing that caught my fancy.

After a quarter of an hour of this I felt a weariness in my legs and a desire to sit. But the only seat in the place was occupied by the now slowly snoring clerk. I was about to walk reluctantly out to the cafe across the street when I saw in the back corner of the store a trunk which seemed as if it would not break if I sat on it. It was an old wooden box, wedged against a shelf, under a sign which read in French, "Mystery Books."

I eased onto the trunk and idly read a book I had picked up off a pile on the floor. As this book also did not appeal to me, I soon noticed lying next to me on the trunk a large leather-bound volume of the type used to keep store records in the 19th century. I picked up this ledger and blew off it the dust of at least a hundred years.

When I opened the ledger I began to read in an impeccably clear handwriting what has turned out to be the first of the diaries of Judah Phillip Benjamin, lawyer, United States Senator from Louisiana, and Secretary of State of the Confederate States of America.

What possessed Benjamin to write at the end of his life that he had no diaries, no letters, and no papers? Well, there is no definitive answer, except, of course, if we take his words at their face value—that he wanted to keep the dogs of biography at bay.

But there is so much more to it. There are so many more questions to be asked about this special man.

Benjamin was one of three men who continued in the cabinet of Jefferson Davis, President of the Confederacy, throughout the entire Civil War. He served first as Attorney General, then as Secretary of War, and finally as Secretary of State. He was Davis' most trusted advisor, yet he was also probably the most regularly and viciously criticized official in the government. Why?

And what, furthermore, is to be made of the Southern criticism, rife throughout the 1850's and 1860's, that Judah Benjamin was a Jew hell-bent on selling out the Christian South?

And what of the Northern abolitionist tirade that in his support of slavery Mr. Benjamin was "an Israelite with Egyptian principles"?

The Benjamin Diaries, published here for the first time, provide some of the answers.

Written in a painstakingly clear hand, with what appears to be the same type of steel-pointed pen, and on the same lined foolscap ledgers year in and year out, the diaries are an amazing account of the very private life of a very public man.

Generally, the diaries are in chronological sequence. There are frequent lacunae, sometimes of months, sometimes of entire years, when the pressure of life apparently left no time for private entries, or when the emotional necessity for keeping a record disappeared. On the other hand, there are other sections in the diaries where the reporting is daily and excruciatingly detailed, such as during the early years in New Orleans and in Benjamin's dealings with his own family. Throughout the diaries there are also copies of letters written, and articles clipped from newspapers, with comments scrawled in the margins.

The diaries begin in the winter of 1828 when Benjamin

was a student at Yale College, and end in entries written upon his death bed in Paris, in the spring of 1884, in the now demolished house across the street from the bookstore where the documents were found.

The only exception to the chronological sequence seems to be a sizable third diary, ripped out and placed in front of all the entries in the first and second. The diaries will therefore, be presented in the order III, I, II and then IV and V, as this gesture by Benjamin seems to call for. His second diary deals primarily with Varinia Davis, wife of the President of the Confederacy. Benjamin must have had some special reason indeed for extracting this material and placing it at the beginning of his personal record of his life.

Were the pages of this third diary ripped from their ledger at the end of Benjamin's life because he wanted to dispose of them? Or, perhaps, was it because he cherished them? And what, furthermore, are we to make of this in the light of Benjamin's own words, nearly his last, that Varinia Davis alone, among his life's contacts, had letters and materials in her possession?

Mrs. Davis, before she died in 1906, said there were never any letters, and she did not know to what Mr. Benjamin had been referring.

Here, then, are the Benjamin Diaries. The time is the summer of 1863, a critical moment for the Confederacy.

I

THIRD DIARY
JULY 6, 1863—APRIL 2, 1865

PART I

July 6, 1863

In spite of all my best intentions to avoid making advances, and in spite of Varinia Davis' best intentions to block and parry them, we are met, we are in love, and we are frequently in bed.

These are days of monumental urgency, of entire weekends spent in conferences with President Davis, with Generals Meyers and Beauregard and Longstreet. These generals like me no more than I do them, but sit we do and plan strategy and the President mediates among us. He gives his complete attention to details, to the exact corps strength, to the rations for officers, to minutiae which I try to free him from. But Davis is fundamentally a military man and is drawn to the details against his better presidential instincts. How many times have I finished my own work in the late hours of the evening, entered his study and found him at his desk, his forehead fallen on the maps open before him, and his heavy sleepy breathing the only sound in the room? How many times have I then gone to knock on Varinia's door, to inform her of the president's condition; and how many times has she told me that he has given orders not to be disturbed, that he wishes to remain in the study for the night, and that an orderly will awaken him each hour on the hour, after these naps, with coffee so that he can continue his work?

And lingering there at the door of Mrs. Davis, she looking at me, and I at her deep blue eyes, how many times have I said, "Varinia, may I?" until one night, until tonight, she said, "The door is unlocked for you, Mr. Secretary of State. You may come in."

July 7, 1863

I have gotten back to my quarters at dawn and have just caught an hour's sleep, when my orderly awakens me and

17

says President Davis requests the pleasure of my company in his office in the capitol. Immediately.

On my arms and hands and shoulders I can still smell Varinia's perfume.

"Go tell the President I will be over momentarily."

I splash water on my face, take my files with me and I go. It is a two-block walk to the capitol office building, and the flies and mosquitoes are rampaging, and the street stinks of urine and just-dead horses.

In the damaging light of the sun I can hardly see, so I close my eyes, shut out the chaos of Richmond, and remember the serenity of last night. Varinia's skin is so fair, so white, just touching it with the slightest pressure leaves marks that last for hours.

Has someone discovered us already? Has the orderly been changed? Did I leave my papers, my wallet on Varinia's table?

Davis is trusting. He is not a suspicious man. He respects me, as I do him. Yet he is so different from me (as are the rest of the plantation men in the cabinet). I love the Confederacy, I love it, I am murmuring to myself as I ascend the capitol stairs. I love it from the deepest part of my heart. And yet there is room left in me for a woman's love, and room to think about the future, no matter the outcome of the Cause. But for Davis there is no other room. For him the Cause is the object of his complete devotion.

Is it any wonder, therefore, that Varinia confided in me last night that the President has not been with her, as a man, in over four months.

Davis' corporal announces me as I walk in. He is standing behind his table, his hands placed on top of it, his head bowed, his great shock of craggy hair ferociously unkempt, his eyes penetrating and full of sadness. Yet his mouth is set, his jaw, as usual, firm, and his presence steady.

"Mr. Secretary," he says, "I have just received definitive dispatches from Lee. The Army of Northern Virginia is in retreat. Pickett's corps is decimated at a place called Gettysburg."

18

"How decimated?" I ask in disbelief, for this was the most splendid army we had ever assembled.

"At least 15,000 dead or wounded, and that is not the whole of it. Jeb Stuart is dead. Longstreet is wounded, and General Lee crosses the Potomac to tender me his resignation as commander of the armies."

"And do the Federals pursue?"

"The Federals, thank God, are too busy burying their own."

"And yet we cannot be sure, Mr. President. They may surprise Richmond."

"Although I doubt it, I have given orders for a siege alert. You will communicate with Slidell and the other agents in Europe, Mr. Secretary. Do the best you can with it, but I fear the effect of the news on our chances for recognition."

"I shall have them stress the severe losses on both sides, the lack of pursuit, and the daring of Lee in that he was but a stride from Philadelphia and the Union heartland."

"I am afraid, Mr. Benjamin," he said, sitting down in his chair, "that this time I can give you not the stuff of good news, but propaganda."

"We had our Chancellorsville, Mr. Davis, and they will not so quickly forget it in the English Parliament, in spite of this Gettysburg." Yet even as I said this, I knew there was something definitive about this recent battle. Early casualty statistics, I know from when I organized the Department of War, reflect exactly half as much damage as, in fact, has been sustained. The motion on the floor of the English Parliament for recognition of the CSA is in deep jeopardy. But I shall not tell this to Mr. Davis. Not now.

"We shall have another Chancellorsville, Mr. Benjamin. Mark my word. We need only reorganize and re-group. . ." and then the President raised his hands to his eyes and did what I had never seen him do: he wept.

I immediately dismissed the corporal, who had been in attendance, and stood by the President, my arm on his shoulder. He sighed deeply and then said, like a father, "I have lost this day so many fine young Virginia men."

Today Vicksburg is fallen.

Thirty thousand soldiers, one hundred and seventy cannon, sixty thousand muskets of an improved make and bore which cost us dearly in Europe. Grant reigns like a king, the Confederacy is cut in two, General Pemberton is stoned as he leaves the city.

It is a grim day for the South. I have seen neither Mr. Davis nor Varinia at the capitol.

•

July 17, 1863

I have not seen Varinia in over a week. She is in retreat with the President. And then, much to my surprise I receive an invitation to dinner for tonight.

"We must pick up our spirits, Judah," she writes on the bottom of the small card, "for we are not defeated as long as there are ardent men and women of the south. Come, it shall be a most patriotic evening, with readings of poetry by several of our writers, including Mr. Sidney Lanier and Mr. Francis Orray Ticknor." And on the other side of the card Varinia wrote the first stanza of Ticknor's poem, "Virginians of the Valley."

The Knightliest of the Knightly race,
   That since the days of old
Have kept the lamp of chivalry
   Alight in hearts of gold

I went to the party, in spite of an urge not to. For at such official occasions I am the Secretary of State, I am not Judah to her, and during these days I find this intolerable. And yet, how not to attend!

The menu consisted of oyster soup, roast mutton, ham, boned turkey, wild duck, partridge, plum pudding, sauterne, Burgundy, sherry, and a sixty-year-old Madeira. I enjoyed the Madeira most of all.

The party was held on the veranda of the capitol. There was poetry and music, and during the interludes of entertainment some of the ladies of the government sat and sewed flags. Varinia hostessed the affair and was so busy that she and I were able to obtain only half a breath alone together.

"There is life in the land yet, Mr. Benjamin," she said.

"Indeed there is," I acknowledged to Varinia and to the wife of the Secretary of War, who happened by just then. "To the ladies of the Confederacy," I toasted.

"And to the men," Varinia politely replied.

July 18, 1863

We have several reports of widespread rioting, lynching, and mob violence in New York City. Protest is being made against Yankee conscription. Regiments of Meade's army are being sent to maintain civil control. Lincoln is treating these events as full scale draft riots and insurrection. Landing of troops is expected within thirty-six hours at the Battery.

These reports from Belle Boyd. Who else! She is the best agent I have in the North.

When I convey this news to President Davis, we agree that those regiments would have been used to pursue Lee. The seige alarm here is, therefore, lifted as of six this evening. But the city is generally in a grim mood. I feel they have never recovered from the death of General Jackson, who was truly like a god. Yet in all, there will undoubtedly be a few *soirees* tonight. And tomorrow morning the first of the ambulance trains from Pennsylvania will be arriving from the field hospitals.

July 21, 1863

The President asked me to meet him today for a short

walk about the capitol. It was an unusual request, as we had always met in his office or, even more frequently, in mine. And it was especially unusual because the sun has been extremely bright these last several weeks, and the President cannot take the sunlight. He squints badly in his left eye, injured in the Mexican War.

On the steps of the capitol he introduced me to a Mr. Thomas De Leon, about whom I had heard much from Davis but whom I had not met. Not until now did I place him. De Leon is from one of the very prominent Charleston families; he is the son of the surgeon Dr. De Leon, who once treated either my sister-in-law or our friends, the Seixas. In any event the De Leons come from a different crust of the Jewish society in Charleston, much higher up than mine, and he did not know me.

No matter. De Leon is a close friend of the President, from connections I know not of; and I am asked to send him to Europe to replace, or rather to supervise, John Slidell.

"I mean no criticism, Mr. President, towards Mr. De Leon, nor do I mean to question your judgment, but Slidell has done excellent service in Paris. He knows some of the top people, and I may add, he has done it all on a small budget."

"Mr. Benjamin," said the President, "it is not to supplant Mr. Slidell, but to expand the scope of his activities for all of Europe that I am asking you to empower Mr. De Leon. We must start a massive propaganda effort for recognition in the press and among officials in France. We must offset the barrage of Yankee lies and we must do it quickly."

President Davis has such a way of speaking that the words are slow and in the deep Mississippi drawl which means the matter is not subject to discussion. Much is subject to discussion, and he leans on me in many matters, but I am quick to perceive that there is no talking permitted on this point. I am offended because this is my direct responsibility, but Mr. Davis is the President, and I am his employee. So, I graciously shook Mr. De Leon's hand and concurred with the President.

The light was very strong and Davis was taking his time in the walking. He said good day to the dozen people who recognized him, and then he stooped to pick up some blades of grass which he placed in his mouth.

"Join Mrs. Davis and myself for dinner on Friday night, will you please?" he asked me.

"I'll check my calendar, Mr. President, but I believe it is free."

"If it isn't, please make it so."

Later in the day I composed a letter for Mr. De Leon to carry to Europe, addressed to John Slidell: "Mr. De Leon possesses a high degree of the confidence of the President as a man of discretion, ability, and thorough devotion to our cause. He will bear to you this dispatch and I trust you will give him all information you may think it expedient to make public, so as to facilitate him in obtaining such position and influence amongst leading journalists and men of letters as will enable him most effectually to serve our cause in the special sphere assigned to him."

I must protect Slidell for personal reasons. He performs private service for me in Paris in that he looks after my wife and has been doing so since his arrival. Even if Slidell turns out to be a lesser diplomat than De Leon, he is still a greater friend.

July 22, 1863

There is a new man in my department, a clerk named Beauchamp Jones, recently transferred from the Department of War. Since he is known at War for his efficiency, a commodity I value highly, I shall give him a mountain of work to do immediately, if he is so disposed. He can make copies of several dispatches, as well as my letter which De Leon is carrying. It will not hurt at all for Slidell to get the letter first through the regular mails. It will clarify to him how I feel, and he will also thereby have time to muster up a gracious reception, if a false one, for De Leon.

Later: Jones has finished his work early. As it is still

23

possible to put the dispatches on an early boat, I have asked Jones to take them personally to the mail barge at Norfolk.

July 26, 1863

I have had the most delightful dinner with President Davis and Varinia and the family. Before we sat down to eat, the President's son, Jeff Jr., climbed up on my knee and the two of us must have played for an hour. He has the president's deep-seeing eyes but Varinia's light skin.

"I'm going to be a soldier when I grow up, Uncle Judah," he says to me, "and I'm going to kill all the Yankees."

"By the time you grow up, little Jeff," I told him, "the war will be over; the killing done."

"Indeed, I hope so," said Mr. Davis solemnly.

"But if it's not, daddy, will you let me go after them?"

"How do you advise on this matter, Mr. Secretary?" the President asked. Varinia came in just then from the parlor, beaming, I believe, and I may be wrong (indeed I hope I am completely wrong) that she beams even more when she sees me and her husband together than when she is alone with me in my arms.

"I believe," I said looking at Varinia, "that the matter for the moment is out of the jurisdiction of the men. I would advise, Mr. President, that a memo be sent to Mrs. Davis' department. For although we may consult on the issue, the ultimate decision is hers."

"Well done, Mr. Secretary. A masterful job of family diplomacy," said the President.

"What did Uncle Judah say, daddy?" the boy persisted.

"He said," the President explained, as he brought the boy over to him and snuggled him in his arm, "that you had better listen to your mother."

"And she says," Varinia answered, "that you had better wash yourself up, little Jeff, or your nanny will be on you quick as a duck on a June bug." And then she turnef to us. "Dinner is served, gentlemen."

And it was delightful. "Mrs. Davis cooked the partridge herself, Mr. Benjamin. One of her secret family recipes from Mississippi," Davis said. "The first time I had it was when I came courting her and her daddy said he thought I was too much of an old man to have an abiding interest in his daughter. Well, I did; and after I tasted this bird, I said to myself, that woman is going to be my wife, no matter if I'm fifty years older than she is. This food'll put years onto your life, Mr. Benjamin—eat away."

"Oh, stop all this formal talk, will you two? Little Jeff's got the right idea when he calls your Secretary of State 'Uncle Judah.' Listen, Jeff," Varinia said, "this man's your best friend in this hornet's nest of a government. Least you can do is call him by his given name. This is not the Senate, after all. Now I want you two to talk like a couple of boys just met over fishin'. Here, I'll introduce you: Jeff, I'd like you to meet Judah. Judah, Jeff."

Thus the informality of our evening was assured, although I was much troubled by Varinia's behavior, and did not know if she herself knew what she was about in this evening.

"I have quite an outspoken wife . . . . Judah," the President said.

"You may call me any way you please, Mr. President. But as your cabinet member, I will address you formally. Our friendship and my usefulness to you need not be affected by such protocol."

After dinner we adjourned to the parlor. Varinia said she was not feeling well and went upstairs. The President was solicitous about my family.

"And Mrs. Benjamin continues to reside in Paris?"

"Yes, sir, for a goodly number of years now."

"If I could spare you, Benjamin, I would tell you to go abroad to visit her or to combine the visit with some diplomatic affairs. But I cannot spare you. Varinia is right. I cannot imagine keeping a grip on Richmond without your wise counsel."

"I am flattered by your compliments, Mr. President."

"Does the separation wear on you, Benjamin?"

"I am well used to it now. My wife and I have had a

peculiar marriage, sir, and she has always been—well, how shall I put it—an independent woman."

"I have heard this gossip in Richmond, and was not unaware of it when you and I faced each other on the Ssnate floor in Washington."

"And at the Senate parties," I added.

"Yes, at the Senate parties. But I have never once let a man's personal life, within bounds, interfere with my cool and objective judgment of his abilities. They shall not have you out of my government, Benjamin, no matter how hard they try."

"Is it anyone in particular this time, Mr. President, and is this the specific reason for your invitation?"

"No, it is the usual crew, Foote and General Beauregard, yet Beauregard has let off you since you are no longer Secretary of War. It is Foote, Chilton, and Miles Porcher of Alabama and Tennessee who are maneuvering for a vote of no confidence about the diplomacy. They say recognition could have been had earlier, Mr. Benjamin, if someone more competent were running the foreign policy."

I listened silently. Davis reiterated their claims, which he had to do, I understood, as President of all the states of the Confederacy, so he could go back to tell them he had consulted with me on these points. But Mr. Davis, who did not take these charges seriously, wished to convey them to me unofficially over dinner and dessert. And having done so, he said, "They shall get nowhere."

"Mr. President," I told him, "I have a new tack to pursue with the British businessmen, with the merchants in particular, which I shall tell you about shortly, as it develops."

"Why, it must be the cotton deal you proposed earlier."

"Yes, sir. There is, I fear, a growing official British recalcitrance. But the feeling of the British people, not their officials, is for us. I think time is right to tap this, and so, with your permission, I shall see if we can spur investment by them in cotton, so that they shall have an interest in our national welfare. And I shall do the same in France."

26

"Pursue, by all means, Benjamin, and let me have a report by August, if you will."

Thus, where from this evening I had expected a confrontation, I came away with compliments, promises of presidential defense against my detractors, and new responsibilities.

Yet, even as I take down these notes by lamplight, my thoughts stray to Varinia. It is clear to me it will be necessary for me to see her alone very soon.

August 8, 1863

I am sending thousands of dollars to this new man De Leon in Paris, and for none so far has he sent me any vouchers. I am less disturbed at Slidell's jealousy over having another agent about than I am over De Leon's careless bookkeeping, and I have written him accordingly.

August 9, 1863

I have written Mason to go ahead with the construction of the ironclads in England. If we can break the blockade, then we are an independent country, and others can trade with us. This is the correct reading of international law and the President seems to think it a fruitful course to pursue, without, however, abandoning lobbying with the kings and princes of Europe for recognition.

I myself am partial to this maritime argument, and am entrusting Mason herewith with all the funds he needs to get the ironclads built.

To Mr. Mason I have also written: "Enclosed is a list of ships entering Southern ports; use them to illustrate the ineffectiveness of the blockade. Furthermore, insist as persuasively as you can to Lord Palmerston that recognition by England alone may bring an end to the war and restoration of a prosperous commercial intercourse with the Confederate States."

I have entrusted Mr. Jones with the quick dispatch of

these letters. There is something that bothers me about this man but his patriotism and his quick expedition of business are to be valued.

August 10, 1863

Have just received dispatches from Mr. De Leon from Paris. This is a preposterous amount of time. He uses private messengers, which are not only dangerous, but slow. I have written Mr. De Leon never to give his messages to private hands. Through private hands the dispatches generally take three to six months before they arrive in Richmond. And when they get here they are stale news indeed. Through the English mails to Nassau the dispatches always arrive within forty days.

If De Leon were in contact with Slidell this would not have happened.

Slidell has written that he has seen my wife at several balls, and that Colette looks well. He has not seen Ninette in weeks. However, he does tell me that Colette passed several not-so-obscure hints that she needs more money. I am not surprised at this news, and furthermore I have asked John (Slidell) to keep me informed. But I must tell him not to put such information in our diplomatic pouches. The embarrassment would be ridiculous if they were intercepted by the Federals.

Ninette must be twelve years old already, or is it only eleven? Can I be so occupied as to have forgotten my own daughter's birthday?

I shall telegraph them a thousand dollars this evening.

September 1, 1863

It has finally happened. De Leon has been intercepted. Belle has telegraphed the headlines to me from the New York *Daily Tribune:* "Secret dispatches of Confederate agent in Paris intercepted." Says the French are a far

28

more mercenary race than the English, and France only wants more money.

And so on.

I had made this De Leon appointment reluctantly, under pressure from the President. Now the bird has come home to roost. He will be doing us no more good there. I will recommend transfer. At any event, Slidell will thereby have a free hand.

Also discussed with the President and with the Secretary of the Treasury, Memminger, details of a plan that the Erlanger House in Paris has suggested. We will sell bonds, the funds of which will be used to buy Confederate cotton, and create interest by European merchants in the welfare and recognition of our country. I told the President I thought we should work on scaling down the total amount, and he agreed. Memminger wanted the interest rate cut as well. We worked for several hours and finally agreed upon a plan whereby Emile Erlanger and his company would underwrite at 77 on a basis of 100 par value, and for which a purchaser could pay in installments. The bonds will bear seven per cent interest and they are exchangeable for cotton at six pence a pound which is about four times the price in Europe. The Erlangers' commission is five per cent for selling the bonds.

"Such a commission cannot be helped, Benjamin, even with your connections to this family?" the President asked.

"No, sir," I answered. "I have had them cut it already from seven."

September 24, 1863

A letter from Mr. De Leon:

Dear Mr. Secretary of State:

I am pursuing to the utmost the possibility of obtaining an audience with the Emperor. Next week I am to talk to his appointments secretary, with whom

29

I have dined. He is a delightful man and has spent some time in South Carolina, where he and my father, before he went to medical school, were boyhood companions with Mr. Lopez, and other notables of Charleston, whom I trust you know. I am extremely optimistic about the possibilities of this meeting.

As to the intercepted dispatches, while I understand they unfortunately had wide circulation in the United States, here happily only one journal in Paris has made mention of them in an unfavorable sense, and that one struck them with but a feather.

Sincerely,
Thomas De Leon

Late in the day at the old customs house I ran into R.M.T. Chilton, now a congressman and former assistant Secretary of State. There is some envy in him of me, as can be ascertained from a recent story in the *Enquirer* in which he is quoted as saying, "The entire Department of State will soon be in the hands of Jewish shylocks if something soon is not done." The President had him removed for what he politely termed as "too much yawning on the job."

Mr. Chilton is of extremely rotund dimensions, shorter even than I, with small arms which seem much too small for his body. He has a way of deportment such that even when he is standing still, as he was upon this recent occasion in the hall, he gives the appearance of moving jitteringly away.

"How goes the ship of state, Mr. Secretary?" he asked.

"Smoothly, Mr. Chilton, in troubled waters," was my reply.

"We in the congress are of a mind, Mr. Secretary, that you should give us an accounting."

"If it please the congress," I said, for I see no point in offending this man, or charming him, for his mind seems set, "I shall gladly meet with you."

"Very good then."

"Upon, of course, permission from the President."

"I am sure that will be no problem."

"Simply secure it in writing and send it to me, congressman, and I shall be prepared to answer your questions."

"How goes recognition from the Dutch?" he then asked as I was making my way from his uncomfortable presence.

"At the congress, as you requested, I shall make a full report, congressman. Now, if you'll forgive me."

"Of course," and then he came after me a few feet and said, "Oh, by the way, how is that new clerk Jones working out for you?"

"Very well," which indeed was the case. "Why?"

"Good. Because it was I who suggested he try you. I've got a full staff, and he's always been good to me. A local fellow. Always interested, I am, in having a competent clerk, at least once, in each department of the government. Worked at War for quite a while. Very competent."

Indeed the oblique message of this oaf was clear, that in emphasizing the competence of my clerk, he was diminishing, in his estimate, my own, and the competence of my department. I need not stand about to listen to this tactless criticism, and so I left him standing there and shrieking at me some virulent nonsense. If a man is to criticize me, and that, after all, is an aspect of public life, let him at least have some humor and some charm to his castigations, so that it will be worth my time to listen. We have no time in this government to be the receptacles for each other's tirades.

I am at least grateful to find out who Mr. Jones' benefactor is. In the days before the Secession, when we were all making our speeches, R.M.T. Chilton was so excessively violent in his defense of absolutely everything that even the President joked that if it were up to Chilton he would take a rifle and march alone on Washington to shoot Lincoln dead. I wrote a note back to Davis referring to Mr. R.M.T. Chilton as Run Mad Tom, and the name has stuck. He enjoys the name, I know that. I wonder what he would do if he knew I was the father of it.

In any event, I shall keep a little closer eye on Mr. Beauchamp Jones.

Varinia is giving a party for the Tennessee delegation and for the administration's gadfly congressmen. This includes Chilton. If it were possible to attend this, I would insist somehow on an invitation—to see her. She has not responded to my last two notes. Indeed I wonder if she ever received them, for I remember that it was to Mr. Jones that I entrusted the notes to be delivered to the first lady.

I am beginning to worry.

October 10, 1863

The ironclads! Are they being built or are they scuttled? No word from Slidell except a personal note that Colette received the thousand from me.

"Je suis triste," he quoted her as saying. "The rich Secretary must send more for his wife and his little Ninette."

She has always been extravagant, but this is getting quite out of hand. I shall ask her where all this money goes in such a short period of time, and perhaps to provide some receipts. It is taking a chance, because Colette has never lost her fierce Creole temper. But then again, my own reserves have never been so low. Belle too needs some funds, and as usual she needs them quickly. Bribes do not wait, and she must pay her informants. I have ordered five hundred of my own sent to her in Baltimore. When we win this war—do I dare say *if* we win this war?—I shall recoup my losses.

I am in receipt of disturbing news from Belle. She says she cannot get away to Richmond. Can I come to Baltimore, where she is performing? I have done this once before, when I was less well known. Now, three years later, my face, or rather caricatures of it, are splattered across Northern newspapers. And yet if I wait for her to make the journey here, I may lose a valuable moment. We are poised for action around these ironclads, and I get more information from my spy in Maryland and Virginia than I do from the whole network in Europe, from Slidell and De Leon combined!

I have asked Jones to prepare false papers for me to enter Maryland. I know Baltimore and we have some contacts there. In the meantime I have shaved off my moustache, and put ridiculous French curlicues into my beard.

When Jones saw me in the office, he was first to comment: "You take a big risk for this information, Mr. Secretary. Could not someone go in your stead?"

"No one else knows my informant, Mr. Jones."

"All the more reason another should go. What if something happens to you; how then will this work be carried on?"

"Help me on with this coat, will you, Mr. Jones? And, may I ask, do you expect something to happen to me?"

"Of course not, sir," said he, "but it is, after all, Yankeeland. At least, sir, take a revolver. Here," he said, offering me his navy issue, "why not use mine?"

"I thank you, Mr. Jones, for your kind concern for me, but I use my wits—they are quicker than bullets."

"But not as deadly," he answered, with something of a sneer.

"We could debate that point, but I haven't the time, Mr. Jones. Have you got everything?"

He handed me the papers I would need, and a list of addresses, rooming houses, and so on, where our sympathizers congregated. I committed the places to memory and then burned the papers on which the notes were written. I gave Jones my own identification papers, for I did not want to take anything into the North which might seem suspicious. I think Jones was quite taken aback by the trust I showed him. I, of course, have my reasons.

"At least," he said, "permit me to know where this Belle Boyd resides, and where we might make contact if that be necessary."

"Mr. Jones," I said to him, "there is no Belle Boyd. She is, or rather they are, a completely fictitious creation of the State Department. There are Belle Boyd sightings throughout the South and the border states, but rest assured there is no *one* Belle Boyd, only girls who say they know her and work for her. I don't know if you understand what I mean, but it is for the safety of the individual who is sewing this Ariadne's thread throughout the land, that I do not make her identity known to anyone."

"I am impressed, Mr. Secretary," he said. I took my bag and we made for the wagon to the train.

"I ask you not to be impressed, Jones, but only to be trustworthy, to take messages for me, and to handle my callers until my return. To all others except the President, if he should ask, I am ailing in a quiet room in the city, where I am well cared for and prefer to convalesce without visitors. If Mr. Davis inquires of me, tell him what I have just told you."

By now we had traveled the short distance to the railroad station that would take me to the border crossing. "And what if Mrs. Davis should inquire of you, Mr. Secretary?" Jones asked.

"Expect you that she will, Mr. Jones?"

"I only delivered to her the notes you asked me to take, sir," he said with an obsequiousness which I found insufferable.

"And how is it you know that the notes requested reply?"

"Did I say they did?" he asked without blinking.

"Of course not," I remarked. "I must have been thinking of something else, Mr. Jones. Please do me the favor of sending the wagon to meet me three days hence, if you will."

"I shall drive it myself, Mr. Secretary," he said, again with a servility that made my teeth grind.

On the ride to the border I perused Belle's file and read a recent article from the *Southern Illustrated News* regarding my spy. I, of course, planted the entire piece, complete with details and facts of origin. Even the picture which is included in the article is false, a composite which we threw together from old daguerreotypes of members of the department staff. I think my own mother's nose is in the picture.

This young lady, who has, by her devotion to the Southern cause, called down upon her head the anathemas of the entire Yankee press, was in our city last week. Through the politeness of Mr. Cowel, the artist, at Minni's gallery, we are enabled, in this issue of our paper, to present her picture.

That our readers may have an opportunity of seeing what the Yankee correspondents say about this young lady, we extract the following article from the columns of the *Philadelphia Inquirer,* which was written by the army correspondent of that sheet:

"These women are the most accomplished in Southern circles. They are introduced under assumed names to our officers, so as to avoid detection or recognition from those to whom their names are known, but their persons unknown. By such means they are enabled to meet the officers of every regiment in a whole column, and by simple compilation and comparison of notes, they achieve a full knowledge of the strength of our entire force. Has modern warfare a parallel to the use of such accomplishments for such a purpose?

"The chief of these spies is the celebrated Belle Boyd. Her acknowledged superiority for intrigue has given her the leadership of the female spies in the valley of Virginia. She is a resident of Martinsburg when at home, and has a pious mother, who regrets as much as any one can the violent and eccentric course of her daughter since this rebellion has broken out.

"Belle has passed the freshness of youth. She is a sharp-featured, black-eyed woman of 25. Last summer, whilst Patterson's army lay at Martinsburg, she wore a revolver in her belt, and was courted and flattered by every Lieutenant in the service who saw her. There was a dash about her, a smart pertness, and bearing which were attractive.

"The father of this resolute black-eyed vixen is a paymaster in the Southern army, and formerly held a

35

place that society, position, and education can confer upon a mind suited to the days of Charles the Second, or Louis the Fourteenth—a mind such as Mazarin or Richelieu would have delighted to employ.

"This woman I saw practicing her arts upon our young lieutenants. She is so well known now that she can only practice her blandishments upon new, raw levies and their officers.

"She has a trained band of coadjutors, who report to her daily—girls aged from 16 upwards—women who have the common sense not to make themselves as conspicuous as she, and who remain unknown and effective.

"The reports that she is personally impure are as unjust as they are undeserved.

"During the past campaign in the Valley this woman has been of immense service to the enemy."

October 13, 1863

Baltimore is like any other Southern city, except it is on the wrong side of the lines, and blue coats are a-swarming. I believe from the insignia they are from Rosecrans' Army of the Cumberland. There are three or four regimental numbers I commit to memory, from my view at the rooming house Belle and I have designated across from the Nuart Theatre.

Belle, as usual, is performing tonight. The town is in a frenzy about her *Mazeppa,* but fortunately I was able to purchase one of the last remaining tickets. The show features her in flesh-colored tights riding a white horse across the stage, yelling something acrimonious to the gods. I have seen the show half a dozen times in as many cities, for this is how we meet. Belle Boyd is the actress Ada Isaacs. And although I commit this information to this foolscap, no one else knows this, nor will know of this until this Cause is won. Only this diary has the secret.

As the curtain falls, the Yankee soldiers mob the stage, and the Nuart turns into circus rather than theatre. She is notorious for giving kisses, and her dressing room is draped with Yankee flags and paraphernalia, pictures of Lincoln and McClellan and the like. It is marvelous cover, marvelous theatre, and the idea is all her own. There is never a secret service agent in sight, such a Yankee patriot is she. The southerners in town are in fact ready to tar and feather her, and would do so if the Yankee regiments did not scare them away.

From my window I see Ada kissing some colonel good night on the street. It is half past one and the street is deserted; a slight rain is falling. The stupid colonel is down on his knee in the middle of a puddle with some romantic palaver all over his face. Ada is a consummate actress, and she is playing her best role to the hilt, until she walks up the steps and enters this room.

I sit on the bed, with two glasses of cognac ready and, yes, now I begin to hear her footfalls.

I think of Varinia Davis, and then, as her footfalls grow louder, I think of Ada and her sparkling eyes. In these desperate times, it *is* possible for a man to love two women.

The door is flung open, Ada Isaacs' famous flesh-colored tights are draped over the bedpost. . .

Afterwards we lie quietly. Her head is on my shoulder, my arm rests on her narrow waist. I am amazed how such a small creature can be possessed of such boundless energy. Indeed "creature" is the apt phrase, for I notice when she is naked here with me, how like a little animal she is, how instinctual, how hungry, how satisfied. Where but from this astounding primitive nature comes the cleverness, slyness, the speed and the style of Belle Boyd!

She stands up and walks around the room. She is completely naked except for a garter around her right thigh. Sewn into the garter is a holsterette for her derringer.

"Judah," she says as she pulls on her stockings, "tell me that you love me endlessly and that you miss me. Otherwise you don't get a shred of information out of me about those old boats."

I went up to her, and without saying a word, I pulled her stockings off again, took her a-bed, and showed her

37

how much I loved her and how much I had missed her.

"I came unprepared to make you speeches, Ada—my embraces will have to do."

"And soliloquies without words they are, Judah. It's been a very long time."

"All too long. You know you may stop this business any time, and come to Richmond. I will make a place for you."

"Who then will give you your intelligence? Boys wet behind the ears riding their horses like gallant knights up and down the countryside? The Yankees may look stupid, Judah, but they're not. They put on false maneuvers for the scouts, and Jeb Stuart, may his rebel soul rest in peace, delivered up as many false reports as true ones. The Yankee officers tell the truth to flatter a lady in a parlor, and nowhere else."

"The whole South honors you, Ada, and even the Yankees give you reluctant praise. Have you read the press?" I showed her the article on Belle Boyd.

"And who put in this line here, that I have passed the freshness of youth? If it's you, Judah P. Benjamin, you can go right back to your fancy office, and all your boats can sink to the bottom of Liverpool Harbor!"

We were now sitting by the window table and sipping the cognac.

"And so they *are* being built at Liverpool!"

"On September 4," Ada began her report, "the Yankee minister Adams visited the English court and talked for a good number of hours with someone. The naval cadet who gave me the information, because he happened to have accompanied Adams, wouldn't tell me any more, no matter how much I promised to do for him."

"Spare your lover your professional techniques, Belle," I said, "and get on with the subject of Adams' conference."

"This cadet was positively popping his buttons. He said Adams told the English. . ."

"It must have been Russel, the foreign minister."

"That's right—Russel, the cadet said. Anyway, Adams told him point-blank that permitting us to build the ironclads in Liverpool means war."

"War?"

"That's right, Judah. War, plain and simple, between England and the Yankees."

"And then?"

"Then, on September 5, Russel ordered the ironclads or rams or whatever he called them not to leave Liverpool without his permission."

"At least we know they are finished, or at least seaworthy."

"It makes no difference, Judah, because last week Russel took over the ships, paid the workers off their contracts, and sold the boats to Spain. Rumor has it that Napoleon is going to do the same within a fortnight."

"He has six vessels under construction."

"What has Slidell done? Have you heard anything?"

"Slidell and that new man De Leon both tried to buy off Napoleon, but the Frenchy is scared."

"Maybe Chilton and Foote are right, Ada. Maybe I am incompetent at this job, and another would do better."

"Chilton, Foote and the rest of that bigoted mob are an embarrassment to the whole Confederacy. If you were a military hero, they would find some way to phrase it to make it seem like it came easy to you. They would say 'the little Jew singlehandedly drove back Grant's whole army.' No, Judah, I learned a long time ago to ignore Jew-haters, especially ones in high places. Consider them your inferiors. They are simply jealous of you."

"Well, my dear little Ada, I only do the best I know how. I cannot win battles in the field, and I cannot twist the arms of kings."

"Beautifully spoken, as usual, Mr. Secretary. Have both of us not come a long way from Charleston?"

"A long way, yes, but the future is still uncertain. I want you to be extremely cautious, Ada, even more so than usual. You are playing with treason here, and frankly, things are not going well for the government. I knew we would be in for a long war from the Secession, but how long, we cannot tell. If God forbid we should fail, we must, you and I, have a plan."

"I'll not think of quitting this now. You make the plans, if you wish—I will continue to gather intelligence for you. Shall I continue to be Belle Boyd?

"Absolutely."

"Soon they will be writing songs about me."

"And I shall whistle the tunes in Richmond until I see you there. Goodbye, my Ada."

November 6, 1863

Upon my return to Richmond, I found placed on my desk a white envelope. I opened the envelope and read:

> Did you enjoy the company of the
> First Lady, in her bed chamber,
> at an unbecoming hour?
> An Observer

I quickly turned to the corporal who stands outside my door. "Who brought in this white envelope?"

"I don't know, sir."

"Weren't you on duty? Who has been in the office in my absence?"

"I just came on, sir. In your absence the office has been filled with scores of people, as usual."

"Yes, but who was the clerk who accepted this note? Who is it from?"

"Perhaps it is in the ledger."

I checked the ledger of callers in the office. The usual people, thirty or forty—congressmen, their wives, merchants with cotton interest abroad, some known to me, some unknown, and the purpose of their visit written in Mr. Jones' neat hand.

"Where is Jones?" I turned again to the corporal.

"Why, right here, Mr. Secretary," said the clerk from inside the office, where he may have been standing while I made a fool of myself with my inquiries.

"Who brought this note, Jones?"

"I have not seen it," he said. "All the correspondence and materials brought by hand to you are as usual in your basket. May I read the note, sir? Perhaps I can help you determine. . . ."

I cut him off. "No, it's not important. I'm making more of this than there is."

I read and reread the note behind my closed door, but there was no hint in it of who the author might be. And who could have seen us? This information is the beginning of blackmail. I wonder what is going to be exacted from me. And I wonder if I should tell Varinia—and how.

Suddenly I, who am never tired, feel exhausted. And I, who am known not to take ill, feel dizzy and nauseous.

November 8, 1863

There is a letter from Ada:

The show has gone to Ford's Theatre,
Washington. Playing to packed houses,
quite a thrill. Lincoln and that ugly
wife of his were at a matinee on Saturday.

With love,
Ada

P.S. Nothing more on the ships for now.

Davis looked like a ghost this morning when I saw him on my way to luncheon with David Yulee of Florida. I did not know why, and as the President seemed deep in conference with the Vice President, Mr. Stephens, I did not ask.

The morning newspapers, frequently employing quicker and speedier correspondents than our own communications corps, had the answer to Davis' disgruntled expression. The army, the paper announced, is beaten at Chattanooga. Sherman seems to have outflanked Bragg, the most overrated commander of all the armies. Ten thousand are killed, wounded, or missing, and Bragg is driven off Missionary Ridge, the heights over the city. He is put to rout, the whole of the trans-Mississippi is endangered, and we are to brace again for another round of making bandages and making room in private houses for the badly wounded. After each battle all of Richmond becomes one large ward. I wish to the high almighty God that I could get 2,000 Parrott cannon from those English shopkeepers, but they will not sell a thing, not when I was Secretary of War, and not now in spite of all my efforts. Longstreet said the Parrotts were the best cannon he ever used, but were twenty enough to stop the Yankees? Hardly.

I meet Yulee at the chop house where we frequently have our large meal of the day at around noon. Yulee is a friend from the Senate, when he was Senator from Florida. He is now, for bad or for good, a Representative from that state in the Congress and one of my few constant supporters. I say for bad or for good, because there are times when Mr. Yulee's support is a mixed blessing. I am constantly being defended by him in response to the Jew-baiting attacks of Chilton and Foote and the others. And whereas I would choose to ignore these idiocies, Yulee, a Jew himself, *né* Levey, responds to them point by point.

He is a tall man with an extremely aristocratic bearing, and could pass himself off as a plantation man. Why he chooses to parade his Jewishness around at a time when it serves neither the Jews nor the Confederacy, I do not know. God knows I have tried to talk with him many times about it. It has practically become a subject known to us like a chess game we have been maneuvering about for years. Yet Yulee is a good friend, and an informant, who frequently brings me word of the diatribes while they are still being written by congressional staffs. We had our discussion today over a bowl of oysters and a mutton leg.

"That fat general, Wise, has gotten to Foote again, Judah, and you are going to be taken up on charges of incompetency from the Roanoke business. Pass the lemon, there."

"Roanoke! Yulee, that was a year and a half ago."

"Wise doesn't think the investigation was complete. You know his boy was a lieutenant killed in the engagement. He thinks you are responsible."

"I held a gun to the boy's head?"

"You didn't put a gun in the boy's *hand,* will be what they argue."

"But that was already settled when I went before the joint session. It's all in the *Congressional Record.*"

"Wise says you didn't answer fully enough as to why reinforcements were not sent, when they could have held the position and beaten Grant back with ten thousand more men and a hundred cannon. He says you sat there and absorbed the censure. But he doesn't want you being a sponge. He wants you telling why, so it won't happen again."

"Will it get out of committee?"

"If that bastard Foote has his way."

"And will he, Yulee?"

"Not if I have any power."

"You don't have much, my friend."

Yulee, who has a gift for ignoring irony but not insult, went right on. "Look," he said, taking out some notes scratched in a pad by an aide of his staff, "Here is what he said in the last session: 'The illicit trade with the United States has depleted the country of gold and placed it at the feet of the Jew extortioners, some of whom have even invaded high government ranks. They are hoarders and inflaters of prices and speculators with the hopes and dreams of true Southern patriots. They are retailing necessary goods at five hundred to one thousand per cent above ordinary prices. These Jews have injured the cause more than all the armies of Lincoln. If we gain our independence, instead of being vassals of the Yankees, we shall find all our wealth in the hands of the Jews.'"

"David," I said to my friend, who was red in the jowls with outrage, "I want to tell you the truth of Roanoke. And I want you to listen carefully. I went before the Congress at the express order of President Davis. I consulted the President whether it was best for the country that I should submit to unmerited censure or reveal to a Congressional Committee our poverty and my utter inability to supply the powder and reinforcements that were requisitioned by Wise, and thus run the risk that the fact should become known to some of the spies of the enemy of whose activity around the capitol we were all assured. Davis thought it best—and I concurred—that I should suffer the blame in silence rather than reveal the terrible dearth of our supplies. Get the information to Foote any way you can, and spare me and the country this needless waste of precious energies."

"And if he doesn't listen, Judah?"

"If he doesn't listen, tell him that the Yankees are a more suitable subject for his hatred than his own Secretary of State."

"Will Davis back you on this?"

"One hundred per cent. But I'd prefer we did not bother him with it. And, David, I want to tell you again that I will not be part of your campaign to reform this Foote into a lover of the children of Israel. Tell him what I have imparted to you as an issue apart from his distorted sense of economics, race, and history."

We finished our lunch and walked around the complex of government buildings, under some of the magnolias positively rotting in their sweetness, and we fell into a silence which was not characteristic of our meetings. We finally found a vacant bench in front of the customs house; we sat and Yulee spoke.

"Of course you've read of the Chattanooga business."

"Yes."

"I shall not go into detail except to say that Longstreet has also, as a result, abandoned the siege of Knoxville, and is in full retreat."

"What is your special news, Yulee?" I finally grew impatient. "Any clerk in the War Department could tell me as much."

"Could any clerk tell you that before Longstreet retreated he captured a small band of Union spies trying to inspire desertion among the troops?"

44

"Yes—and what is new in that, Yulee? It happens at every battle. Come. I must be going." I stood up and began to move back to my office, where a dozen dispatches and drafts of letters awaited me, epistolary infants to be delivered, and no one there to do the midwifing but me.

"What is special about this group of spies, Judah, is that they are led by David Seixas of Charleston."

"I sat down. *My* David Seixas?"

"Is not your Seixas the one who was with John Brown in Missouri?"

"Yes," I answered, stunned. Seixas, my best friend from my youth! I had, as a Senator, intervened on his behalf when Brown burned down houses in Missouri. Seixas, an accessory, had gotten off with but a rap on the knuckles.

"Then," Yulee said, "It is the same man. They were in the employ of that abolitionist paper from the Piedmont."

"The *Emancipator?*"

"Yes, that's the one. Longstreet's going to try to hang them from the first tree he can find. I hope for your friend's sake that the Yankees chase quick and Longstreet won't have time to pick the bough."

"Thank you, Yulee, and God bless you."

"God bless *you,* Mr. Secretary."

I made my way quickly back to the office and, putting all other work aside, drafted a letter requesting special dispensation at least temporarily for David Seixas. Then I sealed the letter and found an idle corporal whom I dispatched with the greatest speed to meet Longstreet. I pray to God it is not too late.

November 10, 1863, 3:00 A.M.

The President has gone to meet the soldiers coming back from Lookout Mountain. He is to be gone two days. Little Jeff has been sent to Atlanta to be with relatives for three weeks, and Varinia and I are together in the interim. We are met at a rooming house on the outskirts of town, and outside the window the crickets are chorusing in a sea of jasmine.

Without her bonnets and bodices, without her petticoats and furbelows, she lies beside me, Varinia is regal. As regal as she is at state functions, as prepossessing, as long and slender and aristocratic.

How strange I feel lying here beside her! I in my coat of Hebraic hair, I, in my body that has grown no thinner with use! I lie here with my dark arm about her lily waist, feeling like a borrower whose term may soon be over. I am overwrought by this note of the other day. I must tell Varinia. I know not how she will respond. Yet the words of this revelation are not the first words out of my mouth.

"My darling Varinia, I now know why we are drawn together."

"But, Judah, it is of course the fire in the flesh. There is no great mystery in that."

"But there is, Varinia, for consider how we are such opposites. We are opposites in such basic aspects as stature, physiognomy, coloring. We are opposite in our background. You are an aristocrat, the daughter of landowners, and I am the son of a poor merchant. You are a Christian and I am a Jew. You are. . ."

Varinia turned on her side and put her finger on my mouth.

"Why, Judah P. Benjamin, what brings over you this fever of comparisons and contrasts? And what of it, anyway? Even if you were to prove your case, as if this were the Supreme Court and not a bedroom, what then would you do? Would you leave?"

"Varinia, you prove to me that in love there is nothing so stupid as a lawyer who cannot suspend his insufferable logic."

"And yet, Judah, we do have much in common. Did you hear what Mrs. Johnston said to me the other night? You weren't at the party, but she opened her mouth, which Jefferson once described as bigger than a shellhole on a sandy beach, and called me Queen Varinia. How do you like that! Queen Varinia. I pity that poor General Joe Johnston who has to listen to such claptrap every day of his married life. It's no wonder he's always nagging Jefferson to send him to trans-Mississippi, where that tattle-mouth bitch'd be too feeble to follow him. Judah P. Benjamin, you and I are the two most maligned people in this government. The only difference between us is that you get maligned publicly, and I am maligned at parties. I don't know which is worse!"

"Queen Varinia," I said kissing her, "meet Judas Iscariot Benjamin," for so Foote had referred to me on the floor of the Senate.

"I like your kisses, Judah, better than your jokes. I like how you suffer this long war along with me. Judah, they wouldn't dare attack the President as they do you and me. We take it on the chin for him. In the woman closest to him, and you, the man in the cabinet closest to him."

"It is most perceptive what you say, Varinia. You and I are true natural targets."

"And I confess, Judah, I don't know how much more of it I can take. I give my parties, I give my husband such comfort as I can, but I am not doing enough, for he gets weaker and more distraught every day. When he thinks he has some control, it begins to slip from him. He is awake two and three nights without sleep."

"Shall I tell you, Varinia, the secret of bearing up? It is, as far as I can tell, the knowledge that even if we fail and the War is lost, after this there will be more of life, that this is not the end. Without this hope each day becomes a nightmare, for we are not doing well. If we were, the President would not be in the field with soldiers."

"Are you saying, Judah, that if we were doing better on the battlefield, we would have less time for each other?"

"Perhaps we would have less need," I answered.

"Perhaps," she said, and then our arms were about each other again. The thin blanket was kicked off the bed and a cool wind covered our bodies.

I did not tell her about the white envelope.

November 12, 1863

Longstreet's column has reached Richmond, according to my corporal, who has returned. He gave my note regarding Seixas to the General, who, according to the corporal's description, was much harried, and not in any mood for dispensations of any sort.

"And what was his response to the note, corporal?"

"He read it, sir, and told me to tell the Secretary of State that, begging his pardon, but in accordance with military procedures, all spies, including Mr. Seixas, were hung at Kingston on the night of the eleventh."

"The bastard!"

"Sir?" said the corporal.

"Dismissed," said I.

I left word with Jones that I would be away for the rest of the day. I contacted Yulee at the Congress office, commandeered a wagon and picked him up in half an hour.

It was easy to follow the haggard column out of Richmond. The walking wounded moved slowly on the side of the rutted road, so that wagons could pass, and the complete disorganization of the army became clear to me as never before. In my days as Secretary of the Army I had never got the view I was getting this day. The rain was pouring down steadily and the soldiers covered themselves with blankets or fragments of tents torn off in the bombardments they had just undergone. We stopped at the hospital on the outskirts of the city, and Yulee went in to get two blankets which we would need.

After driving for several hours with the team getting mired in the mud, we finally reached the village of Kingston. The houses were shelled and beaten into broken walls and the trees all about were singed. When the road at the east entrance forked left we came upon a grove that was the object of our journey.

Hanging from a large maple were three bodies. I slowly raised my eyes and recognized the one in the middle to be that of Seixas. I climbed on Yulee's shoulders, cut the body down, and wrapped it in the blankets in back of the wagon.

On the way back to Richmond the pouring rain had let up.

As we neared the city I asked Yulee if he had made the arrangements I had asked.

"Michelbacher is waiting for us at the graveyard. The ground is prepared."

And so this day, upon arrival of the body in Richmond, I buried David Seixas, spy for the United States, dear friend of my bosom. Born, Charleston, South Carolina, May 5, 1808. Died, November 11, 1863, Kingston, Tennessee.

In attendance were David Yulee, Rabbi Maximillian Michelbacher of Beth Ahaba Temple in Richmond, and myself. We three of us in the rain, covered the body, and then said in unison the prayer for the dead: *Yisgadal v'yiskadash, shemay rabah.* . . .

I was surprised with what ease the words came back to me through my tears.

December 1, 1863

A light snow falls on Richmond this morning, and it is just the gift we need to purify the city of its blood and wounds. The snow settles on the trees, powdering them lightly, and even the government buildings take on a look of gaiety.

My office has resumed its efficient running; the corporals and clerks are no longer needed in the hospitals, and the dispatches now come and go with regularity, the drafts of the new cotton deal are well underway, and I feel once again in control.

I feel that, without too many words spoken, Varinia is withdrawing from me. Whether it is temporary and she will be back when the oncoming Christmas season of family conviviality subsides I know not. But for now it is all well and good, as I have before me a second note in a white envelope, which was not here when I left the office at seven last night.

Your lewdness with Mrs. Davis

is no longer subject to doubt.
If you want to keep this information
secret, you will have to pay for
the silence. Send one thousand and
five hundred dollars immediately to
Box 11, General Post Office, General
Delivery, Amiens, Republic of France.

This note, like the previous one, is printed. The stationery is white and undistinguished, with not a clue to its origin anywhere. I can think only of Thomas De Leon; of all the people in Paris, he was in Richmond last. He could have seen us—but why would he do this? He is a wealthy man, and a friend of the President's. He would not bribe me. My intention of removing him from his position has been vetoed by the President. Because of their friendship his position is secure, regardless of whether it helps the cause or not. I cannot understand De Leon doing a thing like this. And furthermore, why Amiens?

I shall not respond. There is no evidence, no testimony, and how can I be sure there is anything more to this than a vulgar prank? I did not tell Varinia, and I am glad of it. I shall let it go. If this extortionist really has something he will raise the fee, because if he goes to the press with such stories, without proof, even my enemies on the *Enquirer* would not publish it. Thereby would disappear all his leverage. No, there will be no revelations without another opportunity to pay for silence. I run no risk now, except to tell Varinia. Again, I will not tell her. Little Jeff is sick with fever from a fall, and she is up with the nurses all night. It would be cruel to burden her with this as long as it is not necessary. As usual, I will accept it in silence and see what will be.

December 7, 1863

Dispatches today from Slidell. He is attending many parties and doing much in the way of political talk with the court of Napoleon, but everything seems, he says, inconsequential. It is clear to me France waits upon the decisions of England. Mason reports the same type of wait-and-see attitude in Holland and in Belgium. To both these men, and to De Leon who plans a trip to Moscow soon, I send this dispatch, which will be a major step in a change of our policy.

When an appeal to the common sense of justice of the nations has failed to elicit any further response than a timid neutrality scarcely covering an evident dread of the power of our arrogant foe, the United States, we prefer speaking in other tones and insisting that an admission into the family of nations is a right which we have conquered by the sword. In the code of modern international law, the nation which presents itself with an organized government and an obedient people, with the institutions created by the free will of the citizens and with numerous armies which crush all the attempts of the most powerful foe to subjugate it, which is aiming at no conquest, seeking no advantage, and steadily bent on securing nothing but the inherent rights of self government—such a nation may insist upon, and with some degree of stern self-assertion demand its right of recognition. It is preferred therefore that in any communication you may now initiate with the English, French, Dutch, and Russian courts, while the utmost deference and courtesy are observed, the tone of official correspondence be placed on the high ground above indicated rather than on any argument in support of the justice of our cause.

In the same pouch bound for Europe I include a note to my friend Baron Erlanger, a financier of some importance. I have asked him to check on the address given in the previous note from Amiens.

Later today over lunch I have taken Yulee into my

closest confidence regarding this matter of the white envelopes. He is shocked, but, as I expected, sympathetic, and swears to secrecy. A man of bombast and passion, he himself has had three wives during his legal and political career. His present lady is of Seminole blood, but she prefers to live in Tallahassee, where, Yulee says, she tends the garden. I believe he is coaching his Indian wife in the art of Jewish observance. I have more than once blundered into the subject of the lost ten tribes of Israel with Yulee. It is a blunder, for Yulee insists the American Indians are indeed the descendants of Gad, Naftali, Dan, and the other seven. He is convinced, he says, that he is not teaching his wife anything new, but that he is reviving deep-seated but long-forgotten knowledge. Next to defending me on the Senate floor, proving this point of dubious historicity is David Yulee's other passion. In any event, he has given me an insight into these notes, which I have apparently overlooked.

"Just because you are asked to send the money to Amiens," he observed, "that does not mean that your white envelope necessarily resides there at the present time."

"You mean it could be a convenient way to disguise his identity?"

"Of course, Judah. If he asked you to deliver the money somewhere here in Richmond, what is to keep you from observing its being picked up?"

"Clever indeed. Yet the man could be traced from Paris. I have asked Erlanger to look into it for me."

"A touchy business because Erlanger is involved with their finance department."

"In a way, yes, Yulee. But he is going to be floating us a big loan while his government turns its back. He's going to help the merchants buy cotton and store it here."

"Why would they want to store it here?"

"They normally wouldn't, of course. That is to be part of the deal at purchase. It will be a stupendous price, at seven per cent off the going rate, but the catch is that the bales remain in Charleston and in Savannah, in warehouses along the coast."

"I don't get it, Judah. What good does that do us?"

"The merchants then will have an interest in taking good care of us. They will push for recognition even if Louis Napoleon does not. They will hammer on his door and plead with him to recognize the Confederacy in order to protect French merchandise. They will pester him night and day with this, as will we with planted newspaper articles. We are underway already."

"Extremely unorthodox, Mr. Benjamin," Yulee said, as we awaited the pudding. "And if it works you will not get one nod of approval, but it will go direct to Davis."

"I am not in a popularity contest, David. I am a cabinet minister in this government. Who cares where the laurels lie, as long as we get the recognition?"

"And if you fail and this Erlanger business gets known, you will be skeet for the shooting, Judah. Foote and Chilton will take all their delegation a-hunting."

"This Foote who obsesses you, Yulee, will one day step all over himself. Mark my word, he will do himself harm without any assistance from us."

We stood up, Yulee stretched his full six and one half feet, and then said, "You stay away from Mrs. Davis, Judah. It will be a mess."

"It is now. It won't make any difference if I see her a hundred more times, or never again."

We said good day, and I went to meet with my old Louisiana delegation to brief them on the Erlanger business, which would soon be known in the press. In my pocket I carried the white envelope. As I walked I crumpled it ten times over before I arrived at the caucus room.

December 9, 1863

I have just received a letter from my sister Becky. She and mother are safely ensconced in the house I bought for them in Savannah. I am much relieved they have left Beaufort, for the reports are that the Yankees are ranging the Carolinas under Sherman.

53

I think this has been a bad year indeed for our armies. I knew at the Secession that this war would not end soon. Senator Jeff Davis said to me then that the superior Southern horsemen would drive the shopkeepers and peddlers of the Union armies into a little circle and then dance around them to the tune of Dixie. But it has not worked out as he dreamed.

I have read in the *Southern Review* their annual summary of the year. I read it with a suspended optimism.

The old year has whirled into the grand mausoleum of eternity, but the ties which united the living pages of its glory to our hearts have not been sundered.

We look back with pride, it may be mingled with some sadness, to the brilliant victories at Fredericksburg, the capture of Winchester, the magnificent though indecisive field of Gettysburg, the coming repulse of the enemy at Charleston.

I wonder if this "indecisive field of Gettysburg" is in fact so indecisive. Our enlistments are down ten per cent and the governor of Virginia said today that his state's regiments would only defend their native ground, and only under Virginia commanders. We must solve these problems, and solve them yesterday, if we are to win the war.

December 18, 1863

The annual Christmas tree is put up this morning in the middle of the square. Inside a nearby tent, the ladies of the government are gathering Christmas gifts for the soldiers in the hospitals. Mrs. Joe Johnston is organizing this activity, usually one of Varinia's favorites—but Mrs. Davis cannot do it, as she is in mourning. A terrible thing has happened. A nurse left Little Jeff Davis unattended in his room and the child, still delirious from fever, fell off the balcony. The President ran out and picked the dying

54

boy up in his arms. Varinia began to sob, a doctor was summoned, but the boy, whom I loved, expired within minutes. It is a Christmas of dubious joy in Richmond.

I received at my office this morning a third white envelope. This note was briefer than the others:

> Pay or I shall write immediately
> to Mrs. Davis.

It would be an intolerable burden for her to bear right now, so I draft the $1500 and send it away immediately. Perhaps this will keep the dog away—at least for a while.

In the meantime I am overcome with a great feeling of wanting to go home. Or maybe it is a feeling of home-lessness—I cannot be sure. In any event, I have written my mother that I cannot come to Savannah for the Hanu-kah celebration. She is aged, and my farewell to her last year I felt perhaps to be the last. I do not know. At least Becky is with her, and they are handsomely provided for.

Last Christmas I spent as a guest of the Davises, but not this year. I am drawn to being with Belle, but as she is still touring around the Yankee capital with her *Mazeppa,* it is quite impossible.

Just where home is for me I know not. It is not with my wife, it is not with Varinia, and it is not with Ada Isaacs. My home is here in this office with all this work, and the better part of wisdom is to throw myself into it as I never have before.

And yet I cannot escape the knowledge that I am as split asunder within myself as is the North from the South. Such a warring I have not felt in many many years. How can one man be drawn to two women as completely different as Varinia is from Ada? One is dark and the other is fair. One is the bohemian who takes off her clothes down to her tights in front of yelping soldiers every night, and the other is the sedate first lady of the Confed-eracy. One a Christian, the other a Jew. One an aristocrat, one a peddler's daughter, even lower born than I. Varinia is the consummate wife, the mother (bless her in her suffering!) of children, while Ada will never marry, for she considers the institution repressive and demeaning to women. Varinia is exceedingly mannered, and Ada smokes cigarettes. All they have in common is my desire for them and the fact that they are for me both unreachable.

"There are two wars for you, Judah," Ada said to me as we lay together in Baltimore. "There is the one out there, and there is the one here in your heart." I shall never forget this.

As I compose these remembrances by dimming lamplight in my office, I hear footsteps down the hall. As it is past midnight, and no one is in the building except for a guard at the front door, I turn off the lamp and sit in the darkness to see who approaches. Who knows, perhaps it is White Envelope, and I may discover his identity by fluke instead of intrigue. The steps grow louder and when they reach the door to the office, they stop. I can see a form silhouetted against the glass pane. Is it Chilton, is it Foote, or Jones, or perhaps De Leon returned from Europe the other night? I cannot tell by the silhouette. My lips grow dry as I wait.

The figure turns to face the door, the tumblers of the lock click, the door is pushed ajar, a leg enters the office, but then, to my surprise, is suddenly withdrawn. The door is closed, and the figure moves down the hall without entering.

"Who's there?" I shout, my heart pumping. "Who's there? Identify yourself."

With no answer forthcoming, I jump out of my chair and race down the hall. The figure is disappearing out the back door and into the darkness across the capitol lawn.

"Halt!" I shout. When the figure keeps moving, his walk turning into a run, I yell for a guard. A sergeant of the capitol police arrives and I direct him to pursue the man.

"What man, sir?" he asks me.

"Why, that man there, in the frock coat, running. Idiot, chase after him!"

The sergeant takes a step in the direction of where I point, hesitates, and then runs off. He returns in five minutes. I am breathless. "We found no one, sir. Are you sure there was someone a-running? Seems pretty quiet, and there was no signs of running, sir."

"Of course there was someone running, sergeant. I chased him myself from the office building. I followed him down the hall and the steps." But I could see the sergeant was incredulous. I dismissed him. I stood breathing out plumes of misty air in the night. Of course there was a man there. It was White Envelope. There was a man, was there not?

I walked back to the office and resumed my work until the sun rose and filled up the dusty eastern windows. There were footsteps of the clerks and attachés coming in to work, and myriad figures passed by the door to the office. I was extremely tired. Jones walked in and said his usually chipper good morning. I walked out against the flow of people entering the building. I said hello to all who nodded to me. I walked across the grass to my apartment and climbed the stairs to my bed. What time is it, and what day? Could I have been dreaming?

December 23, 1863

"Some good tidings for Christmas, Mrs. Secretary," said Vice President Stephens as he came into my office today. "General Early has struck a surprise blow at Grant at Murfreesboro courthouse. He scared the pants off that whiskey-guzzler of a general, he did, and the week before Christmas, too, when no one was expecting it. Praise the Lord, Mr. Secretary, that Jubal Early has got little respect for religion."

"I praise the Lord, Mr. Vice-President, that he has such generalship. How goes it with Mr. Davis?"

"Why, I was going to ask you the same question, Mr. Benjamin." I like Stephens. He is as tall as Yulee, but with small thin arms and hands as delicate as a woman's. He is pure energy.

"I have not seen the President in almost a fortnight. His grief is great. Mrs. Davis is with him constantly."

"Between you and me, Mr. Benjamin, I think he should send Mrs. Davis to Brierfield for a rest. The Mississippi air will do her good, and he may be able to resume his work, with his wife's grief not constantly before his eye. Will you make this suggestion to him? You are closest to him of us all."

"I shall try, Mr. Vice President. But you know that the President is of his own mind about such matters."

"Of course. And a pleasant holiday to you, Mr. Benjamin, and to your family."

After Stephens left, I was given recent dispatches from Europe. Erlanger writes that the sale of cotton goes well with the merchants, and buying has also begun in earnest in England. So far there is no acknowledgment of this from the government, but Erlanger feels more time is necessary for the goods to accumulate. As to the subscriber to Box 11 in Amiens he writes:

I went, at your request, to the small post office which is around the corner from the Amiens Cathedral. I made inquiries of a postal clerk in the office who excused himself to get permission to tell me the information you require. When the clerk returned, he said he had been given permission, and he began to go through a box of cards on the desk, in which, so it appears, the subscribers are listed. "Ah," he said, "here is Box 11," but then, just before he was about to read the name to me off the card, his supervisor approached at what can only be described as a gallop, and yelled "Monsieur Montague, you cannot give the information requested. I am very sorry. I made a mistake in telling you otherwise." Then the supervisor turned to me and said, "I am sorry, Monsieur Erlanger, this information is to be kept confidential at the request of the subscriber. And in spite of our desire to be as helpful to you as we can, we must honor such requests from regular citizens just as we

58

would honor them from you."

Such, dear Benjamin, is the gist of what happened. Why permission was given, and why it was then withdrawn, I cannot say. I will say, however, that if you wish me to pursue this further, I believe I can. This Monsieur Montague, the clerk, looks to me like a man whom a few francs could influence. At your wish, I shall proceed.

Affectionately,
Erlanger

March 11, 1864

"Lee has given it to Grant and Meade at the Rapidan," said Mr. Davis to me in the war room of his office. The spirit of the President has returned.

"Grant thought he could catch Lee at Culpepper, but Lee outfoxed him and caught him when half his army was bathing in the river at Wilderness. We have sustained only half as many casualties as the Yankees, and they are dug in trenches waiting for another attack. But Lee is too smart. I have instructed him to hold for now at Spotsylvania, while I send supplies to him up the Chickahominy River. Can you use this to sell your bonds?"

"Indeed I can, Mr. President. But I must take the opportunity to tell you I do not believe the plan is going to work, and it has nothing to do with the sale of the bonds or cotton, which have gone well."

"Be more plain for this Mississippi boy, Mr. Benjamin."

"I mean, sir, that the governments are not taking any action. Emile Erlanger and the Emperor of France are as close as you and I are, sir. The Emperor is not taking any steps whatsoever. They will let their merchants scream until they are blue in the face. The government will take no move in Paris without a lead from London, and as we have talked of so many times before, the English fear only a war with Lincoln. London will not risk war, it seems, over Southern cotton bales."

"How long have we been selling the shares, Mr. Benjamin?"

"Some six or seven months now, sir."

"In that case continue for a while longer, and perhaps we can whet their appetites with a few more victories in the field."

April 1, 1864

I have known for two weeks now who the subscriber is to Box 11, Amiens, France. I am a little surprised, and then I am not surprised at all, that the box belongs to Colette Mazareau, my wife. It is only fitting, I suppose, that I have waited until this first day of April, a day dedicated to fools, to make this entry in my diary.

After identifying Colette, Emile Erlanger went on to write:

I must also inform you, as a friend, Benjamin, that your Slidell, who has given me so much trouble in resisting the buying of your bonds, contrary to your own order, that your own Slidell has also been seen very many evenings with Miss Mazareau *sans famille*. To make the point which I am aggrieved to convey, let me simply state that according to my informants your minister and your wife are having, and have had for some time now, an *affaire de la coeur*.

It is terrible what wars wreak. Perhaps after this is over and done with you and I, Mr. Benjamin, can have ourselves a pleasant walk on the Champs Elyseés.

What kind of man am I, I wonder, who will marry a woman who prefers to live across the ocean for so many years, who, no matter how much I have given her, could never find satisfaction, who said everything was *banal* or *triste* and suffered from what she called *ennui* six out of seven days of the week! What kind of woman is this who bears our child alone, and when I arrive, insists upon raising her as a Catholic without consultation with me! What kind of woman contracts to bribe a man his entire life, and gives to this enterprise the name of marriage!

And what kind of fool am I to have suffered this so many years?

I confess that I must have been an easy mark, young and alone and exceedingly ambitious in that Creole town. In the space of a month that family had me overwhelmed with charm and manners and promises for the future, for a life in the family of that elegant gravel-voiced Creole lawyer, the great Mazareau.

Who could have resisted evenings spent under the sultry stars of New Orleans, listening to Colette play at the pianoforte? The ice cubes clinked in the glass on the mahogany tables, the slaves walked in and picked up each napkin that fell from the trays, the admiring parents, the giant Mazareau and his wife, made their phantom chaperone appearances and then let us alone to talk of love.

Who could have resisted her perfume, imported even then from Paris, that filled the night with the promises of deep kisses? Who could have resisted the cool security of that ancient decaying house on the nights of all those months when the yellow fever raged in the southern part of the city? Just over the courtyard wall we could hear the groaning of the wheels of the wagons, loaded with the dead and the dying.

Who could have resisted her, Benjamin? Why, you could have! After all, the entire population of Creole men in New Orleans did. Had you not been so easily overwhelmed, had you learned by then the secrets of the *patois,* had you understood the subtle ways at the balls and the parties, you would have seen that Colette Mazareau, spoiled and not a virgin even at sixteen, was the only unmarriageable Creole girl in New Orleans. For the Mazareaus you were a find, Benjamin—and you have always known this. No one else would have taken their daughter to wife but you and one other man. That man, ironically enough, is now her paramour. They chose you above John Slidell because you were deemed more ambitious. How right they were! Here you are the Secretary of State and Colette's lover is but your minister. Slidell always wanted a Creole woman, always told you how lucky you were because there were no race of females on the planet who made better wives. It is touching indeed.

You married into the world, Benjamin, you married to leave Charleston permanently, and to leave your clerk's job, and to become not just another lawyer but the best and the best-connected attorney in all the parishes of that new state. You married because you wanted aristocracy (as perhaps you want it now with Varinia) and land and wealth. And you are an unqualified success, Benjamin. Look at yourself. You are a man of wealth and power, and the Yankees even have wanted posters of you printed up, lying alongside those of Jeff Davis, ready to be used. And while they are offering a $10,000 reward for the President, they are offering $5,000 for you, which is nothing to sneeze at. Anybody such as yourself who appears on a wanted poster is either a great success in life or a great failure, but surely not part of that mediocre breed in between.

You are a fool indeed, Benjamin, to have become the cuckold; but it is nobody's fault but your own.

April 8, 1864

It is lucky for me that beyond the mountain range of my anger there usually lies the practical plain of lawyer's logic.

Why, I questioned, could Colette not ask me for these amounts of money herself? Why does she resort to this local man, this White Envelope? And who is he? I still do not know. There must be more involved here than just money for her to dine at Maxim's.

And what need has John Slidell of money? He has a wife who happens to be the daughter of August Belmont, the biggest financier in New England, and by her he has three daughters. I do not think that for him the amounts I send are of any significance. If, after all, he needed money, what is to keep him from using the diplomatic funds I mail to him regularly? And yet his vouchers are in perfect order. On the other hand, it is true that he has always lusted after a Creole woman—any Creole woman. Perhaps he has felt the need of late to fulfill this desire. After all, to be the complete continental, a man must have at least one mistress, and Slidell has chosen my wife. There need be no connection between this and the White Envelope. Facts! I need more facts.

Late today I attended the unveiling of the stone on little Jeff's grave. There was much pomp, a riderless horse, and a salute of eight guns, one for each year of the young life cut short. Varinia and the President bore it all in stoic dignity. There is a rumor that now the first family will resume some of the entertaining the idle generals about Richmond need to keep their legs in shape. Beauregard and Meyers, who are in town of late, shared a luncheon with me the other day. It was a stiff affair.

April 9, 1864

I saw Varinia at length this afternoon at the luncheon entertainments which indeed have resumed. The President was conspicuously absent. Mrs. Joe Johnston, Mrs. Beauregard, and several others not held in the first lady's highest esteem, were there, putting in appearances. It is such with us now that every party seems to be a political function, where the wives represent their husbands. Husbands to the field of combat—wives to the field of gossip. Perhaps I am lucky not to have a wife in Richmond.

"Judah!" she said to me as we both stood behind the table to serve punch, "Jefferson is distraught with all this carping at him. It is without end. He is sleepless and irritable, and cannot see people."

"What are you telling inquirers of your husband's health?"

"I tell them simply that he is out of sorts."

63

"Tell the President, Varinia, that his Secretary of State has some opinion to render on the subject."

"And what is that, Judah?"

"Tell him that if he feels he can perform either one duty or the other—either give entertainment or administer the Government—tell him I fancy that he is expected to perform the latter service in preference. If there are complaints about this from the bored officials of the capitol, tell him the Secretary of State shall issue, if he authorize, a few broadsides indicating that pursuit of the war effort against the Yankees is deemed by the President a fine antidote for boredom as it peculiarly affects soldiers and bureaucrats of this Government."

A look of relief moved across Varinia's beautiful face. It was relief, it seemed, for more than her worries about her husband.

"Judah," she said, "I think we must stop. Jefferson needs me, and the Cause needs me, and they need you also. At another place, at another time, in another world, Judah, who could know what we might share. . ."

"Darling Varinia," I stopped her talking and we moved to the seclusion of the veranda, "I've known that we must stop for some time now. What would it benefit anyone for me to proclaim my love for you from the rooftops? They would tar and feather us both, and this war which goes none too well for us now would go, I fear, even worse."

"This double life bears heavily on me, Judah."

"But have I not already agreed that we should stop?" I asked, taking her tightly by the shoulders. "Why do you speak as if we are going to continue?"

"Because I am drawn to you like fire. The words No, No, No, come out of my mouth, but at night as I lie in bed alone, and know that I shall lie alone the whole night long, as Jefferson torments himself about this damnable war, I think of you, Judah, and I have more than once found myself with my dress on, my shoes on my feet, my shawl about my shoulders, and my hand on the doorlatch on my way to you. It is then that I must catch myself and repeat No No No, you cannot go to him anymore. You must stay here, for this is your lot. You must be a woman.

64

You must return to your cold, cold bed!"

I decided this was an opportune time to reveal to her the business of White Envelope. "Varinia, listen carefully to me, and do not shriek or faint, for I have some bad news for you."

"Yes," she said, leaning for support against the parapet.

"I cannot be sure, but I think we are found out."

"Oh God! No, no!" she clutched my hand tightly.

"But it is not revealed—I do not think. I have been paying off a bribe for this for six months now."

"Who is it, Judah? Who is it? I shall punch the eyes out with my thumbs, I shall. . ."

"I have not been able to identify the party yet." I tried to speak with utter calmness, to use my voice instead of my arms to keep Varinia under control. Officers and their wives walked by and they all looked through the glass panes at us. I found a corporal nearby and sent him for wine mixed with potent French brandy. The corporal came back directly; I gave Varinia the drink, and under more tranquil control she was able to listen to me further. I gave her the old blackmail notes and let her read them.

"The subscriber to this Box 11, Varinia, is none other than my own wife."

She looked at me in disbelief mixed with pity. "My God, Judah—she cannot see us from Paris. Who are her eyes here?"

"That is precisely what we must find out. Will you help me?"

"With all my power."

"Are you sure you are strong enough? You must conceal this from your husband, completely. What he would do if he found out—we can only tremble at the prospect."

"Tell me, Judah, has this White Envelope any proof?"

"What might proof consist of, Varinia?"

"I am not the lawyer of the two of us. All I know is that I have always been most discreet, have never let a word about our liaison drop in public, not even with a servant."

"I too have not said a word of this, except to one confidant, David Yulee, and that subsequent to receipt of the first blackmail notes. He is trying to trace something down for me, but so far we have come no farther than identifying my wife at the receiving end of the funds."

"But then there may be no proof, and we are safe from this scandal."

"This White Envelope doesn't need proof anymore. Don't you see, Varinia—my paying him is proof enough; it may be construed as admission or partial admission. It confers much power upon White Envelope. I am afraid we are at present in a very bad position, and we must negotiate our way out. But we can do nothing. Our hands are completely tied until we find out the name of this nefarious bastard."

June 5, 1864

We are in receipt of reports that Grant, who must be a complete madman, has already lost over ten thousand men at the town of Cold Harbor on the Chicahominy River. And yet he still does not leave Lee alone, but batters away at the tired Army of Northern Virginia. Davis has asked me to expedite the purchase of more powder in Europe, for our reserves, which he must send to Lee, grow dangerously low.

In the meantime I have met with the President and Vice President Stephens again about the bonds, which have fallen once more. Davis was wearing a high collar, which, I commented, must be very uncomfortable in this humid weather.

"What the weather is like, Mr. Secretary, and what the day of the week is have no meaning for me any more. Tell me what your counsel is on the securities. Do you still think we should discontinue sales?"

"We have no choice, sir," I responded. "All eyes are on London, and yet she remains intransigent and gives it the name neutrality."

"The English bedevil us more than the Yankees," Stephens said. "If we delivered a hundred thousand bales to them all wrapped up neatly with a bow, they'd send the package back and say no one was at home. Abraham Lincoln might take the gesture of acceptance the w[...]

"So, shall I, sir?" I turned to Davis, who wa[...] in a deep pensiveness on his briar pipe.

"I suppose you shall have to, Benjamin, but continue to pursue recognition, for winning in th[...] of Europe is as important as winning battles in th[...] fields of Virgina."

"Perhaps more important," said Stephens.

"What is clear, Stephens," the President said, "is that the two go hand in hand, which is what Benjamin, here, has been telling me for three years."

"Just so, Mr. President."

"And what will then replace our cotton diplomacy, Mr. Benjamin?" he asked.

"Have you had the opportunity to read my memorandum on the subject, which I had Jones bring over to you the other week?"

"I have," he said, with much reluctance.

"That, in my estimation, is the only card we have left to play, sir," I told him soberly, for so I thought—and so it was.

"What memorandum?" Stephens asked irritably. "Why don't you two ever remember this government has a Vice-President! And although he may be old," (here Stephens ran his hand through his tousled white hair, which made him look a little like President Jackson), "he's not so old he can't read."

"It's a proposal, sir," I clarified, "for a government position advocating the abolition of slavery in the Confederacy. To be presented at the Court of Saint James by private envoy extraordinary. It will force the English hand into recognizing us."

"Over my dead body," Stephens said, rising in place. Stephens is one of the major slave owners in Alabama.

"Relax, Mr. Vice-President," Davis said with a wry smile on his withered face. "We will footnote the proposal and make an exception of your plantation!"

But Stephens was fuming through the plumes of his long white hair. "Begging the President's pardon, sir," he said, "but I do not consider this a matter of any levity.

.oposal of abolition, if laid before the individual ꞓ legislatures, would be knocked down quicker than a Ꞅammer on a nail."

"That is why," the President responded, "the proposal is not going to the states. We are a government here, and it will pass the Congress in Richmond."

"I should hope, sir," said the still irate Stephens, "that there will be no secret machinations with the English; and no proposal presented without first the Congress being consulted."

"I would not advise it in open session, Mr. President," I offered, for so the proposal would be in the papers more quickly than our man could get to London.

"Of course not," Davis concurred. "You, sir," he said to Stephens, "will brief the Congress in the most discreet manner possible. All we want is that they will not be able to hurl at us that they were not told."

"But they are *not* told," Stephens shot back, "according to this talk."

"You tell the leaders, tell Foote and Chilton and whoever we can trust. That will be sufficient, I believe."

"I beg to object formally to this entire procedure, Mr. President," said Stephens.

"On personal grounds, or on principle?" said Davis, his pipe out, and much irritated already.

"I am insulted by the question, sir," Stephens puffed.

"Then be insulted, sir." Davis rose from his chair. "But we are running a Government here, not a plantation. I want you to remember I have Brierfield and 43 slaves, and so does every other member of Congress. We must all make sacrifices, we must all give in to what the moment calls for."

"And if," said Stephens, "the English bite, and comes the recognition, and then comes the end of the war, do you see, sir, that we might find a way, within, of course, constitutional methods, to restore the institution which has made our country what it is today?"

"Mr. Benjamin," the President turned to me, somewhat amused by Stephens' inquiry, "what say you to the Vice President?"

68

"I say it is a series of very big 'if's' upon which the Vice President bases his question. I say that it is hypothetical, that we cannot give definitive answers about this, and that it would be a mistake indeed to cover the bitter pill with this kind of sugar in order to make the swallowing easier."

"Quite so," said Davis. "Don't play poker with the Congress, Stephens. Lay the cards, as presented, on the table for them. If you feel in conscience you cannot do it, tell me so right now. I have accepted resignations enough in this cabinet already so that another one will not surprise me in the least. I have had so many men leave, Stephens, that we will survive, although I want to tell you that in presenting the issue to you in this way and in calling upon you and Benjamin here to do the hard dirty work of being the messengers of bad news, you should therein realize how I value you. And as such, your departure, if that is what you propose, will be deeply grieved by me." Upon saying this, Davis sat down to await a reply.

Stephens, all six and one half feet of him, went to the doors of the office and opened one of them and took a step to leave. But then he brought back his foot, slammed the door loud, and turned to the President. "All right, goddammit, I'll do it," he said. He opened the door and left.

Not a minute could have gone by, during which Davis and I were talking, before the Vice President stormed into the office again and shouted at me. "Next time, Benjamin, make sure I get the goddam memorandum." Then he slammed the door for the second time and stormed down the corridor.

"He's a good man, Mr. President," I offered.

"Indeed so, Mr. Benjamin, as you are."

"And may I compliment you, sir," I said upon leaving the office, "on your effective, if not subtle, powers of persuasion."

I worked on the drafting of the proposal for the remainder of this day and night.

June 6, 1864

After a quick breakfast with Yulee, who said he had been able to unearth nothing more about White Envelope, I go to my office and find there upon the desk another note from the skillful anonymous blackmailer. As I expected, the ante is raised.

You will cease and desist immediately all dealings with the jew Erlanger and the jew millionaire Rotchild[sic.] in Paris. You will carry on all business of this sort in the future with the firm of August Belmont, Inc., New York City.

If you fail to comply with this directive, the complete record of your intimacies as well as your steep financial investment in keeping these intimacies secret, shall be known to all of Richmond.

Same stationery, same printed script, no clue in this— but there is the first mistake of the blackmailer. That he is aware of our financial involvements with Erlanger indicates he is clearly a member of the government, privy to information. That he refers so unkindly to the religion of these two fine gentlemen indicates White Envelope's identity may be sought among the Jew-baiters of the capital.

Since the decision to terminate the bond agreement is approved by the President, I immediately write a memorandum repeating the decision and circulate it about the offices in the government building, so that the demand is met. I am fortunate I can do this, for if the demand were of some other kind, over which I was powerless, then another more drastic approach would, and may have to be, taken. For now, the blackmailer is happy, and this gives me some time to work with Yulee and with Varinia.

Later: I summoned Yulee and discussed with him the above.

"I keep a file," he said, "called 'Enemies of Israel.' I shall make a copy of this note and compare speaking style with speaking style of each of the characters I have. Perhaps I shall come up with a match."

"My hunch, Yulee," I told him, "is that our man is someone *powerless* in the government, not a mouthpiece in the Congress. This enterprise is being conducted by a man with no other outlet."

"Nevertheless, I shall check all that I have."

Even later: I have taken myself about the city for a tour of the newspaper offices. I want to determine if the editors have any scent whatsoever of this story. I went in to the *Examiner,* the *Gazette,* and into the editorial offices of the *Southern Review.* Even Pollard, the editor of the *Enquirer,* seemed to have nothing cooking on the fire.

White Envelope, I concluded, must feel secure indeed, but in that security he may make another mistake or two and be caught. If we catch him in time and in the right way, we shall spare ourselves all disclosure. We are without bishops and without rooks but we may yet check this character with moves of our pawns and our queen.

In the meantime, the movement of the troops indicates that my Ada was right again about Grant's designs on Petersburg. The generals, including Beauregard and Meyers, are bestirring themselves to counter a possible seige of the city and are at work in positions south and east of here for fifteen miles. One cannot walk down the street without seeing all wagons commandeered for the purpose of dragging logs down for the defense of Petersburg. The long wagons, loaded and creaking with the weight of the lumber, remind me tearfully of the wagon David Seixas and his father used to drive along the forested road I loved to walk in Charleston. Had he only stayed in the lumber business and left the business of freeing the slaves to others, less loved by me, I could have him near me today!

June 9, 1864

I meet Yulee for breakfast in the Congress Pub. He is astir and brandishes a Tennessee newspaper which I have not read, although it is my habit to read at least one paper daily from every region of our country.

"Well, Yulee, have you found something?"

"There is another article here by that Reverend Day, you recall him, Judah, from three years ago, when you were in War?"

Yulee showed me the article in which Day, former dean at Yale, purports to have testimony from an unnamed classmate of mine, from 1829, in which it is asserted that I, a needy Jewish student, in order to defray costs of the expensive schooling, had been both a gambler and a thief. One night, this so-called testimony continues, he, the writer, went to bed and when I, it is said, perceived him asleep, I went through his pockets looking for spare dollars. He claims to have caught me red-handed. Thus, to avoid exposure and summary expulsion, I was asked to leave Yale.

"Totally preposterous, Yulee—all wrong. Even the date is erroneous, for I had left Yale in '28."

"Yes, but you must answer his charge with refutations, Judah."

"Why should I? This man is still trying to repay me for not making him a martyr in '61, when I got the Federals to free him. Between you and me, he prefers to be in the North, and he will end up there one day. In the North he has more people to attack—the Germans, the new immigrants, and so on. As to answering him, let others do that if they wish. I will let my career of service and honor and integrity be all the silent and contemptuous answer to his attack."

"I shall answer him for you, Judah."

"I would much prefer you to attend to my local troubles with White Envelope. What you cannot get through your Florida hide, Yulee, is that as long as there is ink, bigots will use it."

"But that's my point. This Day is a west Tennessee steward for Henry Foote. They are well connected."

"That is nothing, Yulee. Give me something to hang a lead on."

"Day has of late been to Europe through the blockade."

"To France?"

"Yes—to Amiens."

72

As the seige continues at Petersburg, food stores are scarce in Richmond. But words cannot describe what I saw today. After days of complaints in the press and milling about by distraught citizens shouting that non-soldiers had to eat to live, too, full-scale bread riots broke out in the southeastern quarter of the city. I was returning from my bank when I heard what sounded like the rumbling of thunder clouds. Two blocks to my left I perceived hundreds of people, mainly women and young girls, running as if being chased.

I made my way toward the tumult, and in so doing tried to call the attention of some young officers. When I got to Phillips Square, renamed Jackson Square, I saw the women storming the bakeries and shops on both sides of the mall. I had never heard such shrieking, and windows were broken in several stores and the trees newly planted in honor of the victory at Spotsylvania, were trampled. I could not tell if any one was hurt.

Fortunately Mr. Davis was about in his carriage with a small escort. He stood up on the seat of the buggy and yelled at the disorderly crowd. "Return to your homes, citizens, or I shall have all looters shot on sight." The President meant business, but just to make his point clearer, he reached down and his lieutenant handed up a revolver, which the President shot off into the air three times. The crowd dispersed, but the President, whom I joined for the trip back to the capitol building, was visibly shaken.

"I am only glad," he said to me, "that Varinia is at home this week visiting her father. She is spared the sight of this."

I am in receipt of another note from White Envelope.

Pay $3,000 to the same address as always.

In addition you will use your influence to have General Armistead's appointment to head the Trans-Mississippi Department blocked.

This is what I was afraid of. I can pay the money, but I have almost no influence about generals. And why, indeed, should I? Armistead is a fine general, and his appointment is undoubtedly assured. I believe he is to meet Davis later in the week, when he comes up from Petersburg. It is Armistead who is engineering the stalling of Grant so brilliantly to the south.

I have gone to the bank and written my bank check in the amount indicated. My funds are low, however, and I may have to ask Varinia if she can contribute to this effort. I know the complications are great, as the President is scrupulous about the spending of each dollar of his salary, and has his wife give him an accounting of the household budget on a monthly basis. But where else can the funds come from, unless I sell what land I have left? What good would it do to arouse suspicion by devoting my energies to the sale of personal property at a time when the capital is practically under siege? Yet I begin to feel the pinch of this blackmail business. Perhaps the bank check will hold them off. I must talk to Varinia.

For my part, I have decided to pursue the Slidell angle. That White Envelope wanted government business thrown to the Belmont, Slidell's father-in-law, indicates a strong connection.

And yet there is something askew about this theory, for Belmont grows richer by the day. He practically clothes and tents all of Lincoln's armies. What need has he of a few Confederate dollars, and obtained by such treacherous means?

I confess that when I lie down to sleep at night I am not completely free from the notion that I may put a quick end to this affair by eliminating my wife.

If it were not for my little Ninette, of whom I have heard nothing in six months, I would pluck this idea from the realm of fantasy and see more closely what it looks like. Though she is a blackmailer and an adulteress, whose infidelities may be the source of my own, she is also a mother, and my Ninette needs her mother.

June 22, 1864

The President is struck down with exhaustion and severe bronchitis. The doctor feels it may be the acute result of the bread riots, which deeply affected Mr. Davis. He is gone to Brierfield to rest for two weeks.

The appointment with General Armistead is therefore postponed, though not cancelled. And although Armistead's appointment seems certain, I have at least another two weeks to see if I may head off this catastrophe.

There are also two interesting communiqués today, which throw much light on this business. First, Erlanger has written from Paris that Mrs. Slidell has apparently put her foot down, and has made John choose between Colette and herself. According to Erlanger, John has made his choice, because the trysts with my wife have stopped. I wonder if Slidell has any notion that I know of the whole affair. However, the White Envelopes still continue. This leads me to conclude that Slidell is *not* the connection.

Second, I have received a response from Ada to my last letter.

Enclosed is the list of ships that have run the blockade, according to Yankee sources. The list naturally is not printed anywhere up here because they don't want to admit how many holes there really are in their socks.

I hope it is useful to you.

My *Mazeppa* is still the rage, and we are two weeks in Philadelphia, then two weeks in New York. The blue coats still hound me, and I can tell you a few new things about Yankee recruiting, if you do not know already. Recruiting officers took a fancy to my histrionics and insisted on taking me out to every tavern in Philadelphia. They have sent whole groups of professional recruiters to Europe, principally Ireland and Germany, to get enlistments for the Yankee regiments. I don't know if it means they're running low here, or desertions are on the increase, or what. But they pay in gold, five dollars per recruit, passage included, and uniforms and citizenship papers efficiently executed on the other side. Quite an operation. No more for now. The curtain goes up. Adieu—Ada.

I have spent the rest of the afternoon carefully checking the list of blockade runners which Ada supplied. The list is complete, as usual, with ports of call and final destination. I went to check out Yulee's lead, and we, strangely enough, have no record of one of our own blockade runners which made port in France recently, near Amiens. Perhaps it is a privateer, and sure enough, even this list of privateers in the past months has ships bound only for England and Germany. I have my doubts about the good Reverend's trip to Amiens, a city and a country of Catholics, for this man is hater of Romanism as well as Judaism. In any event, I have written Yulee a note to recheck his sources in the Tennessee delegation about the Reverend's recent itinerary, and to get the name of the ship and all the details.

It is a blistering hot day, and the mosquitoes seemed to have been reinforced of late. There is a grim joke about that the Yankees will have to leave off the seige of Petersburg less on account of our troopers than because the yellow-jackets are eating them alive. I have studied this question at great length and have come to the studious conclusion that a mosquito cannot tell a Yankee from one of our own. Witness the salve of calomine which I daub daily on my neck, and the towel wetted in water and camphor that I place under my collar, as do all the men of

Richmond, before they venture out at midday.

"I apologize to you," Yulee says to me, barging into my office, "I erred in that Day information. He went to Frankfurt-am-Main, not to Amiens."

"Quite a difference," I said.

"It doesn't hurt to keep track of these fellows, though. I have all his movements on file."

"Tell your informants in Tennessee that their efforts are appreciated, but I would ask them to use any spare hours they have to practice their reading."

"So," Yulee said, seating himself across from me, "where does that leave us, Judah?"

"We have ruled out Jeremiah Day, and I have ruled out Slidell, and any of their staff."

"So we are back where we started from."

"Not completely. We still have this Armistead business to go on. Who, we have to ask ourselves, could benefit from the denial of the appointment of Armistead?"

"I'm not privy to that kind of intelligence, Judah."

"Nor am I, my friend. But I know who is."

"Who would that be?"

"Varinia Davis knows more about what general is up for promotion, and what wife is already sewing brevet-general bars on the uniform. Believe me, she is a walking compendium of the files in the War Department. The President takes particular interest in this and they discuss it much."

"Then you have your next course to follow, Judah."

"I do indeed. I need only worry about time now. I don't know how many more weeks Varinia will be at Brierfield, and the President is due back in Richmond within two days. When he returns, Armistead will come for his appointment, and I am liable to wake up to a banner headline of gossip, scandal, and outrage."

"I think," Yulee observed, "the blackmailer would only leak out a little at a time. For what advantage accrues him if he were to tell all at once?"

"An astute point, my friend. Nevertheless, I see no advantage in delaying in finding this man before he does us more damage. I simply must hope that Varinia will return to the Capital soon."

"Could you not write her in some discreet way, Judah?"

"That would not be seemly. Simply tell me, Yulee, when you hear, as soon as you can, the time of the general's call on Mr. Davis."

July 4, 1864

Grant celebrated this day with a timely assault on the Petersburg breastworks. He lost five thousand more men, and although our losses were by comparison negligible, General Armistead, in rallying his men, received a mortal wound from a large mine which exploded to his left.

July 7, 1864

Today I attended the general's funeral. His noble form was attired in full uniform, with sash and sword. The coffin was silver mounted, and there was an inscription: "General Lewis Armistead, Brigadier General, died July 4, 1864, at Petersburg, Virginia, aged 42 years, Bravest of the Brave."

After twelve noon the coffin was closed and borne for more than a quarter of an hour in front of the cavalry escort, after which the coffin was transferred to a caisson covered in a magnificent Confederate flag, a wreath of lilies, and the cap and sword of the deceased. The members of the general's bodyguard, who had accompanied him to the city, walked with his remains to the railway station, where the body was placed in a special car which left, under escort, for Lynchburg, Virginia, the place of the general's birth.

Fate has intervened on my behalf and has prevented General Armistead from obtaining the promotion to head of the trans-Mississippi.

White Envelope, who has been quiet for three weeks, will undoubtedly remain so for some time to come. I nevertheless continue regular payments to my wife, at the Amiens address, as per instructions.

EDITOR'S NOTE:

From July 7, 1864 on, there are scant entries in the Benjamin Diaries until February and April of the following year. Union troops surround the remnants of Lee's Army of Northern Virginia and place a stranglehold on Richmond.

With the exception of two entries in the winter of 1864 we hear nothing from the Secretary of State—either about the progress of the War or the blackmail plot against him and the wife of Jefferson Davis. Why the silence? No definite answer is available except that we know of Benjamin's disposition to throw himself into the breach in a time of crisis and work ceaselessly until resolution. During this period Sherman's massive pincer movements in Georgia and the Carolinas presented an imminent threat to the Confederacy and particularly to the diplomacy of recognition which Benjamin worked so painstakingly upon. It may be wise, therefore, to review briefly the military aspect of the war in this period.

From May 2 through September, William Tecumseh Sherman marched 100,000 Union troops from Chattanooga, Tennessee to Georgia. At Resaca, New Hope Church, and Kenesaw Mountain, General Joseph Johnston fought a series of defensive actions against Sherman and tried unsuccessfully to cut off communications. Sherman repulsed him and crossed the Big Chattahoochee River, only eight miles from Atlanta.

President Davis, impatient with Johnston, replaced him with John Hood, and gave Hood instructions to be more aggressive. Hood attacked Sherman's superior force on two occasions, but was hurled back with heavy losses to the entrenchments of Atlanta. Within the ensuing days,

Hood evacuated Atlanta and Sherman occupied the city. Northern morale, previously shaken by Grant's losses at Petersburg, was lifted, and the Southern armies moved full swing into a defensive posture, contributing to the Republican Party's success in the presidential campaign.

November 8, 1864

Lincoln is elected again. It is of course no surprise, but his majority is only 300,000 votes. This is heartening to the President, who feels there is strong support among the people of the North to give us our independence, even if their leaders won't.

But this optimism seems to me belated, for we are eating mule meat in Richmond.

December 12, 1864

Savannah has fallen to Sherman. My mother, may she rest in peace, died of natural causes before the bombardment. Becky is unscathed and works at the Abercrombie Hospital.

"There are no sides in this hospital," she writes, "and a wound is a wound, and Yankee and Confederate bleed both the same."

White Envelope has lain low, as have we all, during Sherman's maneuvers. Lee is down to 60,000 men, and the Union ranks continue to swell in recruits, the tide of which we are unable to stop. Their bellies swell, too, on Southern pork and poultry. Yet Hood did sting Sherman at Peachtree Creek, and if their lines of communication and supply can be cut, the Yankees could still be driven off.

There is still no recognition coming our way. The English were pleased by Ambassador Kenner's proposal for the abolition of slavery, but they said it would not affect their neutrality regarding our civil war.

These days my thoughts turn more and more to Becky and to Ada Isaacs.

In mid-December, Hood, under instructions from President Davis, changed his strategy and tried to prevent Sherman from leaving Atlanta. But the boxing tactics did not work, and Sherman moved out with 60,000 troops in his march to the sea. Before leaving Atlanta, however, he destroyed or confiscated all supplies useful to the Confederates. On his march across Georgia, his army cut a swath to the sea, 300 miles in length, 60 miles in width. Factories, cotton gins, warehouses, bridges, railroads and government buildings were systematically destroyed. The soldiers of his army were ordered "to forage liberally on the country," and wild looting ensued. But the march to Savannah was virtually unopposed. From these positions Sherman sent out small armies to seize food-producing and munitions-producing outposts of the Confederate army.

The Benjamin Diaries resume with some consistency early in February 1865, at which time Lincoln offered President Davis a peace conference at Hampton Roads aboard the Union transport *River Queen*. President Davis agreed to send Vice President Stephens to confer with Lincoln and Union Secretary of State Seward, but he insisted on recognition of Southern independence as a basis for the conference. On this point Benjamin had some reservations, and thus his entry of February, 1865.

February 1, 1865

After a long and welcome absence, White Envelope has emerged again, and upon my desk I find his note and a threat.

You will oppose every way you can the proposed peace conference with murderer Lincoln. If President

Davis wishes to attend, you will counsel against. We will have no defeatism now. Just because you have been between the sheets with first lady of the confederacie, [sic.] you do not have the power you think. The ragpicker in you will not infect the fighting spirit of the South. You will be held personally responsible if a cowardly peace is signed.

Send $1000 in silver certificates immediately.

Perhaps I made a mistake but I showed this note immediately to Varinia.

"We must find this skunk, Judah," she said, as we walked down the corridor of the customs house. We have taken to being seen only in public places. "This will break Jefferson, if ever he sees it."

"And us," I said, with the slight irony which always seems to surface when I am in a drowning pool. "For us the printing of this virulence will attach us years hence. If it is ever printed, although we shall labor to prevent it, you may deny everything, as I will. I have faith in the vindication of time."

"Judah Benjamin," said the first lady, "you are a godsend to me and to this Confederacy. Although you have not fought in the field, you are my much decorated hero, Mr. Secretary, and you shall always be. No matter what happens between us from now on, no matter what happens between you and Jefferson, if God forbid this information leaks, I want you to know that wherever you will be, Jefferson and I will always be thinking of you."

And then she kissed me. And when I tried to stop her, because some officers were right then walking by, she said, "Their peeping-Tom eyes can rot in their skulls for all I care, Judah. If I were the Virgin Mary they would find some fault with me."

We embraced with strength and a conviction that it was our last.

Before parting, I said to her, "We might head off some of these disasters if you get me that information I requested on Armistead's next-in-line."

"I have finally talked that Mrs. Johnston into letting me have tea with her in her husband's offices, where I think I shall find what you want. You'll have the information in a matter of days."

In this matter of the Hampton Roads conference, however, I have no choice but to pursue what my own best thinking is for the sake of the country. I will make my proposals to the President without regard for personal considerations. When I explained this to Varinia, she instantly concurred, and we parted, not knowing what the next few days would hold for us, but with the knowledge that in these hours of trial, the needs of the Confederacy take precedence over our own.

February 12, 1865

Today for the first time I argued vehemently with President Davis.

He had asked me to draw up some simple instructions for the guidance of Vice-President Stephens for the meeting with Lincoln, and I did so gladly. My instructions read: "You are hereby requested to proceed to Washington City for conference with Mr. Lincoln upon the subject to which his (Lincoln's) note relates."

Davis asked me if I had read Lincoln's offer carefully.

I admit to being somewhat insulted by this inquiry, as I always read *everything* carefully. I told him I had read the note several times.

"Then what make you, Benjamin, of this phrase of Lincoln's that he is willing 'to bring peace to the people of *our one common country*'?"

"I make out, sir, that Lincoln still feels, as he has said so many times, that he is engaged in fighting a *civil* war, and he perceives one country still intact."

"So do you not see opportunity here to push for a recognition of these States as separate, as basis for this conference?"

"There is opportunity, I suppose, Mr. President," I answered him, "but I feel that the vaguest of phrasing in our return note is needed, lest they cancel the conference, which we could not benefit from."

Davis sat down and all the weariness of fighting this long war sagged into the chair with him. "But Benjamin, do you not think that if we respond to this note as it is, that Lincoln may construe it as an admission that peace would be made on the basis of one common country, that is, a restoration of the Union?"

"I have no objection, sir," I answered him, "to have the conference convened on a one-country basis, if that is what is required to bring the parties to the table."

"But after your herculean labors to gain recognition, you are willing to send Stephens and the others as 'rebels' facing their President Lincoln? I confess I do not understand you, Benjamin."

"What think you, Mr. President, that Lincoln will offer us, and think you that it will be any different if Mr. Stephens is, on paper, rebel or Vice President of a sovereign country?"

"It is a matter of pride and honor, Mr. Secretary."

"That may be, sir, but it is also a question of tactics. According to my thinking, we are going to be offered unconditional surrender, no matter what wording. We may yet benefit from the conference, however, if we show a willingness to negotiate. Let Lincoln say that we must surrender. The South's answer may be to stiffen resistance, to rally against Lincoln's uncompromisingness, and the people of the North themselves may sicken of prolonged war and put pressure on this new and yet untried administration to sue for peace on better terms—at the *next* conference. This is the way, sir, that I see it."

The President rolled the model cannon across his desk, then rolled it back again. "Your remarks are appreciated, Mr. Secretary, but you shall send Stephens with the following instructions: 'In conformity with the letter of Mr. Lincoln, you are requested to proceed to Washington City for informal conference with him upon the issues involved in the existing war, and for the purpose of securing peace to the *two countries*.

"Please read it back to me, Benjamin, for accuracy."

I read the instructions back to him just as he had dictated them, and then, without any amenities, I left his office.

March 4, 1865

The conference has failed.

I have read newspaper accounts of Lincoln's second inaugural address with a sickening feeling in my stomach. "With malice toward none; with charity for all . . . let us strive on to finish the work we are in; to bind up the nation's wounds . . . to do all which may achieve and cherish a just and lasting peace."

All I sense about me is malice and wounds and war, continuing as long as there is one Confederate boy still to bleed.

Late today I received another letter from Becky. It is, I fear, the last I shall get for some time, considering what the Yankees are doing to cordon us off here in Richmond. But it is a source of quiet joy for me to read:

Savannah, Ga.

Dearest Judah:

I hope this letter finds you well and that you are not troubling yourself with the poison the newspapers are printing about you. Every public official, Christian or Jew or Brahmin, if there was such, would at a time like this be most vulnerable to personal attack.

Momma is finally at rest, and she lies now next to Father whose remains, according to your instructions, I had brought from Beaufort. They share a single stone, and the inscription you requested from Exodus, "And they went forth into the land," is handsomely done. I pray that some day you and I may pay our respects to them together.

To change from this solemn subject, I wanted to tell you that I met an officer, whom I believe you know, when the Yankees occupied the city. Upon

85

their arrival the officers began to hunt up comfortable quarters, and I found myself under the necessity of either taking three of them in as boarders or submitting to the confiscation of our house for the purpose of sheltering the foe.

Much to my relief, one of the officers, a colonel, turned out to be exceedingly polite. Not only did he go out of his way to prevent the confiscation of my silver and jewelry, which has happened to many others, he escorted me on a number of occasions outside the perimeter beyond which civilians are not allowed to go, for the purpose of decorating Momma's stone. He accompanied me most nobly, and at the house, over dinner, made polite conversation, and even complimented the southern soldiers as the bravest in the world, although he claimed for himself and his peers the credit for possessing more strategic ability than our generals. 'You can beat us in fighting, madam,' said he, 'but we can out-manoeuvre you; your generals do not work half enough; we work day and night, and spare no labor, nor pains, to carry out our plans.'

Who does this noble Yankee colonel turn out to be, Judah, but Colonel Samuel Porter, your classmate from Yale! He sends you his deepest and warmest affections. He is a fine example that our barbarous foes are not entirely lost to all the dictates and impulses of humanity. Would to God exhibitions of kindness, such as Colonel Porter's, were more frequent in their occurrence.

> My love to you, my brother,
> Becky

As I worked late tonight in my office Yulee happened in. He looked haggard, as does everyone on this diet of mule stew and hard work. Only I look good, they always say, and I wonder what is the secret of my constitution. Except perhaps that I stimulate my system regularly with French brandy and Havana cigars, which no war or block-.

ade could prevent me from obtaining, I have no secret.

Yulee has some files under his arm and he asks me to send over some cigars to the Tennesseans in Congress. "It'll make them mighty happy, Judah."

"Long have I known, Yulee, that the Havana cigar is the secret to success in politics. But come, let us not discuss tobacco. What have you there tucked away?"

I noticed a stirring in the recesses of the office, beyond the last desks, but ascribed it to mice or rats. Yulee, absorbed in the cigars in my humidor, noticed nothing.

"For you, from Mrs. Davis. She asked me to bring them to you, with her compliments."

The files were indeed what I had been waiting for. I combed Armistead's file, Beauregard's, Johnston's, Meyers', and those of all the men who had put in for appointment to the trans-Mississippi department for a clue to White Envelope. Beauregard and Meyers, who are among my bitterest public foes, apparently have no interest in the position.

"Let us then rule out general officers, Yulee," I concluded. "You take these," I handed him half, "and I shall go through the others until we find some connection."

We were thus engaged in these files for some time by lamplight. I found nothing in what I read, just names of officers, positions interested in, backgrounds in the Federal army, grades, recommendations from superiors, and so on.

"Here's something strange, Judah," said Yulee between puffs of his cigar." This Lieutenant Colonel Joseph La Rue, who had been on Armistead's staff."

"Yes—go on, Yulee."

"Well, he was dismissed last year, before the seige."

"Yes, so what? So were Hooker and Kenner and Richland."

"But this La Rue has papers from the Virginia Military Institute in the name of Jones. Yes, look, Judah! Joseph La Rue Jones. Isn't that the name of the clerk they sent over to you from War?"

"Indeed it is," I said, jumping to my feet and peering over Yulee's shoulder at the file. "Born, New Orleans, that checks out, same age more or less."

"Could it be a brother, Judah?"

"Indeed, Yulee, it could be a brother, a discredited officer whom Armistead dismissed, and whom Jones is trying to bribe back into line for promotion. I think. . ." and just then a chair was knocked over in the back of the office and the clerk himself, Mr. Beauchamp Jones, went running down the aisle past us at a tear. "Grab him, David!" I shouted, and in the dim light Yulee reached out his immense arms. I blocked the door, and David had my slick clerk by the neck.

"Look, Judah," Yulee said, immensely pleased with his catch, "this guttersnipe has made me ruin my cigar." I think I shall light him up and smoke him instead." Then David began to squeeze the clerk's arm until he screamed.

"Enough, David," I said, "turn the light up so we may spend a few minutes talking with Mr. Jones."

But just as Yulee leaned over the desk to reach the lamp, Jones pulled out of his coat pocket his navy revolver, which he had loaned me months before when I went to Baltimore.

"You made a mistake in returning me the gun, Mr. Secretary," said he. "Now both of you keep your distance. That's right. I will leave now," he said, somewhat breathless from his tussle with Yulee, "by this door. If either of you follows me, I will have no qualms about shooting."

Yulee lurched toward him, Jones withdrew, and I shouted at Yulee, "For God's sake, don't! What does he have to lose now?"

"That's right, Mr. Secretary," he said, "you are one smart Jew. I shall see you tomorrow morning in the office, bright and early, and there will not be a thing you can do to me. Figure that one out, Mr. Secretary, if you will. Now don't follow, and keep this hairy ape from chasing me, d'you hear?" He made his way out the door, as Yulee and I stood there, realizing that we had identified our blackmailer but had not stopped him.

After Jones's footfalls became inaudible and we could relax, Yulee collapsed on my divan. "I could have broken the arm of that trash," he said bitterly. "Your politeness to a criminal has done you in, sir."

"So you could have broken his arm, Yulee; he still could talk."

"Then you should have let me break his mouth, as well. The source of such foulness as he puts into those notes deserves setting aright."

"And I suppose you could have broken every bone in his body, but think you this man a fool? Think you that my wife Colette herself is not poised in Paris to give such information to Federal ministers as could appear in a month's time in Northern papers and then make its way into press? And think you that this man has no accomplices here? What of Lieutenant Joseph Jones? Blackmail, Yulee, is like an evil root that has many branches. To stop it, all the branches must be found and cut off. Cut one root, and it continues to grow. This Jones is the instigator, but he is now just one part. I wanted to use some savvy on him, convince him I am intimidated, to find out who else is aware of this business."

"I still say he should have been given a good taste of my knuckles."

"The screws will now tighten, Yulee, but we have at least identified the enemy. Be so kind as to inform Varinia Davis when you have the opportunity. And do not assault Jones if you chance to see him in my offices, for surely he will be here, bright and early, as he promises."

As Yulee looked glum, I gave him half a dozen cigars and thanked him for his labors.

March 5, 1865

Just as he had indicated, Mr. Beauchamp Jones was in the office at half-past eight. As I had not left (I have a divan to sleep on, and a washstand in my alcove), I was there when he entered and took his stool. I had spent the remainder of the night pondering just who this man was, for the name of the brother, La Rue, had echoes of familiarity for me. I stared at Jones for some moments trying to fix his character by staring at the eye, which after all is the door to the soul, but much as I stared I could not get beyond a surface glaze and my stare was richocheted off. It was Jones who began the long awaited tete-a-tete.

"Oh, we do indeed know each other for quite some time, Mr. Secretary," said he. "But perhaps you were not as aware of me as I was of you."

"Mr. Jones, I have been paying you a great deal of money."

"You have been paying me *and* your wife a great deal of money," he corrected.

"Yes. May I now for all that expense be spared your circumlocutions?"

He sat there with an impish smirking on his face, expecting me, I suppose, to squirm or to be restless. He took out his handkerchief and patted dry the sweat on his neck. Anyone who would have happened in on the office then, either an orderly or the President himself, would have had no reason to suspect there was anything more going on than a usual business exchange between the Secretary of State and one of his clericals.

"Do you recall New Orleans, fall of 1828, Mr. Benjamin? Do you recall Madame Roselius?" he began.

This was, of course, when I arrived from Charleston, and Roselius was one of the Creole ladies I tutored to learn the *patois*. I had not at that time yet decided to study law. "I have a reputation for some feats of memory, Mr. Jones. Of course, I remember."

"Let me see, then, how good your memory really is. If you remember the madame, then do you also recall any of her. . ." Here Jones stuttered somewhat, as was his wont. "Do you remember any of her servants?"

"By face, I suppose, Jones, but not by name."

"Look well into this face, then, Mr. Secretary, for you are looking into the face of Madame Roselius' coachman, who drove you back many times to your rooms after your little lessons with the lady."

It was hard to believe. Could it be a fabrication, a well-researched plan to make me think him familiar with my entire life, and thus have me in a weaker position? I paused, trying to go rapidly through the file of my memo-

90

ry. There of course was a coachman; there were always so many servants.

"Perhaps, Jones, I only saw your back as you sat on the box of the carriage. A face like yours one does not easily forget. And, sir," said I, growing angry even though I tried to keep it controlled, "if I have my way with you again, it will be only your back, if that, which I shall want to look at, as you walk out of my life."

"It will not be so easy, Mr. Benjamin," he said. "Shall I then tell you some more about that period in our lives, my role in which you have either conveniently forgotten or were never aware of. Shall I?"

"Have I any choice, Mr. Jones?"

"None whatsoever."

"Then, pray tell, Mr. Jones, proceed with your extortion. I only ask that you bring to it the same expeditious dispatch which you show in your other work."

"I shall be brief." Here he took a long breath, in which much of the past was summoned up. "In addition to having in common Madame Roselius, for whom we both worked, we also have in common a man you may recall as John La Rue."

"Dr. John La Rue?"

"The same," said he. "Dr. John La Rue's baptized full name is John La Rue Jones. He is—he was—my father."

This was an extreme strain on my credibility, but as I stared at Jones, I found in his face a vestige of the smile that was John La Rue's. John had been one of my earliest and best friends in New Orleans. Others had called him a charlatan and a mountebank, a veterinarian who treated people when he should have cured horses, but I found him to be a talented, fascinating and kindly character. If this blackmailer before me, who has been the source of so much misery, is indeed La Rue's descendent, I can only stand in wonderment at what things must pass between fathers and sons.

"I loved John La Rue, Jones."

"Very touching. I suppose he cared for you much more than he did for me. Certainly more than he cared for my mother, whom he abandoned. And more than he cared for my brother as well. Every time he talked of you, Benjamin, I cringed. 'A smart little Jew that Benjamin is,' he would say. 'I think it profitable that I make of him a good friend.'"

"And so he did. Is your father dead, Jones?"

"The pox took him before the war. But I am not here to have you eulogize him, whose libertine and unvirtuous life found its appropriate end. I'm here to talk about you. They had no right to invite you to join their society, the Roseliuses, the Mazareaus, and the rest of them. You were a tutor, and I a coachman. We were on the same level. I by birth, however, am much higher than you, who are a Jew. I am at least half Creole. But they overlooked me and made the grievous mistake of taking you in. Why I shall never know, except perhaps that they were fooled by the change you jangled in your pocket or by your Jew merchant connections. They may have been fooled, but not I.

"By every right I should have been invited to the Creole balls, not you. I loved Colette Mazareau with a love you never had, and which you are not capable of. And she loved me—she told me as much, Benjamin. Yes, Colette Mazareau, your wife.

"She loved me and would have married me, but her parents had chosen you and she could not go against their wishes. Ever since then I have taken a particularly keen interest in the development of your career. You and Colette have never strayed too far from me."

"I am," said I, "flattered by your obsession. But if you did not know it already, I want to inform you I am no naïve man. My wife has for many years lived her own life. We have an understanding."

"You have it no more, Mr. Secretary. For your information, when I was with the Department of the Navy, before the war, I had opportunity to travel and to visit Colette many times in Paris. We began the relationship that had never been, and our plan—this plan—has been in the making for some time."

"Let me stoop to your level for a moment, Jr. Jones. The fine Creole wife you think I got upon marriage was already damaged merchandise, sir—if you get my meaning. If this was not done by you, as apparently it was not, my virtuous friend, then it was done by another, less virtuous soul. Or maybe it was several souls that the inimitable Colette had already attracted to herself by the tender age of sixteen."

"I won't let your disgusting glib tongue deflect me from my tasks. I want to meet with you and with Mrs. Davis, here in this office, at this same hour. You two must be here without fail," he said. "And should anything happen to me, should I be arrested or detained in any way, a packet containing the complete history of this little affair, along with documents, bank drafts and so forth, is at the office of a colleague of mine, who has instructions to open them and print them immediately. Do I make my meaning clear, Mr. Benjamin?"

"Crystal clear, Mr. Jones. But what, sir, makes you so certain I shall do what you ask?"

"You will do everything I ask," he said, "because you want to save your swarthy hide."

"Then are we through talking for today, Mr. Jones?"

"For today, yes," said he.

I went immediately to Yulee and asked him to call on the first lady on my behalf.

March 6, 1865

This morning, dressed as usual in his neat black suit, the punctilious Mr. Jones made his demands.

First, the $3,000,000 in gold bullion now in the trans-Mississippi Department, and designated to be moved to Richmond, is to be placed in the command of Lieutenant Colonel Joseph La Rue. The shipment will be diverted to the port of Corpus Christi and placed on the ship *Norfolk* bound for France.

Second, subsequent to this appointment, all telegraphic communications from Richmond to the trans-Mississippi department shall cease.

Third, rail transportation and passes shall be provided

for both Mr. Beauchamp Jones and for the Lieutenant Colonel. If there be any pursuit, hostages will be taken along the route and, if necessary, executed.

Varinia, who had sat and listened with an astonishing tranquility, spoke, when Jones had finished, in the tones of a mother to a child who has a hot poker and does not know how dangerous it is. She was very calm. "You're aware, are you not, Mr. Jones, that the $3,000,000 has been set aside for the treatment of Confederate war wounded, for hospital supplies and rehabilitation?"

"Yes, ma'am, I am," Jones replied.

"Then what soured your patriotism to perform a deed like this?"

"What use our patriotism, madam, when these shy-locks," herein he honored me with his glance, "have our government in a stranglehold from all the way back in 1861. What use my patriotism, madam, when he hoards his millions and makes bargains in Confederate blood with his banker friends in Europe?"

"And yet do you not emulate this," Varinia reasoned, "by the very enterprise you pursue?"

"No, indeed. When I get to Europe I shall set up a Confederate government in exile. I want you to tell Mr. Davis, madam, that he may join me there to serve the Cause."

As Varinia's attempt to deal with this man seemed to be foundering, I decided to use a different tack. "And will Miss Mazareau be your first lady, Mr. Jones? I would not advise it, sir. Take it from her husband. She will be about as faithful to you as a sieve is to water."

"Judah," Varinia whispered with alarm, "he'll kill you."

"He can't," I answered. "He needs us."

"Shut up, you little rabbi," he said. "If I do not see action taken on the demands which I've outlined, I will do the following:

"One, release the packet of documents concerning this affair to the newspapers.

"Two, release to the Northern press the complete file on the Jewess spy, Belle Boyd, otherwise known as Ada Isaacs. She is in Washington right now, is she not, Mr.

Benjamin? If that material is released, she ought to be picked up for treason in the time it takes to make a noose. Wouldn't you say, sir?"

"I should have had you drafted and stood you in front of a Yankee bullet when I had the chance, Mr. Jones."

"Well, you have missed it, Mr. Benjamin, and now you have three days to put into operation all that I have outlined. Good day, Madam First Lady, and good day to you, Mr. Secretary of State."

March 9, 1865

We are being shelled daily here, as are Petersburg again and Fort Steadman to the east. There is rumor that Lee will be trying to break through at Steadman, but he holds no advantage whatsoever over Grant. The only way out of Richmond now is by way of Lynchburg. The stores are empty, people pack their belongings and leave every day in spite of government proclamations to stay. The war has finally caught up with us in Richmond.

Communications are skeletal. Late today I sent a message to Ada Isaacs. It is in cipher, a code we have prepared for just such an eventuality. I want her gradually to move south, by certain steps, so that I can keep track of her and know more or less where she shall be on a given date. She also has instructions to burn all papers that would identify her or her work as Belle Boyd. I earnestly hope the message gets through.

I have not seen Varinia in the three days given us by Jones. Nor has Jones made an appearance in the tents now being used for the Department of State. Our offices at the Customs House were vacated as we had intelligence they had been targeted for shelling.

Davis has issued a brief resolution calling on the soldiers and citizenry to carry on the struggle. This paper is now posted on what trees remain standing in Richmond. At the President's request, I edited the proclamation, and with his permission I added the brief epilogue; lines which, from the very first I read them as a boy, never cease to stir

95

me:

To submit to our enemies now, would be more infamous than it would have been in the beginning. It would be cowardly yielding to power what was denied upon principle. It would be to yield the cherished right of self-government, and to acknowledge ourselves wrong in the assertion of it; to brand the names of our slaughtered companions as traitors; to forfeit glory already won; to lose the fruits of all the sacrifices made and the privations so long endured; to give up independence now nearly gained, and bring certain ruin, disgrace and eternal slavery upon our country.

I call upon you, soldiers of the Confederacy, to fight on!

Therefore, unsubdued by past reverses, and unawed by future dangers, we declare our determination to battle to the end, and not to lay down our arms until independence is secured. Is life so dear, or peace so sweet, as to be purchased at the price of chains and slavery? Forbid it, Heaven!

Only the *Enquirer* and the *Gazette* continue to publish abbreviated editions of their daily papers. The other papers have ceased work, either because they have no staff or because their presses have been damaged by the shellings. I have asked Yulee to check with both the editors of these papers. My hunch is that Pollard of the *Enquirer,* long a government gadfly and no friend of mine, may have the packet which Jones spoke of.

"And if he has the packet," Yulee said, "he surely will not admit to it or locate it for me."

"Just establish its whereabouts by inference, if only by that. Is it at the editor's home, or at the office? Get that much and let me know. My hunch is the office, but I need a closer examination of the premises if we are to seize them."

"Seize them?" Yulee asked.

"By government order, Yulee. It is almost arranged. I have found enough good men here to work with me on this."

"Good, then," said Yulee. "I will get my hands on Jones's neck once again."

March 11, 1865

"I must see you at once," Varinia's note read. "I shall meet you at the residence of the Mallorys of the Navy Department at two o'clock today. Be there without fail."

When I arrived, I saw her awaiting me on the veranda of the house, two columns of which had been shot away. By the third the first lady waited in black dress and bonnet.

"Judah," she told me, taking my hands, "I told Jefferson everything this morning."

I was stunned. "I could have prevented it all. I had a plan. I had Yulee secure—"

"Judah, there will be no way to keep that man from telling the world. He is crazy. I wanted Jefferson to hear it from me, not from headlines."

"And his reaction, Varinia?"

"He took his revolvers and put them in his belt. Then he said he had had enough of paperwork for the day and he was going out with his escort to do a little spirit-rousing among the troops." I waited for what I knew would come next. "He also said he would like to see you tomorrow morning, Judah, right here in this parlor. He took it calmly, as I had not expected."

"The war is undoubtedly lost, Varinia, and your husband is many things, but a calm man is not one of them. I wish you had only let me try to contain it."

"As skillful as you are in these matters, Judah, there are some things you cannot touch. There is, for example, the diplomacy of the heart. I am going to be living with Jefferson after this ordeal is over. I must be prepared for that."

I understood fully what she meant and had no response

to make. I left her standing on the veranda of the house to which I would return on the morrow.

I felt that things were slowly slipping from my grasp. At the tent I found dispatches which indicated General Kirby-Smith of the trans-Mississippi Department had assumed full control of the entire area, its munitions, and wealth, including the goldbullion. Even if I were on the terms of conversation with the President, it is doubtful that this assumption of power could be reversed. I do not know if I even want to attempt it. Kirby-Smith may be able to resist the Yankees. This Jones will steal the money and dash our last hopes. If we are to lose the war, we shall lose it fighting, not to the thieves within our own ranks.

Yulee entered the tent an hour after I arrived.

"Pollard at the *Enquirer* does have the packet," he said. "But Pollard said he would not print the rubbish that was in it."

"He read it?"

"Apparently he broke the seal. He said that there was no love lost bestwen himself and Jones, who was always battering him for permission to write articles. Pollard said Jones's style was not good enough."

"Just good enough for blackmail threats."

"He said, Judah, that he had no interest in salting the wounds of the Confederacy."

"And where is the packet now?"

"I gave him one of your havanas, I had one, and when we finished smoking, before the cigars went out, we lit the packet and burned it to ashes."

"And where is Mr. Jones, Yulee?"

"I have not seen him since he drew the revolver on me."

March 12, 1865

There is at least some good news from the field, which is, surprisingly enough, what the President informs me of when I enter his office. Kirby-Smith has given the Yankees a defeat in Arkansas.

"The Yankees must be getting overconfident. They had

98

no intelligence about General Smith's position during the night?"

"Overconfident, nothing! Mr. Benjamin, I can see you are no military man. If I had been there I would have done the same thing as Smith. Maybe I would have been bolder and would have made the maneuvers by daylight. The Yankees were committed to an attack, and Smith knew it. It was just a matter of when."

We sat down after the President's strenuous explanation and then he pulled a cord which hung from the ceiling. An orderly came in and Davis indicated he wanted coffee for two. I would have been more than content to drink coffee and listen to military tactics the whole day. For, in fact, the President often discusses such affairs. He is truly a frustrated general. He would trade his desk and his luxurious comforts, by Richmond standards, for a brigadier's tent. Mr. Davis often tells me how lost battles could have been won. Davis is a straightforward man, and that is why I am somewhat nonplussed with all this militarism when the real target is not the Yankees, but me.

"At Gettysburg," he said, "I would have held up the charge at Seminary Ridge and moved in a pincer action, I with one half the army and Lee with the other half in an immense circle around the Union emplacements. We would have sent them running with their tails between their legs, Mr. Benjamin. We would have!"

I admire the President immensely, but this military braggadoccio is a defect in an otherwise noble character. What head of state puts a revolver in his belt and goes out to meet the troops returning from the field? Is this a Caesar? Does a head of government make himself a target for Yankee sharpshooters covering a retreating Union column? Yet Davis has done this innumerable times, and is in fact refreshed by it. Then he comes back to Richmond, and the business of government goes on. What I admire most about him is that he accepts his position, which he didn't want, and he labors night and day to keep the departments of government functioning.

He hands me another speech and says, "I have to do a little more spirit-rousing for the troops. What do you think?"

Before I can begin going over the prose he says, "Mr. Benjamin, I have always admired your ability to turn a phrase. Mrs. Davis never tires of telling me that you are the most articulate of my ministers. That you are the most trustworthy, most dedicated, and the most wise."

"The lady praises too much, Mr. President," I interrupted. He rolls a miniature cannon across the papers which clutter his desk. He stands up, walks to the window, to the door, back to the desk, and another roll of the cannon. At each point he glances at me out of his deep tired eyes, and his glances encompass me. My hand moves involuntarily to my pocket where I keep the white envelopes. My fingers roll up nervously in my palm.

"If this is all true, Mr. Benjamin, why have you done this thing to me? It must be true that every commander has his Brutus, Mr. Benjamin, for if this is not turning on me, then nothing is. How long has this been going on?"

As there are never words for a moment like this, I was silent. All I noticed was how poor the President's vision was by now, how deeply impaired his gait. He limped as he stalked the room. He was a shattered man. He went to the window seat and pulled the curtains back. The cloudbursts of Yankee cannon balls descending on Richmond could be seen peppering the sky. Then he repeated his question.

"I apologize to you, sir."

"I held you in my estimation, Mr. Benjamin, as a trusted friend," he said with an even tone. "At times, when you joined us for dinners, and stayed late after the other guests had gone home, I felt in the presence of a brother. I felt in my periods of sickness that you could be relied upon to run the government. I also had felt on occasion that it was you who should have been president of this country, not I —you who are never sick, who are always optimistic, whom no criticism seems to touch."

"Mr. President, there is no man such as you describe in this room. Nor, I imagine, does such a man exist anywhere."

"Perhaps not, Benjamin. Perhaps only in the mind of

100

the husband of the woman you've taken. Were I a younger man, and were this Mississippi, you and I would not be talking now but struggling in the dust with a knife flashing between us. Now I have no choice but to challenge you to a duel on the field of honor."

"Mr. President," I began, and I wanted to explain to him that even had I wanted to, I could not have taken his wife from him. I wanted to explain this and many things and talk to him like the brother whom I also felt him to be, but he would not let me speak.

"No words, Mr. Benjamin, but yes or no. I must dispose of this matter. I am a busy man. I have a war to run."

Just then a Yankee shell exploded not fifty yards off.

"You must let me speak, Mr. Davis, because in this matter I am not Secretary of State and you are not President, but I am a man confronting another man. I want to make a formal apology to you. It was your wife's good sense that convinced me of the foolishness we had stumbled into. She spoke only of caring for you. I felt only your surrogate. Her true loyalty and faithfulness never departed. I beg you, Mr. Davis, to see it in this light and to take back your challenge."

"I take back nothing, Benjamin, and I want no more claptrap. I am a lawyer myself, but I know when a simple answer is called for, and not a speech. Here is occasion for a simple answer if there ever was one."

"Mr. President," I said, "the Yankees are breathing down our necks. The cabinet must meet. If you or I. . . ."

"Damn the Yankees!" he shouted, throwing the model cannon from his desk to the floor, so that his whole frame shook.

"And you, sir," I said, "because of your sacrifices, can hardly see out of both your eyes. You can hardly walk."

"That will not interfere with my dueling you, Mr. Benjamin."

"How can I duel with a man in your physical condition? You cannot see," I repeated, "and you cannot walk, sir."

"And you, Mr. Benjamin," he spat back at me, "have undoubtedly never fired a pistol in your whole office-bound life."

"Then, sir," I said, with the greatest reluctance of my life, "I suppose we are a perfect match."

Thus the President of the Confederate States of America challenged me to a duel on this morning, as Richmond was slowly being encircled by a column of Sherman's army. Mr. Davis said his valet would be his second, and I, for mine, offered Congressman Yulee.

March 23, 1865

The government is expecting to flee.

Sherman sues for peace.

The edict to give up the city could come from Davis at any moment. He has abandoned the northern terraces to the enemy to pack the wagons. Varinia has been forbidden by him to see me. That was over ten days ago. But there is chaos here and her will is her own. We talked this afternoon as I packed state papers. My agents in Canada, in their final dispatch, told me I must take the papers or burn them. Contacts in the north could be terribly hurt.

The office was crowded with soldiers removing furniture, files, and records. I packed as we talked. She was in her bonnet and shawl.

"You have to convince him," I told her, "that this duel is idiocy. Use whatever words you must."

"Jeff does not talk about it any more. The last he said was that he would rather kill you than the Yankees."

"That is hard to believe."

"Even harder for me. He is just awaiting the seconds to set time, place, and weapons."

"Idiocy, pure idiocy," I shouted. Any one in the office could hear me. I didn't care. "Dueling! Honor! Is it possible I do not understand this country, in which I have lived and fought all these long years!"

"You have slept with a man's wife, Judah!"

"A dozen men have slept with my wife in Europe these past twenty years! And you know something, Varinia, I pity them all. All of them. I pity them, and that is my

102

weapon, that is how I do my dueling. If you had let me handle this, nothing would have happened. Now you're liable to have both of us killed. And in the meantime this Jones is still at large, a danger to us all. Hasn't your husband taken steps to apprehend him? Has he lost his wits completely?"

Varinia cast her eyes to the floor. I could see that she had come to me for help, and I was giving none.

"He sits in his darkened room, Judah, and cleans his revolvers. He does not eat, he does not sleep. On his desk is the edict to abandon the city. Next to the edict is a pen, and he sits cleaning the revolvers, staring at the edict, awaiting to hear from your second."

"Well, set the goddamn date, Varinia. Find Yulee and set a date for this duel, and let us have done with it. If it's a duel he must fight, he can have one." A shell exploded in front of the building, causing a team of horses to run wild. "See that?" I said. "He wants to fight a duel amidst all that!"

"Judah," she said to me, and I did not look. "Jefferson is a crack shot, and you do not know guns. He will kill you. You must flee now," she said, handing me a passport and papers. "I have had these prepared," she said, "for some time. I knew a long time ago it would come to this. I knew it the first time we kissed."

With amazement I examined the papers. There were two passports, one for me and one for Ada Isaacs. I asked for explanation. "On many a night, Judah, as I lay awake, and you asleep, you murmured her name. I know who she is. I know everything about her. Your David Yulee has told me. He is a good friend. The woman whose name comes to a man's lips in sleep is the woman he belongs with. The papers will get you to England by steamer, if you can make the connections. You need not thank me."

"Varinia," I said. "Set the date for the duel. Do this with Yulee and tell your husband. When he knows that the date is set, he will put down his revolvers until then, and tend to moving this government into exile."

"You will not go to the duel, however, Judah."

"I will not be there," I answered.

103

"Then Godspeed, Judah Benjamin."

March 30, 1865

I have packed all government papers into three small trunks. The rest I have burned. In the trunks are documents that may yet be used by the government in exile. We may try to reach the trans-Mississippi . . . Kirby-Smith's army is still active . . . I have empowered Congressman David Yulee to deliver Ada Isaac's papers to her in Jacksonville, where she should be, according to plan. From there she will take the passport to Nassau and board a British steamer, God willing. Yulee will join the militia of his home state and fight the Yankees as long as he is able.

For my part, I doubt if I will have need for my passport.

April 1, 1865

All soldiers and personnel of the Government of the Confederate States of America:

The abandonment of Richmond is hereby ordered. Maintain your discipline and prove to the world that your hearts have not failed in the hour of disaster, and that you will sustain the holy cause by standing your colors.

The great resources of our country in the trans-Mississippi await us. There our armies, under the leadership of the courageous General Kirby-Smith, await us. Under the providence of God we yet have the means of checking the triumph of our enemy and securing final success.

By order,
Jefferson Davis
Pres., CSA

The green in front of the old customs house is defaced by craters from the shelling.

Here I arrive at one minute to eight, according to my pocket watch. The air is strangely quiet, a lull in the Yankee fire. I stand off behind a large sycamore; I am out of view but I can see them approach.

President Davis walks slowly up the knoll to the top of the green. His valet is with him. Varinia, accompanied by two officers, walks several steps behind. They reach the green and wait. Off several feet to the left of them a small crowd is milling, as if they are not quite sure of the reason for the President's appearance. They are checking the train of wagons which is waiting to carry the government out of Richmond.

Varinia excuses herself from the officers she is with and walks toward the President, who has just been handed his revolver by the second. She is bonnetless on this brilliant spring day, and her hair, which seems to me a more beautiful yellow than I have ever seen it before, blows wildly in the wind.

I know precisely what she is telling the President. She is, however, wrong.

I check my watch. On the hour I step out and walk the hill to join them on the green. Varinia sees me approach, but stands motionless. I walk up to within twenty paces of the President. The revolver I have borrowed from David Yulee is in my coat pocket.

"You have no second, Mr. Benjamin!" the President shouts.

"Gone to fight the Yankees, sir. I shall have to do without."

"Shall we examine weapons, sir?" he asks.

I take the revolver out of my pocket and hold it up to him. I am trembling. Yulee had instructed me in the operation of the revolver before he left. "There is a bullet in one chamber only, sir, as prescribed."

"As prescribed."

The crowd of people in back of Varinia and her escort nears and grows hushed as we continue.

"We have not decided who shall have first, Mr. Benjamin. This is quite unorthodox."

"I am not knowledgeable, sir, in the etiquette."

"Quite so. Let us then, in light of your absence of a second, be fully unorthodox. We will approach, face back to back, with weapons raised, and take twenty paces. Upon taking the twentieth we shall turn and fire."

"As you say, Mr. Davis!" I shouted. My voice was much stouter than I expected.

We walked toward each other, and as we neared Mr. Davis said to me, "The night is long, Mr. Benjamin, but it is part of fidelity to watch and wait for morning."

Then we turned and began our paces. To my left, out of the corner of my eye, I saw milling in the crowd the face of Beauchamp Jones.

At the tenth step the Yankee shelling began again. Mr. Davis yelled, "Continue, Mr. Benjamin, if you please," and so I did, to the eighteenth, nineteenth, and twentieth pace.

I turned, and then three powerful explosions whirled the green upside down for me, and I found myself stunned on the ground, and all over the knoll people began to scream. I looked up and saw the President, lying crumpled on his side, covered in blood. I was knocked down, but uninjured.

Ten yards to the right I heard more screaming. Varinia was being dragged towards a wagon off the road. Beauchamp Jones had her by the wrist. She was shrieking. They were leaning in opposite directions. There was room.

I raised my unfired revolver and aimed at Jones's chest. I fired, Jones staggered, Varinia broke free, and then Jones fell to the ground.

It was the first and best shot of my life.

I then blacked out and found myself, what seemed like days later, riding alone in back of a ruggedly bouncing wagon. I pulled the canvas back. It was night, but next to the wagon riding escort I could make out the fine and beautiful gray uniforms of two Confederate cavalrymen.

EDITOR'S NOTE:

Here ends the third diary. Here also begins the first, at Yale College, about twenty-five years earlier.

It is still unclear to me why Benjamin arranged his journal in this order. One who keeps a diary becomes intimately familiar with all the entries and often opens to a favorite passage. Is it possible that in his final days Benjamin reread much of his works, and did not rearrange them in the order they were written? Was he about to send them to someone before he died?

Be that as it may, we have chosen to honor his format. If such a presentation is mistaken, blame rests entirely with me.

II

FIRST DIARY

DECEMBER 16, 1827—SEPT. 9, 1828

PART II

December 16, 1827—Seven-thirty A.M.

I begin this diary today because I feel the events of the previous evening have, for good or for ill, unalterably affected the course of my life. Whether I shall be a great man or whether I shall be a nothing, whether I shall spend my days, like the masses of other men, in between these two poles, I do not know. I do know that whatever my destiny, my Rubicon has been crossed, and I am on my way.

December 16, 1827—Nine A.M.

I have just returned from breakfast, and the food lies in my stomach like dead weight. I felt the eyes of the other students upon me as if I were a negro out of my place. Rather than submit myself to their gazes, I sat rigid on my bench and contemplated the contours of the morning meat on the dish before me.

Then Reverend Day clapped his hands, the sounds of eating stopped, and grace was intoned. I uttered not a word of that prayer, for all these routines and procedures, which in these three years at Yale college had become part of me, suddenly seemed completely foreign.

The other students shuffled into the back of the hall to get their cloaks and make their way to chapel, but I did not move from my place even when Reverend Day came over and stood, in his gray suit, towering above me.

"Come, Benjamin," he said, "have you lost your love of God, along with your love of temperance?"

"I have lost neither," I made my reply.

"Of that we shall determine when the committee meets," he said, "but for now you are a student in the college, and if you are not ill you have your obligation to go to morning prayers."

Then he turned on his heel and left.

My friend, Samuel Porter, a second-year student whom I had tutored in his Hebrew, heard all. He took some risk in coming up to me. "The old man is taking aim at you, Judah."

"And why should he not aim at you, too, Samuel, and at Dyer Ball, and the rest of them. You are all surely as guilty or as guiltless as I am."

"Judah, we also will be called up for discipline."

"You will be reprimanded, but I will be expelled. I don't deny we had a party and broke the code and deserve punishment. What gnarls me is that the punishment will not be equal. Did I drink more wine out of the lady's slipper? Did I kiss her more than you, or was I more boisterous? It was Dyer Ball who shrieked like an Indian savage when he came out of the lady's bedroom. It was his carousing that brought the sheriff's call to Reverend Day. And what will the Reverend do to punish Dyer Ball? He will rap him once on the knuckles, and with a soft birch rod at that. And then he will say tut-tut, and write the rich Mr. Ball senior and in return Dyer's father will write a long apology to Reverend Day and wrap it around a thousand-dollar contribution to the college before he puts it into an envelope."

"Judah, you're getting livid, and if we don't leave instantly we'll be late for prayers. Not appearing at chapel will not help your case."

"You go, Samuel, and thank you," I told him. "The case is settled at Yale, and I must begin to think of other things. When you are of the Hebrew religion as I am, and when your father is poor, as mine is, then you are here at Yale entirely at the indulgence of Reverend Day. A blemish on your record or on Dyer Ball's remains only a blemish, but with me that blemish grows and blots out everything. No, Samuel, I know I am here on a shoestring, and the shoestring has been cut."

December 18, 1827, minutes of the Yale Calliopean Society

The society proceeded to investigate the charge of ungentlemanly conduct, etc., against Mr. Benjamin, which terminated in a motion that he should be expelled, which passed. It was requested that the charge against Mr. Benjamin be kept secret.

January 5, 1828

After bidding goodbye to Samuel Porter, who traveled specially in from his home in Greenwich to see me off, I got on the stage in New Haven station and, as the horses jerked us forward, to my surprise I began to cry uncontrollably.

Yale College disappeared around a grove of trees, and as I leaned out of the carriage to get a last look, the tears froze on my face in the brisk winter weather. How glad I was that no one else was in the carriage to witness this loss of composure. I pulled out my handkerchief and by the time the carriage had traveled another five winding miles through the countryside, the handkerchief was wringing wet, as if it had come right from the wash. I tried to remember the lessons I had learned and so carefully written down, but they disappeared in the sensations of shame and failure that swept over me.

The trip took several days and I used this time to consider what to tell my parents. I had not written from Yale, although I had no assurance that Reverend Day had not sent a letter to my father. Although I was far from sure of the words I wanted to use, I was sure that I wanted them to come from my mouth in his presence, and not from any other source. On the road going through White Plains the mail courier speeded by the coach and I all but fell out the door leaning to shout to him if he was carrying a letter bound for Charleston from Yale College. I contemplated mail theft for the first time in my life.

Through southern New Jersey we traveled, and down through Camden and across the Delaware over a pontoon bridge, as the wooden one was being repaired. A steamship plying the waters in the harbor sent up its plume of smoke. As we passed into Maryland, the land became wider in unobstructed expanse, large rolling hills of farms and picturesque barns, with their silos fairly bursting with corn, dotted the countryside. Here I got the feeling I was going home.

What a bag of contradictions I am riding in this coach. On the one hand I am elated at my prospects, at the full world passing by the carriage window. Just let me set my sights, choose, and pluck. On the other hand, I have just been ungraciously expelled from college, and must explain myself to my poor father and family. One minute there are tears on my face, and the next minute I am the bearer of a smile big as Kentucky. For all the changing of my moods, it is good I am still sole passenger in this carriage, and the only witnesses to my girlish loss of control are four boxes of freight bound for Charleston.

January 6, 1828

How does a carriage line like this stay in business, I wonder. We are no more than another day's journey from Charleston and we have just picked up a second passenger at the Piedmont Station. Glad I am that I turned down the driver's offer to ride up on the box with him. I don't think I'm one for all the bumping and the sudden ducking for overhanging branches, and, anyway, this coach has become like a home for me. The idea that another passenger could share it occurs to me as contrary to the laws of fair play. The game I have been playing, i.e., Will a passenger get on at the next Station? I have so far been winning. I have bet No, and No it has been up to now. It is no wonder I did not take kindly to the opening gambits of conversation proferred by my new travelling companion, Mr. Greenbury R. Stringer of New Orleans.

"What's a boy yore age doing travelling alone? Gone to visit your kin hereabouts?"

"No, sir," I replied.

"Comin' back from a church retreat, then?"

"No, sir," I replied again.

"Must be somethin' of the kind, as you have on a fine

suit of clothes."

This time I made no reply, as I took offense to his un-called-for appraisal of my clothes. I did not like this Mr. Stringer, tall, lean, with darting brown eyes, and gamey as a turkey. This Mr. Stringer was a man most befitting his name.

"Then the only conclusions I may draw, young'un, are that you are either a poor sad mute or on some secret mishun—let's say you're spyin' for his honor the King of Spain."

This latter possibility appealed to me, and I answered, "If I were indeed a spy, sir, I would not tell you."

"By which admishun," Mr. Stringer answered, "I glean at least that you are not mute."

"Which," I parried, "need not mean that the opposite is true, for I am not loquacious."

"You may not be loquacious," he came back at me gamey as ever, "but you are very precise, it seems, both in speech and thought, especially for a man of such modest years. And, by the bye, how many years have you tucked away?"

"Sixteen," I said, feigning little attention.

"And what have they called you these sixteen years long?" he proceeded tenaciously.

"The name I most frequently answer to," I said, "is Judah Phillip Benjamin."

"Well, Mr. Judah Phillip Benjamin, I am Greenbury R. Stringer of New Orleans," he said, stretching out his long hand to take mine.

Some moments of silence ensued, during which I feigned preoccupation with the countryside as Mr. Stringer talked on about New Orleans, which he called the new commercial hub of the entire South. He said there were more ambitious hard-driving men there, more fortunes to be made and lost in that one town than in all of Georgia, Kentucky, and the Carolinas combined.

"A smart, sharp-witted fella such as yourself," he said, leaning steeply into my corner of the carriage, "could do worse than go to New Orleans to try making his way."

"And what makes you think, Mr. Stringer," I said, sud-

115

denly full of righteousness, "that I am not already making my way handsomely in the world?"

"Well, unless you were the son of President Jackson himself and had already made your million through political connections, given yore tender years, I'd say you ain't hardly begun."

"I have begun, Mr. Stringer."

"And in what field of endeavor, if I may ask?"

"In the dry goods business," I answered, thinking of my father's little store on King Street. "I sell for a large company of which my father is a partner."

"Be this company in Charleston?" Mr. Stringer asked.

"Why yes, how did you know?"

"By your bag there, stickered with the town's name," he said. "'Twas my impression, however, that things are failing bad commercially in Charleston, and business is going southward with the railroad to New Orleans, as I was lecturing you earlier."

"Maybe for some others," I answered, "but my father and his partners have their ways and their connections. They are sending their goods north by way of the steamships now."

"A risky business," said Mr. Stringer with a smile.

"There is no profit-making but in some risk-taking," I quoted from a book I read in my last months at Yale.

"A fine maxim indeed, from someone so young," said he.

"'Wisdom reposeth in *all* men, it says; but it does not specify that they be of a particular age.'"

Mr. Stringer seemed positively taken by all this book learning. "He stings me with a second maxim in the space of five miles! It seems fate has arranged for me to share this carriage with a veritable young genius—a brahmin!"

At this, both of us started to laugh, and all our hairsplitting conversation came to an end. Mr. Stringer described his New Orleans again and described the notarial business which he ran, and he told of the many types of peoples and nationalities that inhabited New Orleans. He spoke of the languages which one hears in the street there, as if at a conference of foreign dignitaries. I told him how

116

I had mastered Latin and Greek and had a small spatter-
ing of Hebrew too, and in revealing this I had to say
something also of Yale College. I stuck to my story, however, of my father's partnership in dry goods and how it
was in working there with him that my future lay. Mr.
Stringer seemed not to push me here but to accept what I
said with a kindly grin, even though my own neck burned
with shame and my mouth felt strange, for all the false
boastful words that had fallen therefrom.

It was late at night and I was dozing when the coach
driver shouted "Charleston Station!" and woke me up. I
could not see anything but for the play of lantern light
outside the coach, and then Mr. Stringer's arm reaching in
to help me out.

"Here you go, boy," he said, and lifted me out. It was
only then in the lamplight that I became aware of how tall
he was, at least six feet and a few inches to boot. As I am
only some five and one half feet tall and have not grown
an inch since my twelfth year, I confess that I am particularly cognizant of stature in men.

"I'll be continuing on to New Orleans in the morning,"
he said. "But I'll be reposing in this here inn for the night.
If you'd like me to meet your daddy, it would be a real
pleasure, and I would tell him how proud he should be for
having a smart book-quoting son such as you."

"That won't be possible," I stammered, as he reached
up to the coach to get down my trunk, "but I thank you
nevertheless, Mr. Stringer, for your kind offer and your
pleasant conversation throughout this journey."

"The pleasure was mine, Mr. Benjamin," he said, and
then he strode toward the porch of the inn, where the
coach driver was raising a ruckus as to why there was no
hot molasses to drink. "And, by the bye, Mr. Benjamin,"
Mr. Stringer said to me out of the darkness, "I think that
you are a young man who, with the proper connections,
could go far. Good night again, young Mr. Judah Phillip
Benjamin."

"Good night to you, and thank you, Mr. Stringer."

As he disappeared into the darkness and his tall silhouette appeared on the porch of the inn before he entered, I

sat down on my trunk by the roadside and pondered, as I sometimes do when I am deeply fatigued, how strange are the comings and goings of men. When I met Reverend Day at Yale College, how wonderful I thought the man, how sophisticated, how ingratiating, and what aplomb! See how it ends up for me! And this Mr. Stringer, who at first irritated me and needled me, and to whom I took a first impression of dislike, see how gracious is our parting!

I checked my purse and discovered but three dollars left in it from the expense of the journey. To hire the station's flat wagon would cost two, but the only alternative is to drag my trunk the five miles or so down the road to my father's house.

I should put down this pathetic lantern by which I scratch these notes, return it to the carriage and be on my way. It occurs to me this nocturnal surprise is not a fit way to greet my father, especially as I am the bearer of bad news. My dear sister Rebecca should by now be installed with her husband Mr. Levy in the new house about which she wrote me. Let me go first to her, on whom I can count for an embrace regardless of how fortune treats me. There is ample time for me to greet my mother and my father—tomorrow.

January 7, 1828

What a beauty is my sister Becky!

She greeted me with such warmth that it instantly bridged the many months I have been away. Her new house is by a pond frequented by sparrows, bluejays, and many other varieties of birds, which her husband, Mr. Levy, takes delight in stalking in the early morning hours. Mr. Levy, however, does not stalk with gun, but with his Audubon tucked under his arm. He is out to identify them and match them with the exquisite drawings detail for detail.

Mr. Levy, whom I did not meet until today, is thus an extremely self-effacing man, a quality which to me does not seem suited for the dried fruit and candy trade which

118

he is in. Yet he seems to eke out a living from it, and the house, although it has a roof still untarred, does have reinforced wooden walls and a fine hard floor. Most of all there is warmth here around the hearth, and Mr. Levy seems to be as thoughtful and careful with Becky as he is with his sparrows. Under his care she seems to me to have grown more beautiful. Her hair is darker, her eyes seem more penetrating and intelligent, although she has little schooling. Bless her, instead of forcing me to talk about what happened in the end at Yale, she asked me what of particular interest and excitement I had recently learned. With quiet diligent listening she let me ramble on about Aquinas, Diderot, Luther and the sundry other subjects of interest which I had touched but did not pursue.

"Mother will be interested in the Hebrew you have studied, Judah. She still does not believe your letters that in this place where they train clergymen they teach the holy language."

"How long, Becky, can I tell her about the Hebrew studies, brief as they were, until she asks me why I am home, if it is a holiday, and if everything is all right?"

"She will know as soon as she sees your face that something is amiss. You will explain, I suppose, whatever you feel appropriate, and there the matter will end."

"Wishful thinking, my sister."

"We never wrote you this, but our brother Solomon's wife did not recover fully from her fever, and it left her paralyzed on one side. Solomon nurses her now most days and helps out father in the business when he can. You alone of us, Judah, have left this place, and I feel you alone will escape it."

"I am home, Becky, not to escape anything but to help out. How are Momma and Poppa, and Penina and Joseph?"

"They are all as you left them when you visited last. Momma and Poppa seem—what shall I say—older. Momma especially has grown more religious, and she was pleased by my marriage to Mr. Levy, who is an assistant sextant at Kehilat Yisroel. The temple has grown somewhat in the last year, but Mr. Levy's job unfortunately is not a paying one, although honors at the reading of the Torah scroll accrue to him, especially during the holiday season."

"And is he a good husband to you, Becky?" I could not restrain myself from asking.

"Such questions from a brother five years my junior are hard to believe! Yes, Mr. Levy is a good husband to me, Judah. You can cease worrying about me. Mr. Levy has a fine gentle soul, only. . ."

"Only what?"

"Only it is the same problem with him as with all the Benjamins and, it seems, those whom we bring into the family. Money. Never enough, never at the right time, investments too late or too early, I cannot tell you, Judah, all the talk of business between Mr. Levy and Poppa and Solomon the last two months. And do you know the result? They have lost their combined investment in the Beauchamps' sugar plantation."

"How much was it?" I asked. I took a seat in the rocker by the fire.

"It was enough."

"How much, Becky?"

"You're a boy, Judah. I feel I've made a mistake in talking this much. It will be settled out of court. They will get by."

"A lawsuit, too!" I could not believe it. "This must be the first time it has happened."

"You're too young to remember, Judah, but it has happened before. This is not a new business for Poppa. He has lost several times already, and it was Mendes money. In St. Thomas and in the little business of cloth in Christiansted."

"And are the Mendeses still giving money?"

"Isn't Momma still their daughter? Of course they give, Judah. Every other boat from England delivers Momma a 'loan.'" She gives the money to Poppa, and Poppa promptly loses it."

"It is not so simple, Becky."

"Of course it is not, but it is nevertheless the way it is with us, Judah. If you stay, perhaps you will bring us a

120

change of luck."

Just then Mr. Levy walked in with a sack over his shoulder. He nodded hello and went silently through to a storeroom in back of the house, where goods for the store were kept. On his way out, clearly to pick up another load, he said, "Boat's in from London. Dates, pecans, and Injia silk. Big shipment."

"My husband is a good, quiet man, and a hard worker. It is good finally to have my own house too, but," and here she raised her hands to her eyes, "I fear Mr. Levy is himself so much like Poppa, I never cease worrying about the next day's meal or what the future has in store for us." As we embraced, she said, "Judah, Judah, how glad I am that you are home."

That night I slept on a warm blanket in front of the fire. At my foot was the chassis of a cradle which Mr. Levy was carving out of scrub pine. Since Becky had made no mention at all of her being in the family way, I, in deference to her modesty, did not ask. Yet the prospect of being an uncle appeals to me immensely.

All night it seemed that Mr. Levy was going in and out of the house. He walked very softly, as I imagine Indians walked, so that it was not the noise of his shoes on the floor but rather the soft gusts of air from outside which seemed to keep me in that strange state between wakefulness and sleep all the night long. It was either on this account or on account of some food I had eaten on the journey that my mind could not find rest this first evening in Charleston, and I dreamed.

Three carriages speeded down the road in my dream. I was in the central carriage and in a carriage on either side of me Momma and Poppa sat, their faces staring at me so that no matter which way I turned I met their gazes. Although we were driving down the Charleston-Asheville road at a breakneck speed, Momma and Poppa's faces seemed to be motionless in the carriage, almost as if they were not themselves but statues of themselves.

At first my carriage pulled ahead, then Momma's; but Poppa's carriage, although it strained and came near to catching us, never quite took the lead. "You're going too fast," he yelled from the window of his carriage. "Slow down, Judah," he shouted, "I can't catch up to you."

My carriage began to pull ahead.

At a curve in the road Momma shouted, "Use the brake, Judah. Climb up."

I made to climb up to the box of the carriage, but the door gate was bolted and it would not give.

"Climb through the window," Poppa shouted, "or you'll spin out at the curve." He yelled so I could see the veins bulge out in his neck. "Climb, Judah!"

"I can't, I can't!" I screamed, but I knew in the dream that no matter how fast the carriage went, it would not spin out.

We began the curve and it went on and on and seemed like it would never end. Dust kicked up in back of me and gradually all I could see was a cloud of dust. I lost sight of Momma and Poppa's carriages, until all I could see was the glinting of the mares' eyes behind me as they pulled on their carriages, gradually losing ground, and receding into the storm.

"Judah!" they shouted. "Judah!" Until their yelling was smothered by the dust and the hammering of the horses' hooves.

I woke up dizzy and sick and my nightshirt was wringing wet.

January 8, 1828

After a good breakfast of chicoried coffee and toast I took my leave of Becky, letting my trunk stay with her for the time, and made my way to my parents' house. I had asked Becky to come with me, but she said a prodigal son could not return home holding his big sister's hand. She would come later.

So the prodigal walked down the road towards King Street. The ginkgo trees still carried the powdery snow of a recent storm. There was a skittering of animals in the woods and a few of Mr. Levy's birds flew across the road in front of me. It was still early morning and no carriages passed. I walked briskly and inhaled the air deeply. How sweet-smelling it is, how different from the stuff that goes into your lungs at New Haven.

The walk completely revived me, and by the time I was half a mile or so from the house I could see the large spruce where I had cut my initials two summers before. Over beyond it, fifty yards back into the forest, would be what remained of my efforts to build a tree house. I have not much finesse with tools and had no great urge to see my handiwork. When my only close friend in Charleston, David Seixas, saw the platform, he bellowed with laughter. If you should open a carpentry shop here in Charleston, he said to me, I would open one right next to yours, and have all your business within the space of a week. Don't worry, I told him, the carpentry business is yours. I've other things to do. Such as what? he asked bluntly, as is his way. I could give him no answer then. Now it is three years later, with Yale College behind me, and I am still not sure of the answer.

Whatever speeches I had planned for Momma and Poppa disappeared when I saw the house through the thicket.

January 10, 1828

I have let two days pass before I come to my diary again. I have needed the time to digest what it is in the nature of my parents' greeting that has subjected my soul to such tempestuousness. In a word, I am enraged. And it furthermore occurs to me as I gather my thoughts to make this entry that I have indeed felt this way before, on many previous homecomings. Homecomings! The word, with its connotations of warmth and hearth, hardly characterizes the way I feel.

Here I am, home. I present to them the book of my life, with its achievements and its shortcomings. Please read along with me, I had wanted to say to them—and did—and help me to see more clearly what is already written there and what may lie as yet unciphered. But see what they do! They open me up at my middle, and each of them takes one half of me, each pulls in opposing directions, and the strain is such that it comes near to breaking my spine.

"Yehuda," Mother said as I entered from the porch. "Yehuda," she said pronouncing my name in Hebrew, "you did not write to us that you were coming home."

"I am nevertheless here, Mother."

"Yehuda," she said, inspecting me, "you have grown no taller."

"I do not expect to grow any more, Mother. I accept my height for what it is."

"You are at least grown taller than your father, but you are a little plumper as well. Have they been feeding you and giving you enough fire in winter?"

"You received no mail from the college, mother? No letter from Reverend Day?"

"Nothing but your latest letter over a month ago about the scholarship prize. We are most proud of you, as I wrote." Mother is a dark woman, with much Spanish Mendes blood in her. Her hair was pulled back in a bun, and her eyes, now as always, radiated determination. She stood by the pantry scouring pots with sand and lye. The whole room reeked of the stuff. "I am cleaning for the Feast of Lights. It comes exceptionally late this year. Is this the reason for your surprise visit, Yehuda—to be with us for the holiday?"

I knew as I stood before her that some process was taking place inside her, some elimination of alternatives. As much as I wanted to state simply and immediately why I was here, I could not do this. Mother had to be allowed to have it her way. I was hurt that I was not allowed to be at least honorable in the admission of what had happened. But she went about asking her careful questions of me, much as she scoured her pots, slowly, deliberately. What a kinship I felt to those utensils!

"Were you given permission to leave for the holiday; perhaps some special dispensation?"

"Have I ever been home at this time of year before, Mother? Was I ever allowed home for Hanukkah?"

"I know you are home for the High Holidays every year. I thought perhaps this year was different."

"It is an expensive trip, Mother. I have used up almost all my allowance to make it. I would not be here only for the holiday, or for some minor reason. I am home because I have been asked to leave Yale College."

She wiped her hands on her apron and sat down in the rocker. In silence she rocked and stared at me, where I stood in the middle of the large room. I would have preferred a wet birch stick on my backside two dozen times to her gaze. To break it off, I presented her with the copy of the minutes from the meeting of the Calliopean Society. She took out her spectacles and held the piece of paper up to the light. Her lips as always, moved as she read the words.

"What does this mean, 'ungentlemanly conduct?'" she asked in a low voice.

I was about to explain when her hand went abruptly up and she said, "Sha, Yehuda, don't tell me anything. Explain to your father, if you like. The father is the man responsible for this. Let him hear explanations until his ears are full. I will talk to you later, Yehuda. For now I want to hear no more."

Then she went into the bedroom, pulling the curtain behind her.

An hour later she emerged. What was percolating inside her had come to its slow boil. She came out to the porch where I was sitting on the steps. The crickets were making their racket, in spite of the coldness, and some raccoon far off in the field was pawing through the snow for a leaf. I felt diffuse and as unconnected to the world as the cloud that was passing above the house.

"Yehuda," she said, "there is pen and paper on the table inside. I want you to write to this man Day and apologize for everything you did. I don't know where you learned to be ungentlemanly, and I don't care for excuses from you. I want a formal letter sent to this man. You tell him you have recognized your fault; beg his forgiveness, and ask for readmittance to the college."

Without answering I pulled my cloak over my shoulders

125

and went into the house. I sat down at the table where the writing materials lay. I would write to please her. But I am resolved no matter what answer I get from Reverend Day not to return to the college. Here, then, is the letter I wrote while my mother stood beside me.

9 January, 1828

Rev. Jeremiah Day:
Highly Respected Sir:

It is with shame and diffidence that I now address you to solicit your forgiveness and interference with the Faculty on my behalf. And I beseech you, Sir, not to attribute my improper conduct to any design or intentional violation of the laws of the college, nor to suppose that I would be guilty of any premeditated disrespect to yourself or any member of the Faculty. I think, Sir, you will not consider it improper for me to express my hopes, that my previous conduct in college was such as will not render it too presumptuous of me to hope that it will make a favorable impression upon yourself and the Faculty.

When I had reached this point in the letter I was satisfied and was about to conclude and sign my name, when Momma, having read the foregoing, stated, "I think that is insufficient. Write more," she said, handing me a packet of letters from the college, "and it is seemly you make some reference to these."

The letters, several for each of the three years I had been in New Haven, were all similar. First there was one letter asking for the full tuitional requirement for the year. Then there was a note to the effect that they had received a remittance from my father, but that it was insufficient. In the light of my scholarship, however, they would allow delay of full payment, and it would not harm my continued study. Then there was a note from my father stating that due to financial setbacks he would be unable to pay for the remainder of the academic year, and would the college be gracious enough to let me stay. In the end of the letter he reassured the college that he would repay the back due amount in the next year. Thus, for three years.

I was not unaware of these matters. However, to read the letters caused me to flush with real, if belated, embarrassment.

With my mother still beside me like a sentinel, I took pen in hand and added the following paragraph:

Allow me, Sir, here to express my gratitude to the Faculty for their kind indulgence to my father in regard to pecuniary affairs: and also to yourself and every individual member of the Faculty for their attention and paternal care of me, during the time I had the honor to be a member of the institution.

With hopes of completing my education under your auspices,

I remain, Sir, your most respectful and obedient servant.

J. P. Benjamin

I looked at Mother and she at me. No more words had to be exchanged between us. Her meaning was clear. I added the following postscript:

May I solicit, Sir the favor of a few lines in answer to this letter, that I may be able to judge of the possibility of my return to the University?

"I will post this for you, Judah, and we shall see what we shall see. In any event I have done my duty," she said. As she called me Judah and dispensed with my Hebrew name, I knew this weighty business was concluded. If she calls me "Yehuda" today, I think I shall make directly for the cellar of the house and close the door.

By way of epilogue I want to state clearly that I take no responsibility for this letter, that I was coerced into writing it by parental pressure. It was not Judah P. Benjamin who wrote this letter. Rather it was Mrs. Phillip Benjamin. It was she who was begging forgiveness, not I. It was she who was asking indulgence for pecuniary difficulties, not I. It was she who most humbly pleaded to be readmitted to the University, not I. I was simply her scribe.

If Reverend Day writes back that Judah Phillip Benjamin is readmitted, I will send Mrs. Phillip Benjamin in my stead. She is intelligent and, unlike her son, exceptionally obedient. I should like to see this, the first female at Yale.

January 10, 1828—late afternoon

An hour ago, in a fit of boyishness, I took the quill that wrote the letter to Reverend Day and broke it to bits. Mother was in the back room drawing oil for the Hanukkah lantern. She did not see me.

January 10, 1828—late, late afternoon

My father is still not home. Becky and Mr. Levy brought my trunk over, chatted for a while and left. Mother says that he may be delayed in town with the shipments and that I should unpack, if only for a few weeks before I go back to Yale.

When I arrange my things I discover, to my great disappointment, that I do not have the psalter or the prize book with me. I must have left them in my room in the college. I feel terrible. I will have to explain to my nephew and my niece. Fortunately Penina and Joseph are asleep now.

No sign of my father.

I wake up feeling totally rested. Everything inside me feels new. The feeling is so wonderful I hesitate to move.

From where I lie I can see the hearth, where the embers from last night have been replenished. My father's boots are not nearby, which means that he has not come home. The new fire means mother is up and about her chores. I have always enjoyed this house in the morning when it is at its most serene. Noontime was always fraught with expectations of turmoil, and evening was the aftermath of their quarrels, with all that low heavy silence. If I had my design, I'd prefer the morning to last twenty-three hours, and I'd allocate a half-hour each to the afternoon and the evening.

"Judah," Mother says invisibly from the bedroom, "Be up and about. Your father will be at the store today."

In a matter of minutes I am at the table having hot milk. Mother, in her robe, has her hair down and there are streaks of grey in the back, which are not unbecoming.

"What books is Poppa reading these days?"

"It seems he is with his Spinoza every spare minute. The men from the temple meet to discuss it every two weeks. He has probably spent the night at the Lopezes' or at Seixas'."

"Poppa always loved philosophy."

"Philosophy, yes, but business, no. The other men leave off discussing and thinking about Spinoza to earn a good living. Your father, it seems, takes his philosopher behind the counter with him. Can a philosopher give change or make a customer buy three items when he has his mind set on two? We do not do as well as we should. Your grandpa Mendes expected more of your father. He expects more of you."

My mother would have made an excellent essayist. No

matter how far afield the discussion strays, she always finds a way to bring the meandering talk back to her insistent theme.

As I pull my coat on Mother says, "I expect you and your father to join the rest of the family tonight at the temple. It is the first night of Hanukah."

Two wagons loaded with lumber and pulled by old sorrels with white feet passed me on the road into town. They crunched the snow under their heavy wheels and the air around the horses' mouths grew smoky with exhalations. I marveled at the sound of their swishing tails and the absolute silence which seemed to surround it like an invisible garland. I never felt so at home with the beauty of the place where I lived. I wondered why I was so at peace with nature and in such turmoil with the people about me.

I suddenly found myself standing on the threshold of the dry goods store. Poppa's back was to me as he was arranging jars on the shelf. I was about to call his name, but I gave in to an impulse just to stand there and observe him. He had garters on each sleeve and the shirts were puffed up almost humorously large in each arm. When I was very young I used to think those were his muscles. Let me feel your muscle, Poppa, I would say. He would pull the garter down his arm, until the shirt puffed up like a balloon over the bicep. When I slapped it down with my hand, he would pull the material in the other direction, so that the balloon of cloth was on the underside of his arm. Here's an upside-down muscle, he would say. And when I finally finished slapping that down he pulled me to his lap and in a very serious tone he pointed a finger to my head and said, "Judah, this is where the real muscle is."

"Mr. Benjamin," I said stepping into the low-ceilinged room, "I would like to buy one of every item you have in the store."

"For you," he said, without turning around, "I could make a very special deal."

"Sold," I said, and then we embraced, with the counter between us. "You look well," I said. "Your mutton-chops are becoming."

"They are only to please your mother, a compromise in lieu of the beard she wants me to wear. It is supposed to make me more distinguished-looking."

"You look noble enough for me."

"Oh, Judah, with such compliments, I know there must be trouble."

"News."

"Important enough for one of our walks?"

"I think so."

"Then let me close the store."

And thus our walk began. It may have lasted an hour, it may have lasted two. Like all the other walks we had taken here and in Fayetteville, when I was just beginning to read the same kinds of books that interested him, the time ceased to matter. Poppa told me about Spinoza, but it was all by way of making it easier for me to talk to him about Yale. Why I ever thought it would be difficult to talk to him, to break the news to him, I don't know.

I then told him about the letter Momma had made me write to Reverend Day.

"Whatever the outcome of this letter business, you may do as you wish as far as I am concerned. Only between you and me, Judah, for the sake of amity at home, I must pretend to agree with Mother more than I in fact do. So that if you hear me parroting her words glibly, do not think this a contradiction of what we have discussed, you and I. In marriage a man must make accommodations— especially so with a strong-willed woman such as your mother. You will find this to be the case too when you wed."

Then we returned to the store.

I sought some place to go in Charleston that would be conducive to my thoughts, so it was to the Harbor I went. No steamships were about, but the schooners were putting into port and some very high four masters, and one of the new U.S. naval frigates, *The Constitution*, was being worked on by crews in dry dock.

Crates of cotton and barrels of sugar were piled on the piers; families of negroes gathered, perching on the boxes, apparently waiting for the agents to arrive. They spoke some high British-accented English and I also heard a rhythmic French being spoken by a second group of negroes. Such light and vitality as presented itself to my senses appealed to me immensely, much more so than the exchanges in my father's store. If one must argue and wrangle and do business, better that it be on a grand scale and out-of-doors. My eyes were splashed by a hundred different colors and the same number of olfactory sensations to match, smells of tar, fish, oil, sweat, sugar cane, and maple.

Then suddenly I heard my name called, as if from a great distance. "Judah, Judah Benjamin."

I looked about but could not determine from which direction the voice was coming.

"Up here, Judah," the voice sounded again, a pleasant booming. "In the rigging."

I raised my eyes towards the heavens, and there, one arm about the mizzen mast of the *Constitution,* was a figure whose arm was waving at me in recognition. My eyes squinted in the bright light. By the shock of black hair and slender frame of the body I thought this might be Samuel Porter, but what he would be doing here in Charleston, when I had left him less than a fortnight ago in New Haven, I could not fathom.

In any event, the figure slid adroitly down the rigging, obviously intent on meeting me. I went to the ship, out of the center of the broil of activity at the harbor.

As we neared each other I saw immediately this was not Samuel Porter approaching, but my old friend David Seixas.

David is the only son of Ephraim Seixas, the lumber merchant, and as David approached I could have taken him for his father, by measure of his build. David has filled out, as our mothers are wont to say, his shoulders are thick and his arms big from work. Seixas is a head taller than I and he strides up to me in a pair of overalls which could have been the sail of one of the vessels in the harbor. He was very large indeed.

"Was it you I saw on the north road early the other morning?"

"It was I, David."

"Well, how could I be sure it was you, wrapped up in your coat as you were? What brings you back this time of year?"

I have been asked this question many times, but Seixas has such innocent earnestness in his questions, I suddenly realize that what is stale news for me is not so for him.

"I have left Yale College, Seixas."

"Without completing your term! Your parents must be —"

"Bearing up well," I interjected.

"Livid, is what I had in mind to say." What I like about him is that he always speaks his mind plainly, even if it hurts.

"You have good reasons, I hope," he said, "because they've made you into the great hope of Charleston."

"Ask me something else, David. I'm sick of explaining myself."

He put his hands in the big pockets of his overalls. "I can understand that," he said. "I only mention it because Moses Lopez, who heard you were about, was wondering out loud. My cousins in Sunday school said he brings your name up a lot."

"I wish he would not."

"You're a model for the younger kids," Seixas went on.

"Now I'm home, a broken idol, I suppose."

Seixas laughed. "Welcome home, Benjamin."

"Thank you, Seixas," I rejoined. It was our manner to call each other only by use of the surname, a habit we picked up when we were together in Fayetteville before both our families moved, along with a number of other Israelites, from Fayetteville to Charleston. Seixas worked for his father, a very old man who was sick and badly ailing. The business would soon be his. How Seixas and I became friends I can hardly remember. Perhaps it was that we are such opposites, he big, boisterous, and physical. I figured a scholar such as I could do worse than having a friend like him.

"Tell me, Seixas," I said, "how goes your life in Charleston?"

"The same as when you left, only much more of it," he answered me. "The town is growing somewhat," he said, directing our looking towards the harbor. "Every time a ship comes in there's a haul of lumber needed for the fixin'." He looked longingly at the harbor and somewhere in his eyes I saw a desire to go to sea.

"Ever get an itch to travel?" I asked.

"Naw," he said, "I got things to do here, Benjamin. You know I'm always doing something. Building a cabin now half a mile from the house. You ought to come see it

"I will," I told him. "I'll be around,"

"For long, Benjamin?"

"Can't say yet."

We ducked as two negro workers came by with a huge beam.

"That's cedar for the foc'sle," Seixas proudly said. "I felled it myself . . . hey, Benjamin, I got a great way for you to clear your head. Come on."

He pulled me towards the *Constitution* and we made our way all the distance to the end of the pier where the ship lay. Up the incline he dragged me, the board that connected pier to ship, and beneath its narrow breadth the harbor water clamored. "Just follow me," he said, "hand over hand, keeping your knuckles turned to the side when you grasp the rope."

"Hold on," I said hesitatingly as he began to go back up the ropes.

"That's right, just hold on, and you'll be aloft in two minutes with a view of the harbor and damn near the whole Carolina coastline."

Seixas' energy was so infectious that I followed. Perhaps timorously, but hempen rung after rung I climbed, until the men below on the decks and piers appeared to me humorous in their minuteness. We finally got to the crow's nest of the ship and straddled the beam. My heart was beating fast as a bird's and the wind was blowing raucously through my hair. The view that I beheld was far more moving than Seixas had promised. I could see South, the gentle coastline, the green fields and the watery inlets, where skiffs which seemed the size of ladybugs moved imperceptibly across the blue-green patches. North the coastline seemed rougher and more adventurous, and against both lay the immense expanse of the Atlantic, on the other side of which were the France and England that I knew only from mother's stories of the Mendes family and from books I had read.

"That's where I came from," I yelled against the turbulent wind as I pointed north towards Connecticut. It seemed as if no coach and horses could have brought me the distance.

"And where are you headed for, Benjamin?" David shouted back at me.

"At this moment, Seixas, I don't know any more than you do. You have a sick father and I have a poor family, so our decision isn't entirely our own."

"Our what?" he yelled back at me, not being able to discern my words in the gusts.

"Our own, own, own."

We were aloft for the better part of an hour and then roamed the pier for another hour, by the end of which time I was acclimated againto Charleston, South Carolina. I took Seixas' leave with a warm handshake. I note that his grip is firm, but not overpowering, a trait I admire in a big man, as it indicates restraint, control, and power in reserve. We will see each other again this evening at Kehilath Yisroel.

January 11, 1828, midnight

As all the others in the house are asleep, I take pen in hand quietly and light a small taper. I do not want to disturb Rebecca and Mr. Levy, who lie in the bed in the opposite corner of the room. In the light that my candle throws I can see how my sister's arm is cast over Mr. Levy's shoulder in the most touching manner. I write very slowly, as I myself am tired and seem to get mesmerized by the shape of the letters in my own calligraphy.

Momma and Poppa fought before the family went to

Kehilath Yisroel. It was about money and what donation we would give to the temple. Poppa said he had little as he had sustained a loss in damaged material this afternoon.

After the services Becky and Mr. Levy came home to spend the night with us.

Father put his book down on the mantlepiece before joining Mother. He never brought his books into their bedroom. While I lay in my blanket and scribbled the first of these notes this evening, Mother came out in her robe and knelt down by me.

"Judah," she said, "you should know now that your father has been unable to contribute even a fraction of the tuition at the University. These three years almost all of the money has come from Mr. Moses Lopez, and from several others, to whom he talked about you. So you see it is more than a personal matter, it is a matter of family pride, it is a matter of much importance to me. I must be able to hold my head high, Judah. I am a Mendes. Do you understand?"

"Why has no one told me this until now?"

"Your father wanted it this way. Mr. Lopez agreed."

"So why did you make me write to Yale, Mother?"

"What do you mean?"

"If the tuition was being paid by Mr. Lopez, why did you make me write for their indulgence of my father's pecuniary difficulties?"

"Because, Judah, it was your father who signed the notes and sent them to the University on your behalf. Mr. Lopez simply gave the money to your father or deposited the money on his account. They thought it better handled that way."

"So what pecuniary difficulties were there?"

Mother paused and said, "Your father could not always send all of the money. Sometimes he suffered a loss in the business, sometimes he needed to pay back a loan, or make good a credit, and there were no other funds, so he borrowed the tuition funds. He never took from the fund without paying back into it, but take he did."

A sense of shame and fatigue swept me, followed by a wave of sympathy for my mother which I had never before

136

experienced.

"I want to tell you, Judah, how many times I wrote to your grandfather asking him for help, so many times that I am embarrassed to tell you. I want you to make a man of yourself so that some day you will be able to pay him back and shake his hand, and I want all of us to live to see that day."

She began to cry quietly, and I put my arm about her. We exchanged no more words, and after a few minutes she composed herself and retired to the bedroom.

I felt Becky's presence suddenly awake across the room. She had heard everything. "Judah," she said, "six months ago Momma sold her china and wouldn't tell me why. Now we know."

Mr. Levy moaned slightly and turned over.

"Becky," I whispered to her softly across the room, "I am going to take care of all of you. I swear it."

January 14, 1828

It is imperative that I find employment immediately. And it is of the most importance to me that I find it on my own. What sense in helping father, when he has Mr. Levy and Solomon assisting him?

I made my way to town and went directly to the livery stable, taking precautions to approach from the off side of the street. I do not ride too well, I will admit, and I prefer passage in a coach or any wagon conveyance to sitting astride a horse. But speed is of the essence, and Seixas' house is a good ten miles away, so that today I shall take my chances in the saddle.

It is enough that the black boy Nicholas laughs at my awkwardness in mounting. No one else in the street need be given similar opportunity. I give the boy a coin and tell him I shall return the mare before sunset. Then I take off by detour on the back road.

I know Seixas' habits and by the time I arrive he should be finished with the chores and tending to his father for the morning. There is no woman at the Seixas' house,

David's mother having died in childbirth, along with her infant, and it is the marvel of the community that Ephraim, the father, and David manage as they do. After the death of Mrs. Seixas, some of the women, my mother included, cooked breads and stews and brought them over, but when the mourning period had ended, Mr. Seixas insisted that they could manage. They have a negro woman in twice weekly to do the heavy washing and cleaning, but she is a free woman and gets paid a wage. Mr. Seixas is an abolitionist in his thinking. At least that is what David tells me. It is not a popular view but it is his view nevertheless.

The trees leap up and down as if they had springs for roots, and my stomach feels as if it is seeking exit through my throat. I could blame the beast for all this agitation, but I fear the fault is with the rider. The clumps of felled trees to my right indicate the Seixas homestead is no more than half a mile away. Thank God!

David is drawing water from the well as I approach him.

"I'm taking you up on your invitation to visit!" I shouted.

He took the bridle of the sweating horse and helped me down. "Do they teach horsemanship at Yale now, Benjamin? I remember when you left you swore you would ride only in comfort."

"I've taken back my oath," I said, trying to catch my breath.

"Well, they did not teach you how to canter the horse," he said, leading it to the trough, "or else you galloped him all the way. What is the emergency?"

"I want to work for you and your father, Seixas. Is that a possibility?"

He was, as I expected, clearly surprised by the request, but he answered, "Anything is a possibility, Benjamin."

"'Anything is possible,' indeed," I quoted him. "Did they teach you philosophy in Charleston?"

"Only what I've learned from listening to you, Judah."

"Good, then," I said, "I shall teach you all the philosophy I know, and you shall teach me the lumber business."

"Sounds delightful, my friend," said Seixas, as he directed the horse into the nearby pasture to graze, "but let us first discuss it with my father. He is not well, but he still knows more about the monies than I do. You talk to him, Judah."

We entered the house. Mr. Ephraim Seixas was indeed not well. He lay on the large sofa, propped up by several pillows, and covered up to his waist in blankets for warmth. He had only his nightshirt on. I got the impression he did not dress as a matter of course, such was the gravity of his illness. But he had a kindly face, much like David's, and a large powerful body which he shifted this way and that, for the reading and signing of papers, only with great exertion.

"This is Judah Benjamin, father," David did the introducing. "He's back from Yale College and looking for work. He's asked me if there's room for him with us."

Mr. Seixas put down the sheaf of disarrayed papers which he held in his large hand. "Welcome, Judah Benjamin," he said, in the friendliest way imaginable. "Come here so I can give you a welcome home shake."

I went over and shook his hand but there was not much strength left in that awesome grip of his. I noticed on the small shelf above Mr. Seixas' head a small memorial candle was lit, and on the candle was lettered a name in Hebrew. From what little I knew of that language I made out the name of Mr. Seixas' wife.

"What can he do for us?" Mr. Seixas asked David. "He's too puny to cut and haul," he added with a laugh.

"And he's too afraid of horses to tend the team," the younger Seixas added. "But he is as sharp as they come."

"And sharpness is a trait," I offered, "desirable in the lumber business. Is it not?"

"It is indeed," said the elder Seixas. "Can you make out these, Mr. Benjamin?" He handed me the sheaf of papers from his bedside office table.

I glanced at them and discerned their import quickly. I had seen the same in my father's business file cabinet. "These are bills of sale, of credit, and invoices," I an-

139

swered.

"And could you scriven copies and keep them in order, Judah?"

"With pleasure, and with accuracy."

"Good," said Mr. Seixas, pulling his son to his bedside. "Then this big lug could deliver the proper number of board feet, as per the signed invoices. Do you know, Judah, this boy is going to inherit this business, but instead of the work of a businessman he prefers that of a day laborer. Just the other day he was duped by one of the ships' captains, who let him climb up in the sails while he, the captain, had the wood unloaded and dispersed before David came down to make a proper accounting." Seixas and I exchanged a knowledgeable glance. "That can't happen any more, David, or you will inherit a broken axe instead of a lumber business."

"No one will be inheriting, father," David said. "You will be getting well."

Mr. Seixas coughed deeply and hoarsely. He was no older in years than my own father, but that cough of his seemed ancient indeed.

"You do have a good hand, do you not, Judah?" Mr. Seixas then asked me.

"They have told me it is tolerable at Yale."

"Take this foolscap and pen and make a copy. Use the light by the window over there, and when you are done, bring it to me."

I copied the bill of sale and brought it back to Mr. Seixas, who had used the interval to catch his breath. He was inhaling heavily, his chest heaving and his hand shaking as he examined the copy.

"What is only tolerable at Yale College is most excellent in Charleston," he said. "Mr. Benjamin, you are hired." Then, turning to his son, he said, "David, we will now open the little office in town. Young Benjamin will take all these papers which are only gathering dust here and transfer them to the office. Assist him at first in getting the office in order.

"America is changing, boys," he said. "There are now insurance companies and agents for insurance companies, and lawyers every which way you turn. Scrupulous men have been joined by men not so scrupulous in business as I. A good pair of eyes and a good head are as important these days as strong hands and a strong back. Charleston is changing. The whole country is changing. The. . . ." He fell to coughing again. David went out and quickly came back with the bucket of drawn water and a wetted towel which he applied to his father's feverish chest.

"And one more thing, Judah," he said to me as I was about to take my leave. "There are six negroes on the payroll of this business. Mark that they are free men all and are to be treated as such, with proper wages, and so on. Mark that they are not slaves."

"I am in your employ, sir," I answered, "and it is only proper that I honor all your instructions."

"In spite of what you yourself believe," he said with laboring breath.

"Don't talk politics now, father," David said. "Save your breath." He looked at me to indicate he preferred I not continue the conversation with his father. "He grows extremely agitated about this subject," said David.

"I have no opinions on the subject." I tried to conclude the matter with Mr. Seixas.

"You will, Judah," he wheezed, "you will."

January 16, 1828

I have spent the day cleaning up the Seixas Lumber Company office. So neglected is this place that in the back room ragweed is coming up from between the planks. Seixas and I have moved in cabinets, a table, and chairs which had been at their house. I found several sets of sleeve garters in one of the drawers, but I prefer not to wear them.

The office is down the street from my father's store.

"How much will you be earning?" was his response after I told him about the position.

"Eight dollars a week to start."

"You will not get rich on that, Judah," he said at the

141

dinner table.

I had no patience for his philosophy and snapped at him, "It is only a beginning."

"A man never strays too far from where he begins," he said.

"That is certainly true in your case, Phillip," mother said as she brought in the platter of chicken. "It need not be true in Judah's."

"Pass the chicken," said Solomon, "I'm hungry."

Becky and Mr. Levy were spending the evening with Solomon's wife.

"We will say the blessing over the bread first," my mother directed. "Since my husband has his silly principles about such things, and since Solomon's mouth is almost full already, will you, Yehudah, do the honor?"

I had forgotten the blessing, once learned by heart in Hebrew instruction when I was very young. As this practice had only been recently revived by my mother, I was in need of the text. My father pointed to the mantle where a Hebrew prayer book lay. I retrieved it and read as best I could. "Blessed art Thou O Lord Our God, King of the Universe, Who bringeth forth bread from the earth."

"I have made special prayer, Yehuda, that we hear favorably from Reverend Day, and I have also made a special prayer for the well-being of Solomon's wife and Mr. Seixas."

I considered these thoughts of the evening before as I arranged the register and the inkwells and the ledgers. I also swept the floors and cleaned the windows of the store which faced the main street. People walked by whose faces were familiar from summers spent by the harbor, but I could recall no names. Some peered into the office to see what was about. I copied some papers which Mr. Seixas had given me when I left and I quite enjoyed the sound of the pen's scratch on the paper. I re-arranged the desk by the window so that I could benefit from direct sunlight. The office was very cold, for there was no wood for the stove. I was expecting Seixas, however, within the hour with a load of wood, both for the office, for storage, and for the harborside shed which the company maintained.

When I finished copying, I took out the Spinoza, which I had borrowed from father, and also *Gladstone's Business Practice,* which I had found among his unused books in the chest. I supposed it was appropriate that I begin a position by reading about it in a book, even as I sat in the office where the business was conducted.

I don't know how long I was reading but it must have been at least two hours, for the light was getting bad and I found myself holding the volume up to the window to make out the words. I heard the sound of the shopkeepers closing their doors, and Seixas had not yet arrived.

I closed the door of the office and went down the street to father's store. I found him, Mr. Levy and a number of other men, all, I believe, of Kehilath Yisroel, conferring with each other. Father saw me through the cluster of men as I entered.

"Judah," he said somberly, "the doctor here just arrived in from the Seixas'. Ephraim Seixas died this afternoon. I was just on my way to tell you." He took me by the arm.

"Let's go home," he said.

January 24, 1828

The feast of lights is over, the funeral is over, the mourning period also is just about completed.

Becky and my mother and Mrs. Moses Lopez and the other women have been attending to the ritual. The mirrors are covered up, sheets are thrown over the furniture in the house, the windows are opened up, as much as the cold will allow, to enable the angel of death to remove himself from the premises.

As I go to the house—I walk to be alone with my thinking and because the weather today permits it—I feel in my pocket the eight dollars which Ephraim Seixas had given me as advance on my salary the day before he died. The coins make a strange music as they jangle in my pocket. The money truly does not belong to me, because I have not worked for it, and I am puzzled over what to do with

143

it. I certainly cannot return it to David, not now. As much as he expected his father's death, as prepared as he confided to me he was, still he is wracked by enormous grief, and he sits in the rocker in the house with the prayer book in his lap, his eyes cast on the floor. I have been to the house once already with some speech of condolence on ny lips. Fortunately I did not deliver it, but rather sat with David and learned the lesson of silence."

Today, as I arrive, he is about to recite the mourner's prayer. I take a place next to him, we face eastward, and although I am not familiar with all the words, I whisper them as best I can along with him: *Yisgadal v'yiskadash shmeh rabah/ v'almah d'vera chiruseh . . . v'imru Amen.*

After a few minutes of silence, Becky comes over to David and me and says, "We have brought a chicken today. You may eat any time you feel like it."

We eat very little but during the meal David asks me to visit Moses Lopez on his behalf. "He was father's lawyer, Judah, he has all the papers and he has the will."

January 26, 1828

Mr. Moses Lopez lives in the most imposing house in Charleston. In addition to being a rich merchant, a scholar, and a philanthropist, he is also a lawyer. The house is gabled on all four sides and surrounded by courtyards where willows grow thickly against the walls and offer much pleasant shade from the sun.

A negro servant lets me in and shows me through the parlor, sitting room, and long hall to the veranda, where Mr. Lopez is sitting at a small writing table examining papers from a packet which lies there. A number of times I had been in this house, and I especially remembered the library, off the hall, with its three walls lined with many books, many tiers high; there is a rolling ladder to enable you to climb to reach them, much as there were at the libraries in Yale.

Mr. Lopez rose to greet me. "Good day, Judah Benjamin. Mrs. Lopez informed me of the pleasant news that you were going to pay me a call."

"The pleasure and the honor are mine, Mr. Lopez."

"Some tea? Or perhaps something cool—some lemonade?"

I explained to him the dual purpose of my visit, the business of Yale and the request of David Seixas. He listened patiently but his answer was something of a surprise. "You mean," he said, "you have not also come simply to talk to me about yourself and the world and what you think you shall do in it, as we used to do, Judah?"

"I have not forgotten our Sunday morning discussions, Mr. Lopez."

"They are among my most pleasant memories. Your wit and acuity have been unsurpassed by the students that followed you in my library." Then he paused. "You won't mind, Judah, if I smoke a cigar? I am cultivating a new habit with these excellent havanas."

When he opened the humidor, the sweetly pungent aroma filled the porch. I think he sensed the delight my nose took in this new phenomenon. He held the humidor up and offered me my first cigar, and then he gave me a few minutes' instruction in how to let smoke fill up my mouth without descending to the lungs.

"These come up on the boats from Curacao," he said, "once in two months. I look forward to them, as I looked forward to your visit, with pleasant expectations. Do your parents know of your call on me?"

"I believe they do."

"Just don't tell them it was I who gave you your first cigar."

"Oh, my father would approve, I am sure," I answered. "It's my mother from whom I must conceal this sin with all my zeal and energy."

An affectionate grin formed on Mr. Lopez's face. I saw clearly how weather-lined his large face was and realized how many hours he must have spent on the decks of ships loaded with his cargo, as he nursed his fortune among the islands of the Caribbean and up the southern coast.

"As to the business at Yale, let me ask you a number of questions," he said, "and try to give answers as precise as

145

possible. First, was your being of the Hebrew religion maligned in any way by the authorities at the college?"

"There was nothing said officially."

"If not officially, how then was it communicated to you?"

"In subtle ways."

"Such as what, Judah?"

"Things said off-handedly, errant remarks at the table, procedures surrounding going to chapel."

"They forced you to go to Christian services?"

"Not exactly forced, but indicated, that my openness to the experience would be looked upon with favor."

"Looked upon favorably by whom? All of your teachers, or some of them, or one in particular?"

"Certainly not all of them, Mr. Lopez."

"I know some of the professors there. Give me a name or two. Perhaps I know the man."

"The teacher I had most difficulty with was Reverend Day."

"The same one who was instrumental in your dismissal."

"The same."

"Well, then, I know him only by name, but a letter to the congregations at Newport and New Haven may reveal more to us of this situation than meets the eye. Yale College may not be entirely rid of its proselytizers, in which case a protest could be lodged and your reinstatement effected by demand, not by supplication."

"I want no part of this business, Mr. Lopez," I said strongly.

"But if you have been the victim of a religious wrong, it can and should be rectified. There is a professor of Hebraic studies there, a Moses Meyer, with whom I have been in occasional correspondence. I could write—"

"I will not go back, Mr. Lopez, and be the center of a religious scandal, marked for the rest of my life as the man Yale was forced to take back because he was a Jew. Furthermore, I believe there is more to it than being a Jew, although that was certainly a part, but only a part. There is also the business of the tuition, for which I want to thank you, and apologize for its misuse. I shall endeavor to pay you back in full when I am able."

"Gracefully said, Judah, but entirely unnecessary. As to investments, the investment was, and is, in you, in whatever you decide to do with your life."

"Then I do not have to return to the college?"

"You have only to realize you have abilities, which I recognized three years ago, and to fulfill them."

"I am most grateful to you, Mr. Lopez, now more than ever."

"Will you have, then, a little brandy with your cigar? I shall show you what new books I have acquired since you were here last."

We adjourned to the library, I, with a cigar in my left hand, and a brandy snifter in my right, fairly tottering. But the sight of books always sobers me.

"I have this new version of the *Pensees,* which is infinitely easier to read than other Pascals. When you have grown and I have entered my deep old age, I should very much like to discuss section 72 of these *Pensées* with you. Let me read to you the most provocative lines."

He read the following with such slow fervor and asked me to reread it to him, so I was able to commit it to memory and herein inscribe it:

Let man consider what he is in comparison with all existence; let him regard himself as lost in this remote corner of nature; and from the little cell in which he finds himself lodged, I mean the universe, let him estimate at their true value the earth, kingdoms, cities, and himself. What is man in the Infinite?

"And here is a new collection of poems by Heinrich Heine and a pamphlet by Lessing, which I find provocative," he went on as we crossed to the other side of the magnificent library. "My German is not so good as it should be, but I can make out that they are much concerned in Europe now with the question of conversion.

This is no new issue with us; our ancestors, Judah, having been either converted or expelled from Spain and Portugal at the time of Columbus."

"Father says," I offered Mr. Lopez, "that Columbus was himself a Jew."

"No one knows for sure," he said, "but look." He scrambled up the ladder to an upper shelf and withdrew a big dusty book in a fine hard binding, which he handed me before he descended the ladder. "This old book has been handed down to me from my father and his grandfather before him." He opened the book up and we walked with it to the reading table in the center of the room. "Can you read this, Judah?"

I remarked on the rococo quality of the large Hebrew letters, and since I had studied the language both with Mr. Lopez and somewhat at the University, I offered that I could. But when I began to make out words by sounding the letters first, nothing familiar came out, nothing sounding of the Bible, the Hebrew with which I had a passing acquaintance.

"It is *Ladino*," Mr. Lopez finally relieved my difficulty and embarrassment, "the language of the Portuguese Jews." I had heard it but never seen any printed book in the language. "It is the old Portuguese/Spanish dialect written out in Hebrew characters, and this volume is a history, in Ladino, by the last of the Ladino scholars. In it he mentions the very story of Columbus that you alluded to earlier. Sit down here, Judah," he said excitedly, "and let me translate:

"'In the same month in which their Majesties issued the edict that all Jews should be driven out of the kingdom and its territories—in that same month they gave me the order to undertake with sufficient men my expedition of discovery to the Indies.'

"That is a translation from the diary of Christopher Columbus, Judah, the closest thing to proof that we

148

have."

"And it is hardly proof at all," I offered Mr. Lopez. "He is simply remarking on a major event, that is all. I do not hear in what you read any special attachment or sympathy for the Jews. Had Columbus departed in the same month as the terrible Lisbon earthquake, he might have mentioned that event instead of the expulsion of the Jews, as Voltaire did in his *Candide*."

Mr. Lopez smiled. "For the very reasons you point out, Judah, the Ladino historians felt they either had to dispense with the idea as apocryphal or find more proof. Hence they expended tremendous energy in finding in the diary of Columbus secret codes in Ladino, and sought to identify among the known members of his crew what conversos and what marranos were in league with him."

"A most dubious intellectual exercise."

"Well, yes and no, Judah. We have, for example, used this text and others like it to trace the families after the expulsion. The Benjamins and the Mendes families, for example, came to England shortly after the expulsion. My family and the Seixases came to the Indies via the Dutch provinces. I will never forget how my grandfather in Curacao lit the Sabbath candles in the basement, even though the regime was friendly to the Jews. What had been a marrano necessity was retained as custom."

Just then the servant entered and announced that Mr. Lopez's business appointment had arrived.

"We have been talking books for over an hour, Judah, and I had not realized what happened to the clock. Now, let me see, as to the Seixas tragedy I will be opening the will and reading the papers next week, as they were just delivered from the bank this morning."

"Mr. Seixas paid me eight dollars advance salary before he died, sir. I should like to render him a service, or render his son a service, by assisting you with the papers, either in copying them or delivering notice of them to concerned parties, or to be in service in any way you find appropriate. Either that, or I shall return the money to you."

"Old Ephraim would not want you to return the eight dollars, I am sure. Be here on Wednesday in the morning, when I attend to the Seixas papers, and we shall see. I have some suspicion that young Mr. Judah Benjamin may, in his own subtle way, be expressing an interest in the legal profession. Might there be some grounds to this suspicion?"

"I suppose there may be," I said.

"Well, then, Judah, make your way home now. Give my best regards to your mother and father."

I went to the door of the library to exit. "And thank you very much, Mr. Lopez, for the cigar and the brandy." I put the cigar out in the floor spitoon, and left the house in excellent spirits.

Feburary 3, 1828

For several days now I have been trying to get Seixas to go with me to Mr. Lopez.

I go up the creek road a half mile and turn off through a thicket of cypresses which eventually leads on the the lip of Barger Lake. Here in a nest of insects even the brisk February weather can't drive away is a shack built of remnants which David gathered piecemeal over the last several years and put together, with his father, on the Sundays they spent together. I found Seixas fishing off the wharf of three pine planks nailed over some old barrels and leading out into the lake. His beard seems to have grown thicker and he is hunched over and pensive.

"Biting or not biting, Seixas?" I said as I approached.

"I heard you a hundred yards away, Judah," he said. His smile and his good humor reassure me for I am the bearer of bad news. "You would make a terrible Indian."

"I am fortunately tending to a career more suitable to the indoors."

"This can only mean Lopez is set on making you an apprentice lawyer."

"He does say I have a tolerable acumen."

"'Excellent acumen' is likely what he said."

"But I have not come out here, Seixas, to discuss my career, but yours."

He pulled in his line. "I have no career as such, Judah. I have a lumber business."

I decided to take a direct approach. "You *had* a lumber business. According to Mr. Lopez the claims of the creditors of the business heavily outweigh present assets, unless there are holdings, deeds, or resources you have which you have not told Mr. Lopez about. He wanted me to ask you, in your own best interests, to tell all that you have, if something remains hidden."

"Will they then have me in the poor house, Judah?"

"If they have you there, we shall share bread and water, my friend."

"But you are going to be a great and famous apprentice to Mr. Moses Lopez."

"I confess he has offered me a position in his counting house at the harbor, but I have refused."

"Why refused, Judah?"

"Because my family is beholding to him for many thousands, and under those circumstances I do not feel I want to apprentice out. I need to make a fortune, not a salary. So the position I spoke of is open. It is yours for the taking."

"Thank you, but I do not want the leavings of Judah Benjamin."

"There are no leavings involved here. Mr. Lopez offered you a job similar to the one he offered me. I have not yet told him that I will not take the apprenticeship. Go, see for yourself if there isn't at this very moment a position waiting for you, too. He does not think you are a slouch, Seixas, and he had much love for your father, even if he disagreed with his politics."

David threw his line out farther. "Everyone disagreed with my father's politics. He was a kind man. He abhorred the plantation owners, Judah. He read to me in the Bible and proved conclusively in it that slavery was prohibited, chapter and verse prohibited. This is one reason God assisted the Israelites to flee from Pharoah."

I was not so sure about these ideas—any of them—so I chose a conversational route away from further discussion. "Will you then," I asked, "earn your way in the world as

151

an abolitionist?"

Just then there was a strenuous tug on David's line. "See here, Judah?" he said energetically. "I've caught myself a big one. A man does not need a career or a job in order to eat."

"Shall you sit by this lake your whole life long catching fish?"

"There are worse things I could do with my life."

He sat there. I gave him fifteen minutes during which I swatted some bugs dead on my neck, and then I gave a yank on his big arm. I was surprised at how easily he rose and accompanied me back. I gave him the final inducement necessary by telling him Mr. Lopez would in all likelihood also honor him with a cigar and brandy.

As we got on the Indian path towards Charleston, Seixas said, "My own father has already initiated me into those delights. There are still some cigars here. If you ever have a strong desire to have one in isolation, you are more than welcome both to the tobacco and to the shack, for as long as I own them."

"I think Mr. Lopez said you could retain some small property and some 100 dollars cash if you liquidate the other assets, and pay the due bills."

"You know, Judah, my father said that he never enjoyed smoking a cigar so much as he enjoyed it smoking with me."

We walked silently the rest of the distance into Charleston and into Mr. Lopez's ante room.

February 27, 1828

I have been home almost two months. The season is beginning to change. I am thinking about leaving Charleston for a place of better opportunity. All the wrangling in the store is maddening. There is only talk, and no income. I have visited Solomon's wife and put compresses on her forehead many nights this week, as Solomon has driven the wagon to Columbia. Nancy needs a good doctor. She should go to Savannah or the doctor should be brought for

152

her before it is too late, but there is no money in the Benjamin household for either of these measures. Becky continues to hold the family together. I can count on her if I leave.

March 5, 1828

First really warm day of the spring. All the men are in their shirtsleeves on the street. Where King meets Harbor there is a little square where the local orators discuss business, politics and gossip. Between doing menial tasks in the store, which I abhor, I go out and listen. One portly man with a tall tan hat today was bellowing:

"And if there ever was a Sin City, then surely New Orleans is it. Why, gentlemen, I tell you the ladies of ill repute line the thoroughfare and compete with each other in sheer audacity. No self-respecting wife of a Charleston man could walk down Bourbon Street without blanching in shame for the very concept of womanhood."

This town of New Orleans interests me.

March 7, 1828

I have induced Seixas to listen with me to all the talk of New Orleans in the harbor. He has a small bank account, which will not last much longer, and Mr. Lopez was able to help him retain the shack on Barger Lake. All else is lost to him, and the business is now just a name on the commercial record books of the city.

"You hear the man yourself, Judah," he says to me. "New Orleans has yellow fever. Why go there?"

"*Had* the yellow fever. It is all but vanished now, I read in the *Courier.*"

"Yellow fever never vanishes. It just lays low," says my naturalist friend.

"And five years ago we had the pox in Charleston, do you remember? The town is still here, you and I are still here. And Savannah has malarial periods, and it's growing

153

and has a railroad now three hundred miles inland."

"New Orleans is six hundred miles away."

"It is a crossroads, a huge port, the touchstone of the world."

"You memorized the fat man's speech, Judah," Seixas interrupted.

"I can't help myself. The place appeals to me. Where there is sin there is money. Where there is money there is business, old ventures losing, new ventures starting up. This is a place where a man could make his fortune. I have decided to go, Seixas, and there only remain two questions. First, will you go along with me? And, second, when shall we leave?"

He sat there whittling a stick with his knife, and I could see there was no answer forthcoming. I thereupon pronounced him the most indecisive friend I ever had. "Go and think about it, Seixas, and let me know by week's end. For I have only to let my family know, and then to check on the coach departures."

"I'll tell you this, Judah," he said to my surprise, "that if I decide to accompany you, it will be on horseback and not with fancy ladies in carriages."

Not wanting to lose this advantage, I agreed that if he would go with me, I would ride on horseback with him all the way to New Orleans.

We decided to consider the journey to New Orleans a temporary trip. For Seixas it would be a vacation from his brooding subsequent to his father's death. And for me I would accompny my friend, and also deliver some papers from Mr. Lopez and Kehilath Yisroel to the rabbi of the temple in New Orleans. The latter papers did in fact need to be delivered, and I seized on the opportunity to have Mr. Lopez entrust me with them.

Thus I decided that this was how I would present the notion to my mother and father. While I emphasized the temporariness of the venture and my eventual return in several weeks, in my heart I knew that going to New Orleans was, for me, to be a move of much longer duration.

This morning the packet of papers for Rabbi Venuevel, a clergyman of Dutch extraction, was presented to me by Mr. Lopez. My father entrusted me with ten dollars in addition to the sixteen which I had saved for the trip. My mother said that perhaps when I returned there would be some news from Reverend Day regarding my readmittance to Yale College.

"Perhaps," I told her, "there will be."

I shakily got on the mount which I had arranged to be brought over to the house from the livery stable. My niece and nephew and Becky were also there to see me off. I promised the children that I would not forget their gifts this time, and that I might even send them from New Orleans, so they would not have to wait for my return. They jumped giddily around the horse until mother pulled them away.

Becky leaned up to me and said, "Remember always, Judah, that we love you." And then she whispered so no one else could hear. "I know I shall not be seeing you for a long time."

I spurred the horse gently off in the direction of the shack, where I am to meet Seixas.

My family will write to me care of this Rabbi Venuevel, until I establish an address.

I also have in my saddlebag a piece of paper which I found, when packing, in the bottom of the gladstone I brought home from Yale. On the paper, which he apparently put in the bag when I had fallen asleep, was the name and address of one Greenbury R. Stringer, 14 Rue Madeleine, New Orleans, Louisiana.

March 20, 1828

I have been riding with Seixas for a day and a half now along an offshoot of the old Cumberland Road.

A short while ago we arrived in Knoxville, Tennessee,

and the feel of my feet on the ground and my backside in a chair is utterly indescribable. I must negotiate with my friend about the next three hundred fifty miles, which now seems like a painful eternity to traverse. We have found an inn on the outskirts of town. While my hardier companion is watering the horses, I am drinking a cool sassafras in this inn house and noting what I see on this foolscap.

Men wear clothes of coarser fashion here in Tennessee. There is more buckskin and moccasin and look of the Indian than one is accustomed to in Charleston. And here there is only talk of the tariff, praise for Andy Jackson and damnation heaped upon President Adams. The men are gathered here talking of politics, and one not conversant in politics is deemed an idiot. Worse yet, one who evinces even the slightest leanings of support for the protectionists is a ready target for tarring and feathering. And yet Jackson supports the tariff, and parades himself at the same time as the faithful son of the South, and he walks this narrow ridge in his public pronouncements, which I take now to be the meaning of politics: that is, to please as many as possible, and offend few as possible.

Seixas now enters the inn and comes over to my table. "You'd think they're electing a president tomorrow," I offered him some of my thoughts.

"Who'd you vote for, Judah?"

"I'd vote for John C. Calhoun because he's got the sharpest mind of any of the politicians. Look here," I pulled out a copy of the *Charleston Mercury* which I had picked up in town before our departure, "Calhoun says that if you look carefully at the figures you see the government is supported in large part by the proceeds of the tariff. Yet the South contributes two-thirds of the exports from this country to England and Europe. Now, they would not send here unless we sent there. So it follows that the southern states, composing one third of the Union, contribute two-thirds of the national government expenses by paying duties on the foreign goods they buy. Highly unfair and prejudicial, he says, and he's right."

"I'd vote for Jackson," Seixas answered me. "I like his looks."

"Fortunately they are of the same party and will in all likelihood be on the same ticket."

Thus we talked and I could see my companion was not catching the political fever of Tennessee. Not that politics were not also on fire in Charleston, but it seems to me that all I read there was my Latin and my Greek. It has taken my departure to leave off the classics and start reading my newspapers.

"Adams is a friend of the New England storekeepers," one of the drunker men at the end of the bar was shouting. "He'd have us pay the duties until we go hat in hand to his Boston banker friends. My brother in Columbia wrote me that South Carolina would sooner secede from the Union than have northern tariffs forced down her throat." Seixas and I exchanged a glance. Then the man raised his glass and proposed a toast. "To Southern rights," he said. All the men near the bar lifted their beer and whisky. As their eyes marked us, Seixas and I too raised our sassafras to Southern rights. The only protectionists in this bar were hiding under the tables.

"Shall we be off then, Judah?" Seixas finally says to me, after the tumult of the toasting dies down. "There's still hours left before sundown, and the horses are rested."

"The horses may be, but I am not." Seixas looked at me with a slight smile, as if he had expected this to happen.

"May I remind you, Judah, of your pledge to ride the distance with me to New Orleans."

"I've ridden in good faith so far, and it's the farthest I have ridden in my entire life. Let's sell the horses and go the remainder by coach."

"You set foot in a coach, and I return to Charleston. You need some toughening, Judah, and anyhow, it's only another week's journey."

"Another week's riding shall find me clinging to the horse's belly, not riding on its back."

"In which case I shall point out the defect of your horsemanship and turn you right side up."

"I am much obliged for your concern for my health. But I guess a pledge is a pledge, even if it kills me. Let's

157

be off then, but for God's sake keep off the gallop. I am no frontiersman like you."

I am glad to leave Montgomery. Never in my lifetime have I felt the bite of a bigger or meaner mosquito. Seixas, as usual, is riding ahead of me, and as I struggle to keep apace, I concentrate, wishfully, on the tail of his mare swinging like a barely hinged pendulum to keep the insects at bay.

Two miles out of Shreveport and my horse goes lame!

"Hey, Seixas," I yell up to my friend, who is about to disappear over the crest of the hill. He rides back at a gallop as if he's just mounted the horse and has not been in the saddle for over a week.

He examines the horse's leg and pronounces her lame. "She's unrideable, Judah. You hop up with me, and she can trail along at her own pace."

Thus we enter Shreveport an hour later, crossing the Little Chattahoochee River. There is a crowd at the far end of the bridge, and at the point where the bridge begins to slope stands a man with a gun.

As we approach, he crosses our path and stops us. "Where do you hail from, boys?"

"From Charleston in South Carolina," I answer him.

"Horse gone bad on ya?"

"Yes sir."

"Planning on staying long?"

"Just the day and the night."

"And then where is it you are heading? New Orleans?"

"Yes sir," I answer him.

"We had ourselves a little trouble the other day and we ain't got 'em all yet. That's why I'm here interrogating all newcomers, by special orders of the mayor. We ain't always so unfriendly."

"Got who?"

"Why, Stephen Vesey and his malcontents, that's who. You mean you ain't heard?"

Just then we heard the neighing of a horse, a quick gallop, and the shooting of several guns from the end of the bridge.

"That'll be the seventh one we hung in half as many days. So be on the lookout, boys, for stray negroes that looks ownerless but not free. And be careful, we caught three of 'em with guns from the arsenal."

We moved on across the bridge. "And if you wanna see Vesey hisself," the man with the gun yelled to us, "he's the big buck hanging from the first tree."

The crowd of people was dispersing from the hanging. As we rode by a young negro who could not have been older than me or Seixas was swinging from the limb of a tree. On selected trees along the roadway from the bridge six more negroes hung, their faces in hideous shapes of bulging. Another armed guard patrolled the road to prevent their being cut down.

When we had put enough ground between us and the hanging trees, Seixas turned and said, "You remember when there was talk in Charleston of the slave insurrection, Judah? My father hid Gloria and the other blacks in the basement of the house, laying the bed across the trap, so none of the hotheads could find them."

"But if these negroes in fact stole guns. . ."

"I doubt if there was a trial, Judah."

"But they are, after all, only property."

"They are people, Judah, just as you and I are."

"They are moveable property, but property nevertheless." And so our argument went on, always at loggerheads on this issue, until we found a rooming house for the night.

We are both shaken by the sights of Shreveport braced for anti-insurrectionism, with men walking around armed with rifles, and with muskets tucked in their belts, and hardly a woman or child to be found on the streets, as if the town were ready for invasion or war. In the town square the local militia is drilling, and as our rooming house is within view of the square, this is where I sit, writing. Seixas has gone off, at the suggestion of the lady who runs this house, to a stable, where we have decided to sell the horses. Even Seixas is willing to give up the animals at this point, for we would have to sell them in New Orleans at a lesser price.

"I never learned to write," she says, coming over to me. She is a big dough-faced woman. "My husband did all the writing necessary for the both of us. If you be a newspaperman," she says, "you are late indeed. For they have come and gone and gotten all their stories on Stephen Vesey, using his very own words, while he had tongue to speak them."

"I am not a newspaperman, madam," I answer her politely as I can. And although I tried to charge my words with a certain inflection, as if to indicate to her that I preferred my writing to her conversation, my efforts seem to have failed, for she kept talking with me. Rather, talking at me. She is one of those people, who, it occurs to me, grow more numerous in the world every day, who ask you a question not to hear your opinion on the matter, but rather to give themselves a pretext for their own endless locutions. Outside the rooming house window a mildly drunk sergeant gave orders to a somewhat less drunk platoon.

"Oh, my husband, he loved to read the newspapers, like yourself, young sir. The *Gazette* was never enough for him. He would pay extra to have the *Telegraph* delivered to him by post from Washington, and then there was always the *Democrat,* from New Orleans. These are my politics, he would say, referring to the editorials in the *Democrat*. He was a well-read man and would have made a fine politician with his baritone. He could talk about any political subject and make it as interesting as the parson's talk of scripture." She paused. "And I had a fine son by him, who looked a mite like yourself, but he died in the fever three years ago tomorrow."

"And your husband, madam, what became of him?" I asked.

"My husband was Purvis Bowie, hero of the Battle of New Orleans, the only American to catch a British ball and die in the engagement."

"I thought that story was apocryphal, madam."

"You thought it was what?"

"I thought it was legend."

"No, indeed. You are making conversation with his widow. As a matter of fact, Colonel Jackson rode right up to this house and presented me with Purvis's body and made a most eloquent speech about his heroism, right out there on that green. I have got some small pension from the government for my husband's deeds, and if Andy Jackson gets himself elected president, I am going to send a letter to him on January 1 and tell him I knowed he would be president the day he came to my house with my husband's body and that I have confidence in everything he does."

One of the other roomers in this house has just come down the steps requesting some hot water be prepared for a bath, which request terminates my conversation with Mrs. Bowie.

Out the window I see Seixas returning by way of the drilling green. The sergeant, who sees him lingering, tells him to pick up a stick and drill along, if he likes. Seixas, to my surprise, does pick up an old tree branch and falls into step. He is big and stands straight, and, not being drunk perhaps, he cuts a fine figure in comparison to the rest of the platoon members. Even at this distance I can detect a slight smile on Seixas' face. We know what the sergeant does not know, and that is that Seixas is drilling in the wrong army. If it's a soldier he is to be, it will be among the followers of men such as this Stephen Vesey.

"Hey, Judah," he yells toward the window seat where I write, "come march around for a spell. It's your horse that's gone lame, or is it you, too?"

I put down my pen and go outside. The sun is brightly shining. It is a bad day for all this dying in Shreveport. "I am going to drill my way over to the stage lines and arrange for our passage tomorrow to New Orleans," I yell. "Drill away, Seixas. I shall see you at Mrs. Bowie's for

161

dinner."

On my way over to the stage office I found myself a secluded tree, in an area where no one seemed to be drilling or shooting or hiding, and I sat down and pulled out of my pocket "The South Carolina Exposition." With what delight I read the compelling words of John C. Calhoun.

The Union is based on a compact between sovereign and equal states. And in accepting the Constitution the individual states have not abandoned their separate sovereignties. They have created a federal government to act solely as an agent to carry out certain specifically delegated powers. The Constitution, instead of creating a sovereign nation, was but the body of instructions these principals gave to their agent. And the people of the individual states—not Congress, not the President, not the Supreme Court, for these are but their agencies—must decide and judge whether their directions are being carried out.

I read, went to the stage office and purchased the tickets for the morrow, then went back to my tree and read again. By the time I got back to the rooming house dinner was over. But Mrs. Bowie, telling me again how much I reminded her of her own lost son, said she had put a portion of stew and cornbread aside for me. I ate my dinner and listened to her conversation, and drank coffee with chicory until I felt fatigued enough to go to sleep.

April 1, 1828

We are arrived in New Orleans at seven in the morning. Seixas and I are crammed into this coach, with a physician, two ladies and their young daughters. The ladies are speaking the patois we had begun to hear in Shreveport, and which has grown more and more common as we descended southward. The ladies speak in a lilting chattering

French in whose words I can only make out the slightest similarity to the French I heard at Yale. We are all smiling at each other, the ladies, myself, and Seixas. The little girls are irritable and are looking out the window and asking, Mama, may we get out now? It is a feeling Seixas and I share, especially poor Seixas, who with his mighty legs crossed and tucked in, looks like a giant in the thimble of this carriage. The doctor, for his part, has a handkerchief out, with which he seems to cover his face as if to breathe in from it some chemical with the smell of brilliantine.

"What, in your professional opinion, doctor, shall we do to remedy this condition?" I asked the good doctor.

"The best remedy," he answered with a cultured smile, "is for us all to exit the carriage immediately."

"It is, however, moving," I pointed out to the doctor.

"As you have observed correctly, Mr.—"

"Mr. Benjamin."

"As you have observed correctly, Mr. Benjamin, the carriage is moving, and thus the remedy now—broken legs, arms, etc.—would cause greater harm than the malady. I suggest we exit just as soon as the coach arrives at St. Peter's. In the meantime, may I propose, as an interim cure, some of this fine absinthe?"

The doctor thereupon withdrew a silver flask from his vest pocket, raised it to his lips and heartily imbibed. He offered it to the ladies who demurely declined, then to Seixas, who also declined, and then to me, who graciously accepted.

"It'll put a hole in your stomach, Judah. I've heard stories about that stuff."

"Quite the contrary, Mr. Seixas," said the doctor. "Absinthe dilates the eyes, aids appetite, makes the head clear as a bell, and is in general a fine physic. Drink away, Mr. Benjamin, and pass on to us your responses so we may solve this scientific debate before—" and here he checked a gold watch big as pear which he withdrew from his pocket—"we arrive at the church in about seven minutes."

I drank, and although the taste of the absinthe was sweet and licorice-like, it seemed to have no special effect other than that of liquid candy.

"Perhaps the dose should be increased," said the doctor, "in the light of your strong constitution."

"Bourbon Street," yelled the coachman from the box.

"Ici, ici," shouted the ladies, pulling on the bodices of their dresses and arranging themselves. The horses slowed down and the door of the carriage was flung open. Someone threw a box on the dirt and the ladies stepped out, bidding us adieu. Their children followed them, giving us gentlemen a little curtsy before they left. One of the little girls insisted that the box in front of the carriage be moved so she could jump the distance from the carriage to the ground. *"Ne tombe pas, ne tombe pas,"* said one of the ladies, or something to that effect in the patois. Jump she did, and fall she did, to the mortification of her mother. The door was flung shut, and the horses neighed under the whip, and off we were to the last stop, our stop, at the cathedral in the heart of New Orleans.

"The creole ladies are most proper," the doctor commented. "I predict that the little girl will be sent tonight to bed without supper, and she will as a result from this day forward always act the complete lady, especially in the presence of gentlemen. Your dose, Mr. Benjamin, is prepared," he said, offering me the flask. "The perfect way to let the body return to a normal state after an arduous journey."

I was enjoying the company of this doctor, and enjoying also Seixas' not enjoying him at all. "Stretch out your legs, Seixas—remember, this is your holiday."

"I think I shall drink to that," said the doctor. "And you, Mr. Benjamin?"

I raised the flask to my lips. I held it there for a number of seconds, emulating the doctor, until the droplets, which slowly trickled out of the container, began to have their effect. "Much better this time, I am happy to report."

"Last chance, Mr. Seixas," said the good doctor, "for me to have the great privilege of offering you your first absinthe in New Orleans. It's a little custom with us, and a great feather, if you will, in the cap of our hospitality. Please, Mr. Seixas, you'd be offending me if you did not, and here's already St. Peter's up two blocks to the left."

"Don't offend the doctor, Seixas," I laughed.

"I'll drink to that, too," said the doctor.

"Well, I'll have just a sip, I guess," David relented. He took the flask, and took what the doctor called a quick nip, then he spit it right out the window of the carriage. Someone who had the misfortune of being in the street at this time cursed as we sped by. "It's wood alcohol," Seixas said, "pure poison."

"A most delicate system," laughed the doctor, "for such a big man. Quite uncommon." We drank to that, too, as the carriage slowed to a halt at the cathedral. As we said our goodbyes, the doctor introduced himself as one Dr. John La Rue and gave me his card. I believe I told him the address of Mr. Stringer. The next minute, the door was open, someone outside said watch your step, and I, marvelling just then at the view of the several spinning cathedrals of New Orleans, promptly did not watch my step and fell decisively on the ground like the little creole girl. I had the sensation of something snapping, felt myself lifted in Seixas' massive arms, and the doctor's voice giving instructions to a place called the Hotel Bolivar.

April 2, 1828

"I am most grateful, Dr. La Rue, but nevertheless still embarrassed. I shall get out of bed now," I said, turning myself, "and go to Mr. Stringer. I have responsibilities. . ."

"You shall do no such thing," the doctor insisted. "You still have slight fever, and a day or two in bed will not hurt. If you had to break your arm, believe me when I tell you that there is no better city in all the South to break it in than New Orleans. We understand such things here as the wages of a good revelry."

"You may come to my office in two weeks, if you like, and I will examine the arm, although I anticipate no problems. My practice, Mr. Benjamin, rarely includes broken arms, as I am primarily involved with the healing of bro-

165

ken hearts."

I believe I slept for about an hour and then woke up feeling fortunate that I had the use of my right arm, and that Mr. Stringer remembered me sufficiently, even in what must have been Seixas' elaborate explanation, to give us both positions in his office. I hear outside the continual patter of the patois, mixed with Spanish, the barking of dogs, shouts of drunken men, and the enticing melodies, in all their forms, of women's voices. If this is New Orleans by day, what, I wonder, can be its character by night?

April 18, 1828

I am very pleased with this position with Mr. Stringer, who is as steady and affable as ever. It is much to my advantage that he finds my work so acceptable, as he evinced in conversation with me this noon hour over some tea.

"I never had a one-armed clerk before, Judah, but if you're a model to go by, I should fill this office up with them and become a rich man thereby. With one arm you do the copy work of two men who have both their arms."

"It's because the real work, Mr. Stringer, is up here," I answered him, pointing to my head. "The formulations are similar even in different documents, and I write frequently from memory, so the work goes quicker without sacrificing neatness."

"So you be learning a thing or two, Judah?"

"Yes, sir, but I don't understand some of the laws quoted in these papers. You know the one where the runaway slave, I think it is the Plaquemines Plantation Case, is shot by the planter on patrol, and the other planter, the one who owns the slave, is suing the first planter on the grounds that the slave was not running away but just on an errand for him. And the property damage is such and such, because the slave can't work any more? You know which papers I'm referring to, Mr. Stringer?"

"Well, of course, boy, I know which papers you're referring to. I wrote 'em up. But I can't answer your questions because, lawyer though I may be, I am no slave lawyer. And anyway, that case is Mazareau's. He's the best of the Creole lawyers. You can ask him all your questions. I can't answer them, and believe me, he can, and he will."

"How do you know he will, Mr. Stringer?"

"Because he's already told me what a damn smart boy you are, that's why."

"But I hardly spoke two words to him."

"Well, those must have been mighty careful chosen words, Judah, because you impressed the pants off Mazareau. I think he's going to try to steal you from me."

"I would never go, Mr. Stringer."

"You'd be a damn fool not to. Anyways, you have to learn the patois first before you'll be any good to him. Most of his cases are the Creole merchant stuff, and if you don't have the lingo, you don't have the case. But I want to tell you something, Judah, about Mazareau, and it applies to Soulé and Grymes, and all the lawyers in this town. None of 'em is really doing you a favor completely." I did not understand and asked him to exptain more. "I mean, they can spot a bright boy right away apprenticed to me, or to anyone. That's how they can find talent and head it off at the pass. I don't blame them, though that type doesn't appeal to me. They want you to work *for* them, Judah, so you won't work *against* them. Won't be competition for them. You work for them, and you'll be under their thumb. You'll never appear in court against them."

"But I'm not a lawyer, Mr. Stringer. I just began working for you."

"Judah, I knew you were going to be a lawyer the day I met you in that coach to Charleston. You'll be a lawyer, mark my words. You're born for it—sharpness, manners, temperament and all. It's just a matter of time. Well, are you interested?

"Interested in what?" I was dumbfounded.

"In what! In my helping you to study law and pass the bar in Louisiana. That's what."

167

I could have jumped straight up through the ceiling. "Of course I am interested. But I'm overwhelmed."

"Well, unoverwhelm yourself, finish copying those Plaquemines papers, and then take these books home with you tonight. Start studyin' and we'll put aside an hour every day to go over what you read. And start learning the patois—and Spanish wouldn't hurt none, either."

"But you don't speak either, do you, Mr. Stringer?"

"No, I don't, but that's because I'm from Pennsylvania originally, where we ain't got any patois speakers, and anyway, language moves across my tongue like heavy molasses. Do as I say, not as I do."

We drank the last of the tea. "And one more thing, Judah, which is some of the bad news I wanted to talk to you about, now that the good is out. It's your friend David Seixas. He is not working out. As pleased as I am with you, that's as *unpleased* as I am with him. I confess that I gave him the position here, which a hundred other boys on the street would like to have, just because he mentioned your name. I would have given it to a negro if he'd have mentioned your name, even though they would have run me out of New Orleans for it. But he don't belong here, Judah. He sits at the desk dreaming and his papers are full of ink blots and errors. I got to go over everything or have someone else do it for me. He's a good boy like yourself, but he don't belong. I don't want to hurt his feelings. You talk to him, will you?

I knew exactly what Mr. Stringer was referring to and decided to speak to Seixas this evening.

"He can finish off the month," Mr. Stringer said, "with full pay, but just talk to him, Judah. He's like a blacksmith in a china shop. I confess I don't even know why you dragged him along with you to begin with."

April 18, 1828, 1:30 A.M.

This evening, after a long slow and silent walk back to our rooms at the Hotel Bolivar, Seixas announces to me that he is going home. The speech I had prepared disap-

168

peared from my lips.

"I am sick of New Orleans, Judah. Sick of everything about it. This afternoon when I was walking over to get the stationery I passed two dead horses on the roadside. When I came back from the store half an hour later, the horses were still there, flies buzzing over them like black clouds, and the smell so sharp even the dogs were keeping their distance. No one was doing anything about removing them. So I took the dollars in my pocket, went to the nearest stable and hired a rig and a rope and pulled them out to the dirt myself."

"But you don't work for the city of New Orleans, David. You work for Mr. Stringer, and that's why he lit into you when you came back at half-past-six."

"I know, I know," he said as he went through the small closet gathering his things. "I'm just not suited and we both know it. I'll find something to do back home."

"With Mr. Lopez?" I asked.

"Naw. What difference does it make with Mr. Lopez or Mr. Stringer? I think I'm going to sell the shack and go north. There's no one left in Charleston for me now."

"Why north? What's there north for you that's not down here?"

"You know we've been arguing abolition for two months running now. I'm southern born but with a northern heart, I suppose. I'll go see what I can find in Kentucky or Tennessee or maybe even further up. My father's cousin works for the *Emancipator,* last I heard. Maybe I'll go nose around there for a while.

"That's a Garrison paper."

"That's right. He does touring and selling subscriptions up and down the Piedmont. It's outdoor work, but of the spirit. It appeals to me more than all this legal notetaking and nitpicking that you're so good at."

"You be careful, David. A lot of hate follows the abolitionists around." He had put all his things in the suitcase and was making to leave. "Aren't you going to wait till morning?"

"What for? I'm going to walk until I get tired, and then maybe I'll buy a horse."

"But I was going to write a letter for you to deliver back to Charleston. I was going to write it tomorrow."

"Better post it, Judah, because I'm not going back to Charleston. I'm going straight north and maybe west," he said. "You take care, Judah."

"I want to apologize twice over, David, for making you come out here and for making you work with me in Stringer's. I feel I put you through unhappiness on my account."

"I wasn't forced into doing anything I didn't want to do. I'm grateful for the little nudge you gave me. Helped me see what other parts of the South are like; helped me, I think, make up my mind about where I belong. It's me who should do the thanking to you. Goodbye, my friend."

"Goodbye, Seixas."

I listened to his footsteps down the stairs and then I went over to the window and watched him disappear out from under the hotel sign and down the street, brightly lit in the moonlight. Seixas was the only part of Charleston I had left with me in New Orleans. I realized that in all my maneuvering him to come along with me, I was doing it in order to bring with me a little bit of home. I had done it for selfish reasons, but somehow a person must leave home, and some of us choose a cleaner, more efficient way to do this than others. I wish him only happiness but I have the eerie feeling we are moving away from each other, like two trains full speed on the same track, but hurtling in opposite directions.

With Seixas' departure I feel a little piece of my heart is chipped off and fallen away.

May 1, 1828

I am suddenly become a very busy young man.

Every night, at least three per week, I am fallen upon the law books Mr. Stringer loans to me. I read and reread them until the points are clear, for as long as the arguments are elusive and vague I am uncomfortable with them, and even with the volume itself, which seems to

170

have an almost physical movement in my hands. When I understand it, the book seems to settle down and I possess it.

Last night I did not fall asleep until the lamplight merged with the sunlight. I was an hour late getting into the office, the first time this has happened, but Mr. Stringer was very tolerant. My eyes experience occasional strain, but this does not concern me, as it seems to go away with some good washing in cold water.

One evening a week and on Saturday I am doing tutoring in English for Doctor La Rue's patients. One patient, an elderly Creole lady, who lost her husband and has not gotten beyond her tragedy, is trying to learn some simple English verbs with me. Although I do my best, I feel my skill is more in the law than in pedagogy. I am interested in teaching her some functional English, words such as "walk," "eat," and so on, and also common phrases usable at the grocer's, the apothecary's, and in the courts. But she is resistant to me in a charming way, and insists on using the Saturday afternoon hour together telling me in quite gory detail of her husband's demise at the hands of the negroes in the Santo Domingo uprising. I gather this episode is a common heritage of the Creole community here. The verbs Madame Roselius requests me to drill her in are "kill," "die," "torture," "maim," and the like. And while I am learning French and the patois through her, I confess to considerable outbursts of impatience. How many times must   listen to the retelling of the same massacre! I feel my mind grasping out for new material. That is why I am so much more comfortable in the law, where no two situations, in spite of similarities, are ever exactly alike. Oh, this Madame Roselius, I must see her again tomorrow! It is all a little reminiscent of the retelling of the escape from Egypt by the Israelites. The story fascinates me, but thank God Passover happens only once a year. If I had to listen ot it every week, and, perish the thought, I believe Madame has requested Doctor La Rue to increase her dosage of me to twice per week, I think I would go out of my mind!

On Friday nights I tutor a little Creole girl named Bernadette. Bernadette cannot be any older than my own dear Penina. She, like all the Creoles, is dark, with burning eyes and the demurest of manners which contrasts so strongly to the flame which seems to glow within. While Madame Roselius comes to Doctor La Rue's office on Bourbon Street, I tutor Bernadette in her home. This home is truly a mansion. There is a magnificent granite facade, and under an archway the entrance through a wrought-iron gate to the courtyard. Here in the courtyard I meet Bernadette punctually at six o'clock. Her mother brings her in and places her at a table where I am seated, as per a plan which was described to me at our first meeting. The table is situated near a goldfish pond, in the center of which is a piece of stone sculpted into the shape of a frog, and through the frog's open mouth water spouts. The goldfish swim by in sprightly procession and effectively distract Bernadette from whatever I'm teaching. Each time she slumps in her chair, over rushes her mother and straightens her out. If the mother is out, there is a negro maidservant who rushes over and straightens the posture of the little girl, places her hands in the proper position on her lap, and then gives me permission to continue with the lesson. With the Creole girls, who are being groomed to be young women and brides, one is struck by the strictness of the training. One is impressed by the greater importance placed upon posture than pronouns in these strange lessons I give. Yet my French is indeed improving, and I test myself always on the servants, butlers and coachmen with whom I talk while my pupils prepare to receive me.

It was during one such interlude, when I was speaking for a moment with Bernadette's mother in the courtyard, that I saw a wagon move up the street. VENEUVEL HARDWARE was painted along the side. Suddenly I remembered the letters from Mr. Lopez which I had been entrusted to deliver to Rabbi Veneuvel. I wondered if this was the same family.

"Pardonnez-mois, Madame Picard," I said, checking my watch, "but I must be off. I've just remembered another obligation, which cannot wait."

"A young man such as you," said Madame, "must have

many pupils."

"Not so many, Madame."

"Enough, however, to keep you active."

"Enough, yes, but none so bright and promising as your daughter, Madame."

"And none of the young men we have engaged has been so charming as you, Monsieur Benjamin."

"I thank you for the compliment, Madame, but truly I must be going."

"Well, then," she said, "in two weeks I am giving a little party, a musical soiree, and I wanted to ask if you might find time in your busy schedule to attend, along with the other young people?"

"I could indeed," I answered, much surprised at the invitation. "In two weeks my cast should be off. It would be a fine way to celebrate the return of my left arm, Madame."

"*Bon.* You shall receive a formal invitation by post. And now, be on your way, Monsieur Benjamin."

I left the courtyard at a brisk walk and then, when outside on the street, I began to run. The traffic was fortunately congested, the wagons were caught at corners, the drivers were cursing the heat and the obstruction, and two negroes were trying to gather a dozen chickens which had gotten out of their boxes and were blocking traffic. One negro was holding up his hand to keep the oncoming wagons back, and the other was on his hands and knees scurrying to get the chickens before they were crushed under the horses' hooves and the wagon wheels.

At the head of this congestion, on the corner of Bourbon and Deauville, I finally caught up with the Veneuvel wagon. A man, even shorter than I, and extremely agitated, was driving the wagon. He held the reins limply in his hands, as if he had given up all hope os the horse ever being able to move the dray amidst the havoc of the street.

"Sir," I said, "would you be an employee of the Veneuvel family connected with Rabbi Veneuvel of the Beth Abraham Temple?"

His eyes flashed at me as if I was the cause of all the congestion. "I would be Rabbi Venuevel himself, young man." The horse gave a sudden lurch forward, and then stopped short. I jumped back to get away from the wheel. "Climb up then," he said irritably, "and tell me your business. I am going nowhere fast." I climbed up and sat next to him. He had the feeling of constant motion about him, but contained in a small space, like a spinning top. "The irony is that the old sorrel is named Pegasus, and every time I hitch her up I seem to get caught in this mess."

"You have not yet taught her to fly, in spite of her name."

"To fly! She barely remembers how to walk." There was a break in the traffic, and room enough to move the wagon. "Get on, Peg!" shouted the rabbi, and we moved into clearer space up north to Deauville. He breathed relief and said, "I think Pegasus and I shall both soon retire."

"Do not do that on the spot, rabbi, because I have some letters and papers for you from Charleston. I am Judah Benjamin. Mr. Moses Lopez entrusted a packet to me. . ."

"Of course, I've been waiting for the papers. What delayed you? I should have received them two weeks ago," he bristled.

"Don't be angry," I said, rolling up my sleeve. "See, I have broken an arm getting them here."

"Very well, then, give the letters to me."

"They are at my room."

"Mr. Benjamin, can't you see I am a busy man! Where is your room?"

"Hotel Bolivar."

"Bolivar! Ridiculous. That's all the way across town, and in this traffic! There's no hope." I had not attached such importance to the packet, nor had Mr. Lopez told me the papers were crucial, so that Rabbi Venuevel's anger and irritability I could only understand as part of his every day constitution. Then he added, "You know what is in that packet, Mr. Benjamin?"

"No, sir. I did not open it. The papers not pertaining to me."

"Well, Lopez did write that you were an honest young

man! In that packet are several bank drafts from him made out to me on the account of Beth Abraham, for rent on the temple space and for the purchase of chairs and furnishings. We barely have a place for people to sit down as it is. Can you understand that, Mr. Benjamin?"

"I can understand it, but I am not responsible for it, rabbi."

"Oh, let's not bicker," he said. "Just get me the letters. When can you do it?"

"As I did not deliver them to you immediately, I could take it upon myself to go to my room and bring them over to you tonight."

"You could, could you?" he said, not quite believing me. I had work to do and commercial law to study this evening, but I did want to fulfill my obligation. "You're not a bad sort, Benjamin," he relented. "Look," he said, "you know the old Lafitte House near the casino of John Davis?" I had become familiar with this spot from the conversation of Doctor La Rue. "The store is on that corner. It says Venuevel, you can't miss it."

"And the temple?" I asked.

"The temple? It's right there, in back of the store for now. What do you think? This town is no Jerusalem, nor is it a Charleston, for that matter. We have maybe twenty-five families here, Mr. Benjamin, and half of them don't want to know the other half." He pulled in on the horse with such a violent tug old Pegasus turned her head and gave the rabbi quite a mean look. "It's a long story."

At this corner I got down from the wagon and promised to return to the rabbi's with the papers in an hour.

Having dug up the packet of letters, I returned by the same route I had taken and found the Venuevel residence without any difficulty. I was surprised to have the door to the house opened by a woman perhaps a year or two my senior. She had on a scarf which covered up her long dark hair, and over a dress of the same dark hue she wore a white starched apron. "I am Miriam Veneuvel," she announced, "the rabbi's daughter. He told me to expect you —if you are Mr. Benjamin."

"I am."

"I am to invite you in. You may give me the letters, and please sit down." She ushered me into a house whose furnishings seemed quite confused, as if the family had not yet completely moved in.

When Miriam Venuevel returned from the far room, she said, "Good Sabbath. My father has asked me to invite you to share the sabbath meal with us. If he had known you were in New Orleans he would have provided a proper invitation, he says, but you will perhaps accept if you have no previous engagement."

Miriam conversed with me for the half hour or so I sat in that ill-lighted living room, but, alas, I don't think we had any common ground upon which conversation might have grown. I felt she was extremely quiet by disposition and I felt my presence was placing upon her the immense burden of small talk. And while small talk comes easily to me, I must have a partner who has at least some capacity to engage in same. The household seemed unhappy without warmth or adornment on the walls, such as pictures and hangings. The only article which caught my attention was a loom off in one of the back rooms, visible through an arched hallway. There was none of the fineness of spirit and decoration here that I had noticed in the Creole homes.

After a long hiatus Miriam spoke again. "My father tells me you plan not to stay too long in New Orleans."

"On the contrary. While a brief trip was my original intention, I now feel I shall stay indefinitely. I like this city very much."

"He said he received a letter announcing your arrival here from Mr. Lopez at the congregation in Charleston."

"I grew up in Charleston, Miss Venuevel."

"And what is it like in Charleston, Mr. Benjamin?"

To such general questions it is hard to give response, for one does not know what precisely is being asked. I tried to give Miss Venuevel some concept of the city, but she sat there listening to me so completely quiet and placid that I felt I could have been reading to her from the gazeteer or the *Charleston Almanac*. I like to be interrupted when I speak, to be challenged, to have myself tested. No such challenge was forthcoming.

"You know that our congregations are part of an association of the new reformed, Mr. Benjamin. What is the congregation like in Charleston, Mr. Benjamin?" she asked. "I believe it is called Kehilath Yisroel, is it not?"

"Yes, but I would hardly say I am involved with it in any way. My mother and father take an interest in it, and the building is quite old and venerable, but I have been away at college for three years and have drifted away."

"You have no religious observance, Mr. Benjamin?"

"Had I none whatsoever," I said, "would I be dining with you tonight?"

"I would just like to know if you are like the other Jews we have met so far in New Orleans. We have been here less than a year, and father is in despair," she said, and then she began to lapse into quietness and to cry slowly.

I was nonplussed by this display of emotion, especially around this topic and in front of me, an acquaintance of hardly thirty minutes. I simply did not know what to say, but fortunately I didn't have to say anything as the rabbi then entered, his irascibility honed to a fine edge. I confess that his nervous, jumpy way of moving and speaking was a welcome contrast to the brooding quality of the room I sat in and to the tears of young Miss Venuevel.

"Benjamin, Benjamin," he said, coming over to take my hand, "I'm glad you could stay. Do you wear one of these or do you not?" he asked handing me the skull cap.

"You are my host, Rabbi Venuevel. As you wish."

"As *you* wish," he insisted, not without charm.

"At my family's house my mother usually insists that the men wear skull caps, and my father insists that it is not necessary."

"And how do you resolve this issue in Charleston?"

"It usually turns out that the food is served, and we sit down, undecided, with the skull cap tucked away in a convenient pocket."

"Well, you may put the skull cap in your pocket if you wish. I am going to wear it. And," he said, turning to his daughter, "you stop this crying and help your mother with the chicken." Miriam went directly into the kitchen. We followed. "A very emotional girl, Benjamin, and pretty,

177

too, don't you think?"

At what point, I wonder, does tact turn into feigning and then plain out-and-out lying? Miriam Venuevel does not move me. I would much prefer to be with my books tonight, or even with Madame Roselius or little Bernadette. "A very emotional girl indeed," I said.

I shall not go into details of the Sabbath dinner, which is an event I have true affection for. This dinner, however, transpired with the pace of the Venuevel wagon and old Pegasus caught in traffic this afternoon. The candles were lit, the blessings were said by the rabbi and the food, very delicious chicken in peas and cashews, was served. "It was one of the few things we could bring out of Curacao," said Mrs. Venuevel. "We too were badly San Domingoized. We got out with barely the clothes on our backs and a doll for Miriam to hug on the countless journeys we have been on ever since."

"Now, Sarah," said the rabbi, "Mr. Benjamin does not want to hear." After tearing off a respectable piece of poultry the rabbi went on, "I will tell you, however, that it was a mistake to come to New Orleans."

"But you wanted your own congregation so badly, dear."

"Oh, let's not go into that at length, Sarah," the rabbi said, "although I will agree it would have been wiser to try going to England. This is too young a country for an old man like myself to figure out. Half the congregants speak German, and the other half are like you, Mr. Benjamin, and like us—American for a generation or two. The Germans ape the Spanish ritual, and the others, instead of being flattered, feel encroached upon, and nobody gives money, and hence we have a synagogue of sticks of furniture and boxes instead of the furnishings a place of worship deserves."

"And we don't even have a proper Torah scroll, Mr. Benjamin," said Miriam, amid renewed sniffles.

"Use a napkin, dear, if you must," Mrs. Venuevel comforted her daughter.

"How is the chicken, Mr. Benjamin? Good, no?"

Thus the evening went. Tears, trivialities, and the affairs

of the New Orlenas congregation. I left before midnight, but not without receiving and parrying a standing invitation to sabbath services, sabbath dinners, and special privileges at the backroom synagogue.

All these did not disturb me as much as the invitation I felt was being offered by Miss Miriam Venuevel. Between her tears there were a goodly number of glances my way which were, if I may put it delicately, invitational in character. It will be easier to turn down an invitation to attend sabbath services than it will be to turn down the offerings of this young lady.

May 10, 1828

Doctor La Rue has removed the cast. How my arm itches! I continue to study law, and to tutor Madame Roselius and Bernadette.

My income is ten dollars per week. Two and one half dollars are for rent, two for food, fifty cents is for tobacco, a habit Mr. Lopez has me well schooled in. Of the remaining five dollars, I have opened an account at the bank and deposit two and one-half dollars each week. The remaining two and one-half I send home.

May 15, 1828

The fragrance of Madame Picard's party is still in my nostrils. Never did I see more beautiful women, never did I see more beautiful dresses, or hear more exquisite music. One girl I was drawn to with particular fervor. It happened like this. The orchestra which was assembled on the courtyard walk stopped, and then Madame Picard announced that the girls had learned a new dance, a variation on the tarantella, and that they would teach the boys. The other chaperones of the party besides Madame Picard were a lady whom I don't know and my Madame Roselius. These formed a line, and down the line the girls assembled themselves. When Madame Picard clapped her

179

hands the girls each went across the courtyard where we young men were standing and each chose a partner for the dance instruction.

Of course each of us had our eye on one of them long before the signal of Madame Picard. So that when she clapped her hands and the girls moved toward us, giggling, because their strict training forbids approaching a man in almost any way except this protected party game, the men began to maneuver to get themselves selected by their choice, a little like ships negotiating the harbor.

I saw mine the instant I entered that courtyard. So that when she started walking in our direction I walked towards her and we met at the goldfish pond, the first couple in the courtyard to be ready to learn the dance.

She has eyes dark as coals and a high intelligent forehead, white skin, white shoulders, and looks altogether like a lily wrapped in chiffon. Her dress was of a flowing red damask and easily the most stunning of all the girls there. There is nothing about her presence that does not exude an aura of romance and even a little intrigue, especially when the light of the candelabra falls on her and is reflected in her eyes. My first impulse was to put my hand on her shoulder to see if this exquisite material was indeed of human stuff.

"And will you do me the honor of telling me your name?" I finally asked.

"You may call me Colette," she said.

"And is that what others call you as well?"

"What others call me, Monsieur, does not matter, does it?"

"I suppose not," I believe I stammered.

"And so, I repeat, you may call me Colette. Unless, of course, you think that name does not fit."

"No, mademoiselle, I think Colette a beautiful name, and you are fittingly called."

We were already well into the instruction of this dance, and I, with my hand on Colette's waist, was like a man transported. She seemed not to look into my eyes but let her gaze glance off mine and then return.

"You are an excellent dancer, Monsieur," she said after

a delicious silence.

"I should do even better if my feet were on the ground, Colette."

Looking over my shoulder as we circled the courtyard, she said, "The others are staring at us. Why is that?"

"I am sure it is *you* they are staring at. The women out of envy, and the men out of desire."

"You are a flattering man, monsieur, and not a little immodest in the presence of a lady."

"I meant not to be immodest. I apologize if I offended you."

"You have not offended me at ·all, monsieur. Quite the contrary. I am completely charmed."

"Judah Benjamin, at your service," I said.

"I know who you are," she answered.

And now, to my delight and amazement, this Colette, this dream of a girl, turns out to be Colette Mazareau, the great lawyer's daughter!

June 6, 1828

Mr. Stringer told me at work today that he has made some inquiries into the background and character of my friend Dr. John La Rue.

"Dr. La Rue is a complete charlatan and a mountebank, Judah. I have done some checking. Not only is he not a people doctor, he's not even a horse doctor as you said he claimed. He is unlicensed, unschooled, unbusinesslike, and uncouth. On the surface he is the opposite of all these things and appears extremely civilized, debonair, and so on. This is called the flim-flam, my young friend, and Doctor La Rue is one of New Orleans' finest practitioners of the art.

"You thought I didn't know this?" I asked.

"How could you know this, Judah? You just arrived."

"I can read character, Mr. Stringer."

"Well, you fooled me. Why are you seen with him?"

"Who's looking, Mr. Stringer?"

"Mazareau, that's who."

181

"Aha! So she's spoken of me to him. How wonderful!"

"I don't know how you do it, Judah. Do you know how close-knit those Creoles are? Why, even to get an invitation to one of their soirees is highly out of the ordinary. And then to charm the old man's daughter off her feet! What did you say to her, Judah?"

"I refuse to answer," I told Mr. Stringer, "on the grounds of confidentiality."

"Well, refuse away, and deny an old man his little pleasures! But take my advice and keep away from La Rue because Mazareau may be a great lawyer, but he's also a Creole father. And if he says no to his daughter, then no it is, and you will not be bringing her ices anymore in the courtyard. And that would be a shame because he likes you immensely."

"He will even more when I am admitted to the bar."

"And that will be soon enough, the way you're learning. Give yourself another year or two, perhaps, Judah. By the way, how are the eyes?"

"Dr. La Rue says they are fine."

"Dr. La Rue my arse!"

Mr. Stringer and I shook hands and he told me he was raising my salary to $13 a week.

June 28, 1828

I received today a written invitation to come to dinner at the Venuevels'. The invitation said they had not seen me at the sabbath services for over a month and were concerned about my welfare. Mrs. Venuevel signed the invitation and on the bottom of it she wrote: "And Miriam asks me to send you her special regards."

I sent back a note politely thanking them but begging their indulgence in that I have so much to study. This is true, as Mr. Stringer and I work on torts and contracts this evening.

July 1, 1828

182

I am pleased to have received today a letter from David Seixas. He is in Missouri of all places. "Dear Judah," he writes, "I am here in a small town the name of which seems to change every other week, as does the population. We have to walk half a mile for water in the morning and we sleep under the stars, as there is a shortage of lumber for cabins. You would love it here! Am working with Mr. Lundy in organizing a society which even you, with all your ease of phrase, would have trouble getting out in one breath. It is called *The American Convention for Promoting the Abolition of Slavery and Improving the Condition of the African Race*. I know we disagree on this subject, but wanted to let you know that a lot of planters here and in Tennessee and the Carolinas belong or at least are sympathetic to doing something for the African. Something short of emancipation for now, something like a gradual tenancy and education. I'll take the liberty of sending you some of the pamphlets when we've finished preparing them.

"In the meantime, I wanted to tell you Mr. Lopez has disposed of the shack for me and I have the proceeds of that, all of fifty dollars, which I am donating for printing costs for the Society. It's lonely and it's frustrating, but it's a mission and a direction in this life.

"How is that ridiculous Dr. La Rue, and are you become an absinthe addict yet under his tutelage?

"I would tell you to write to me but I have no permanent address as I am an itinerant with the Society, so you will have to rely upon me for this period to keep in contact.

> "Affectionately,
> "Your friend, Seixas"

July 4, 1828

The cannon roared, a bonfire was set to float in the harbor, and an old Seminole Indian was dug up and tarred and feathered to celebrate the independence. The Davis Gambling Parlor was shut down by order of the police, who decreed there was to be no blackjack on Independence Day. The defense is going to contend that it was solitaire that was being played, by sixteen men, individually, sitting around a table!

Monsieur Mazareau gave a small party for several of the friends of his family, and he honored me with an invitation. My French has improved so much that I was speaking it the whole evening without realizing it was not my own first language. Mazareau and the other lawyers discussed the trial of Marat during the Revolution in France. He found half-a-dozen flaws in the thread of the Jacobins' argument. He is a brilliant man. I listened in awe, as did the others there in attendance, including the brothers John and Thomas Slidell, both recently passed the bar examination.

As Madame Mazareau suddenly took ill with a slight fever just before the guests arrived, Colette has filled in as hostess in her mother's stead. Half a dozen times I wanted to rise to help her with the chores, but she supervised the slaves brilliantly, and one course followed another, the party moved from ballroom to parlor to courtyard with a fluid effortlessness.

The other guests left early and I lingered to talk to Mazareau. There were so many subjects I wanted to discuss that I did not know where to begin. He is a man of such heady brilliance that he can talk of anything, he can talk about the weather and make it sound sublime. He is like my own father, but amplified one hundred times over. And, *unlike* my father, Mazareau is immensely successful. He sits in a large high-backed chair, in a smoking jacket, his thin cigar in a holder, and his long unkempt hair pushed back behind his ears.

"Did you talk to the Slidells, Judah?"

"Very briefly, Monsieur."

"I review the bar examinations for the state, as you know, and these two acquitted themselves quite well."

"Yes, they told me you were pleased. I myself, of course, am pea-green with envy of them."

"But whatever for, Judah? Together they are only half as brilliant as you. Their examinations were not so much precise as they were clever."

"But you said they excelled."

"I have my reasons, Judah. Look here. These men are both from New York. They passed the bar here only as a stepping-stone to run for political office. I do not quarrel with this at all. I like to have politicians indebted to me in some way. The Slidell brothers know what they did on their examinations, and they know some praise from me, deserved or not, has and will continue to do them well. It is a good position for a lawyer to be in. Would you not agree?"

Of course, I saw Mazareau's point. One grows up very quickly in New Orleans!

Before I had to leave, Colette and I found a moment to be alone. She was wearing red again, not a damask, but rather a scarlet gown with a black velvet belt and shoes with silver buckles. "Will you permit me to hostess a party for you, Judah, to celebrate your admission to the bar?"

"Not only will I permit it," I said after kissing her on her soft lips, "I will demand it."

September 1, 1828

Today I have received the following letter from my mother:

Yehudah:

Here the High Holidays are approaching and we have not received a letter from you whether you are returning home to be with us. While your father and I can accept your moving to New Orleans and approve your study of law, we cannot countenance disregard for tenets of your religion.

I must tell you Rabbi Venuevel, here in Charleston

185

on business, paid us a social call. And I, having only the normal instincts of motherhood, asked him of your welfare and whether he had seen you at the temple.

I confess that his report to me is a cause of much concern. What is wrong with his Miriam, a daughter of Israel, child of a respected and learned man, that you shun her attentions?

Your father and I thank you for the money you are sending home, but we do not want one red cent from an assimilationist!

Mend your ways, Yehudah, and write your mother a letter.

September 9, 1828

I relent and finally give in to what amounts to out and out pleading by the Venuevels to attend high holiday services. It is hardship for me because I am only half way through the French code, and by now I expected to have completed it. Mr. Stringer tells me to slow down, but I know my own pace, and I could get through fifty pages during the time I will be with the Venuevels pounding my chest in atonement.

I skipped the New Year holiday, feeling that celebrating the secular new year is enough. And the September new year on the Jewish calendar is, at any event, an agricultural or seasonal marking point.

The Yom Kippur service is filled up with all the Jews in New Orleans. I realize that except for the Venuevels I recognize no one. I have been spending my time in different circles. I anticipated this to some extent and had asked Mr. Stringer to join me; perhaps he might find the holiday of interest. But, no, he said. "I honor all religions but practice none."

"I'm not asking you to practice," I answered him, "but to keep me company. You see, Mr. Stringer, they are trying to make a match for me, and I need your protection."

"You, my young sir, need protection from no one. And anyway, in affairs of the heart I am the complete fumbler. No one is a bachelor by choice, you know."

"Perhaps I can interest the young lady in you. Miriam Venuevel is her name, and she is dark, not bad-looking. . . ."

"Not so easy, Judah. No new tricks for this old dog. Tonight I shall dine at my favorite restaurant, alone, as usual, and quite enjoy it. If there were a female seated across the table from me, how could I read my paper and my law journal?"

"When I am married," I told him, "I shall ask my wife to leave the room so I can read."

"As you wish, my boy, but for now you go off to your Jewish feast, and I shall go off to my gentile feast. And by the by, Judah, is there any talk yet of marriage with your Colette? Whenever I see Mazareau at the court he is always asking of you."

"In truth all I do with my time is work for you, study for myself, and see his Colette."

"His?"

"His until I pass the bar. I will do no talk of marriage and I even try to avoid thinking about it, until I pass the bar. A man has to have a sense of his profession and a sense of his future before he takes a wife."

"Ha! He's probably offered you half the Creole practice in the city."

"Well, I do feel like part of the family."

"I knew it," Mr. Stringer said, as we locked the door to the office. "You will be the first Hebrew among the Creoles, and your son will be the mayor of New Orleans. Good day, Judah," he said as we parted on the street. "You have every reason to be wearing that smile you have on your face."

During the service, who is sitting next to me? Miriam. I had to ignore her, for politeness on my part might be too easily misinterpreted as interest. I believe also that I had some success at this, for midway through the prayer in which the supplicant (surely not I!) strikes his chest with the enumeration of

187

each and every sin, I could not help but notice Miriam looking at me while I was looking at a striking woman on the far side of the stark room.

What a shapely breast this woman was striking in her prayer! It was all I could do to restrain myself from running over, grasping her hand, and preventing her from doing any damage to her form. My speech was already prepared in my imagination. Some breasts may be struck, I would tell her, but others, yours in particular, should be caressed. For her part, she would respond by being slightly shocked, but also aroused by my lewdness. Not in the temple, she would say. Where, then, madame?

I need not go on with this script, delicious as it is. But the woman, with her curled hair, her delicate nose, and her fine figure, did seem to me a little like a Jewish version of my Colette.

When Miriam saw me staring she, with some reluctance, whispered, "That is Ada Isaacs. She's an actress and a singer."

I was about to ask where she sang and what she acted, and if under her own name, and in which plays, and was she married or engaged, and a hundred other questions, when the rabbi saw us whispering. From amidst the intoning of the prayers, in which he was leading the congregation, I detected a slight smile on his face. How ironical that he thinks, if this be the meaning of his smile, that the object of my whispering is his daughter.

I did not get an opportunity to be introduced to Ada Isaacs, but I shall make a note of her name to see if it appears in any of the plays about New Orleans. Ada Isaacs' nose is more shapely than Colette's. Colette's hair is finer, darker, more lustrous, but Ada's bangs are alluring . . . I wonder if she noticed me. . . .

Editor's Note:

Here, with the conclusion of this entry of September 9, 1828, occurs the first, but by no means the largest, of the many lacunae in the Benjamin Diaries. While there are scant entries written in Benjamin's hand, there are, however, a good number of letters, mainly from his family, which he received and placed in the ledgers of the diary. In some of the letters, particularly the ones from his mother, there are underlinings and circling of certain words, as if Benjamin were going over the letters carefully. Certain letters in which Mrs. Benjamin discusses the family's strained finances, have the amounts of money circled in the bold blue ink of Mr. Benjamin's pen. In the margins of these letters we also find computations, which perhaps suggest it was here he figured out the amount of his income he could spare, over the years, for the support of his mother and father and family. It is well established that he provided not only for himself, but for his parents and siblings in Charleston, and later in Beaufort, South Carolina, where they moved in 1831.

In addition to the letters, the pages of the Benjamin Diaries, subsequent to the September 9, 1828 entry, contain a substantial number of newspaper articles, apparently clipped by Benjamin and inserted as part of the ongoing record. The newspaper articles cover a wide variety of subjects, but feature mainly politics.

We may dwell for a moment on why the actual diary entries do not cover these years. While there is of course no definitive answer, it is clear that Benjamin was studying intensively for the bar examination during the late 1820's. His reputation, obtained later in life, for the prodigious amount of energy he possessed, and for his capacity for sustained legal and political labors, clearly shows its origins in this period of his life. He began to shoulder the responsibilities of a career, a wife, and the support of his family as these years wore on. So that when he re-emerges in the early 1840's he is already established as a rising legal star of New Orleans and Louisiana.

Before presenting a selection of the letters, articles,

and legal papers, let me, for the sake of continuity, simply indicate that Judah Phillip Benjamin was called to the bar of the state of Louisiana on December 16, 1832. Three months later on March 12 he married Colette Mazareau and moved with her to a house at 11 Bourbon Street.

III

SECOND DIARY

MARCH 11, 1834—APRIL 15, 1861

PART III

March 11, 1834

Dear Judah, my son,

I have just had opportunity to read your *Digest of Reported Decisions Before the Supreme Court of Louisiana*, which copy I am appreciative you have sent to your old father. While I know little about the law, and even less about the law in Louisiana (I have, alas, not much mastered even the commercial law of South Carolina, where I do business—or so says your mother), I can at least tell a thorough book when I see one. It was astute of you to write it, and your collaboration with Mr. Slidell seems to have been felicitous. A man must hang a special shingle, if that shingle is to be spotted among the rest. I believe you have done it. I wish you continued success.

Needless to say, what you are able to send us is much appreciated, or so mother has asked me to tell you. I also take this opportunity to write you, man to man, now that you are married, that things do not go well with us—with your mother and me. I have taken a small room of my own now, away from her. Please continue to send what you can, but send it all to her. A man can make his way in the world more easily than a woman, and you have nothing to fret as concerns me. Pursue your career with all the ambition and drive which I seem to lack. You have in your veins not only your own share, but mine, which is unused.

What, Judah, do you make of the politics of our time? The firebrands, the hell-raising speeches I have heard in the square, and all this business of conventions and nullification! I read political sheets, but I am mainly with my philosophy, the mother of discipline. Be assured that in South Carolina there is at least one calm, sane man poring over his Spinoza as the others drill and oil their muskets.

With Love,
Your father

Dearest Judah,

My dearest brother! How wonderful it always is to sit down to write you. I have looked forward to it all day. It is as if I am talking to you with my pen, and I await your letters back to me as I awaited birthday gifts when we were children.

I am sorry to say there is no good news to write of Momma and Poppa. Their separation seems quite complete now, and all my attempts to reconcile them have failed. Poppa has moved out all his clothes, his books, and his pipes. The rest, he says, Momma can have, or burn.

Yesterday the rabbi told them he could have a writ of divorce drawn up, if they both consented. But neither Momma nor Poppa seemed interested. When together, they are stony silent or Momma is shrieking. I wonder if ever a marriage is perfect. If marriages are all made in heaven, as Momma says, then God has certainly blundered in this case. I believe they endured in silence these many years while we grew up. Now that we have our own lives, their patience for each other has run out.

Momma spends almost all her time at Kehillath Yisroel; Poppa has his store and his cronies. Their lives go on, and occasionally someone gossips cruelly, and then it subsides. I look after Penina and Joseph as best I can. God knows I could not manage without your kind help. I hope you get more cases, as you write, and that you are a success in all the ways you want and deserve.

Your adoring sister,
Rebecca

July 18, 1836
Paris, France

Judah,

How marvelous it is in this city! We must go to Europe together some time, but since you must work, as you say, I am so grateful I at least can be here. A thousand thousand more thanks, my husband.

I found the most lovely gown at Tussaud's the other day and had no trouble buying it. I have been actually able to communicate well with the Parisiens. Our dialect is not so strange here as you told me it would be.

I am newly coiffed, and you would find me radiant, I am sure. My father's cousins, the Martinets, are wonderful hosts. They have given me my own room, a large chamber with two double windows which look out upon the Place Clitchy. The bed is so comfortable, pure goose feathers, that I sometimes spend the whole day lounging and reading.

It rains here twice a day, at noon, and just before dinner. The air in the city is thus cleansed by Nature herself. How much more beautiful than New Orleans, where I feel I must hold my nose with each and every junket into the streets!

Oh, Judah! I feel I was born out of my time. The old world is for me. Mr. Martinet took me to the salon of the cousin of the second cousin of the Emperor's assistant for American affairs. I believe I was the prettiest lady there, or so I was told. But you cannot believe a word of this world-famous French flattery; so says Madame Martinet. I told her I could choose to believe it if I wanted, and perhaps I would want to, as I am so far from my dear dear husband.

Please write, and send me 1,000 more francs.

Adieu,
Colette

January 5, 1837
Richmond, Va.

My Dear Son-in-law,

It is like a summer's day here, and I am through with my meeting at the attorney general's earlier than I had expected. Do you know what he showed me, Judah? It was a copy of the *Reported Decisions of the Supreme Court of Virginia Commonwealth*. Does it remind you of the title of any legal tome with which you are familiar? You are slowly but surely becoming a well-known name outside our home state, and this is to your credit. Your book apparently is becoming the model for similar state books throughout the South.

But it is really not the law about which I wanted to write you. It is the subject of my daughter—your wife. It is amazing to me how men such as myself, who make their living with words and speeches, find it difficult to express themselves in person on delicate matters. Thus, this epistle.

It concerns me greatly that Colette and you spend so much time apart. It is not only that I rarely see her, although that is part of it, but it is also unseemly that a young married couple should have such an arrangement. If there are troubles between you, you may come to me about them. What is a father-in-law for? And your own father is so far away. Judah, a marriage without trouble of some kind hardly deserves the name of marriage! My door is always open for you.

If Mrs. Mazareau, however, seems at times curt, as I know she was when we dined together at the Roseliuses, please forgive her. She tends to lay all blame on the husband, as she is a mother and blind to any faults whatsoever in her daughter. As a man, I can appreciate that a woman, even my own daughter, may have a shortcoming or two. But can these faults be so grievous that you spend with her only one or two months a year?

P.S. The brief you and Conrad wrote for the Robinson case was excellent. I did not change even a comma, but sent it on to the court clerk.

August 11, 1838

Dear Judah,

I want to put on paper (is it so I can get the credit from posterity?) that you should begin thinking about a career in politics. The speech you gave last night at the Boston Club was among the most eloquent I have ever heard in Louisiana in the twenty-five years I have been here. And I have heard many a travelling orator work over the silver bells in his throat to make a point, and a dull one at that! But never have I heard such music and subtle logic as you graced us with. I pointed you towards the law, and was not wrong. Mark me when I say that politics is for you.

I agree with you that the Whigs deserved their loss and that Hugh Lawson would have been the candidate to defeat Van Buren; that New Yorker ought to go back to his farm in Albany. I would keep an eye on Harrison, however. He has a position on the rights of the states just as solid as Lawson's, and Harrison has wider appeal. You performed a service by underlining their positions and showing their similarities.

I cannot stomach Van Buren. I miss the good old days of General Jackson. This Van Buren is ridiculous, and some say it is because he may be a relative of Aaron Burr's.

Remember that the 1840 election is not so far off. I nominate and second YOU.

Your friend,
Greenbury Stringer

May 5, 1839

Judah,

As I told you last night, I have left for New York City. I have been waiting three long months, and now that the weather is fair, why should I delay?

You say your work does not permit you to accompany me. Well, I cannot help that, nor can I complain. I simply must get away.

I am staying with a niece of the New York philanthropist, Mr. August Belmont, whom I met in Paris and whom I told you about. Do you remember? Did you listen to me? Do you ever? I could swear that when I speak to you, you have your mind on your cases.

I know you are thinking of your career and, in that, you are working also for me. When I return I shall make a party for all the lawyers and politicians, to whom you are beholding for return invitations.

In the meantime please send funds as requested.

Colette

P.S. I do not believe I am pregnant, but as I do not trust the doctors in New Orleans, I am going to be examined by Miss Belmont's personal physician.

March 1, 1841

Dear Judah,

Enclosed please find one box of fine Havanas. You may ask what they are for, and I will surely tell. They are by way of congratulations. I had to find out from the proud grandpa, Mazareau, that you and Colette are blessed with a little girl. I will therefore accept one of these cigars from you any time within the coming year. You fool! Don't you know you are supposed to celebrate things? I never thought I would meet a man who works harder than I, but in you I have found him.

The other purpose of the cigars is also congratulations and thanks—mostly thanks—for all your help organizing the club for Harrison. He made a good speech at the inaugural, which I attended. The man, however, looks very sickly, and I hear tell we may have elected a tubercular to be President of the United States. If this is so, Clay will have even a louder voice in the government than we had expected.

My regards to Mrs. Benjamin.

Yours,
John Slidell

November 1, 1842

Dearest Yehudah,

It were not bad enough that I have not seen *you* in so many months. Now I have to beg that I may be permitted to see my grandchild, who is to be two years old without having been gazed upon by me.

It may be true that I have been hard with you, but I have my principles, to which I must be faithful. Nevertheless, I would like to see this child of yours. Have you so little say in these matters that you cannot have your wife journey home from Paris for at least a month? I should like to see this Ninette, who will live on after I have died, with Mendes blood in her veins.

I surely am too old to go to France myself, and although your offer is appreciated, it is as unfeasable as it is generous.

When you left Charleston I told you that marrying outside your religion would bring nothing but trouble. And now you see how true a mother's prophecies can be. You have position and wealth and fame, but where is your happiness? Where is your family life? Can all your "substantial fees," as you describe them, give your mother the joy she seeks in heirs?

Momma

199

December 3, 1842
New York

Dear Benjamin,

Your disposition on the runaway slave case is being distributed in pamphlet form in every major port and city. You, who never owned a slave in your life, are now the legal authority to whom the slave lawyers are all turning!

Congratulations! If you do not accept the club's bid to run for Assembly on the Whig ticket, you are a fool. Even Cicero served in the Roman Senate.

Yours,
John Slidell

March 15, 1843

Dearest Brother, J.P.,

I write to thank you from the bottom of my heart for the beautiful doves you had delivered for Mr. Levy.

After he was lowered into the ground, Mr. Lopez released the doves, just as you requested, and they flew straight up into the blue sky. As I watched them grow smaller and smaller, until they became specks, I thought of the gentleness of Mr. Levy and the good years God granted that we could spend together.

I wish you could have been here, but your doves, your gift of perfect thoughtfulness, made me feel you were right by my side.

Forgive Momma, who has written you a scathing note, which I read on the desk before she posted the mail. I understand that you are a busy man. Only God can explain how your first day in the Assembly coincides with the funeral. Is the good never unmixed with the bad? I think I grow philosophical and more like Poppa in my middle age.

Please do not take heed of Momma's recriminations. I

doubt whether she believes them fully herself.

As for your suggestion: we are selling the house, which is too big for Momma alone; she will be moving in with me.

Rebecca

September 12, 1843
Norfolk, Va.

Dear Judah Benjamin,

I was passing through Charleston, when I met your sister. I was shocked and saddened to hear of the death of your brother-in-law. Mr. Levy and I had spent many a wonderful afternoon in the woods, and if ever there were a man who could be returned to the earth in peace, as the Bible says, he was the man.

Becky also conveyed to me the good news of your first political victory. I say "first," because I know it will be one of many.

I have been working with Birney of the Liberal Party, which you may have heard of in Louisiana. Birney ran on the Abolitionist ticket.

I am enclosing some copies of *The Philanthropist* for you to read. As I wrote you last, I have given up working with Garrison, because he talks more than he does. Birney gets votes while Garrison gets applause. I myself hardly make speeches any more, and only to old friends, like you and Mr. Lopez, read some of *The Philanthropist* with interest, and then launched into a speech of his own. He quoted chapter and verse to show how slavery was sanctioned in the Bible, how you couldn't have your slave work on the Sabbath, and you must free him every Jubilee. As you know, Judah, almost no one is as learned in the Bible as Mr. Lopez, so all I could say in response was that we didn't have time to wait fifty years to free the slaves. Not a very good answer, I admit! I was told, later, that the Bible can be understood to be anti-slavery too. Broth-

201

erhood is not only for whites.

You may be interested in knowing that I was selected to present Henry Clay our petition, which requested him to free his own slaves, as a gesture for the rest of the South. He wanted to find out precisely where this Democrat stands. You know what Clay said as I approached him? I think I can remember exactly.

"I've read your petition carefully, gentlemen," he said. "And I want you all to know I condemn slavery. If I had my wish I would have every American slave sent back to Africa."

"So, why will you not sign this petition, Mr. Clay?" we pressed on, "and emancipate your slaves? You own over one hundred, we know."

"One hundred and three, to be precise, young man," he said with a charming smile. "And have you any idea," he asked, "what would happen to my one hundred and three slaves, if they were given their freedom immediately? Do you think any of them can read and write? Do you think any of them know a profession? No, sir. Much as I condemn the evils of slavery, I condemn even more the greater evil that would result from immediate abolition. We would have on our hands a contest between the two races, civil war, carnage, conflagration, devastation, and the ultimate extermination or expulsion of the Africans."

"What, then, do you propose, sir?" I asked him.

"Gradual freeing of them, and some education to boot."

"Then," said I, "if we change the wording of this petition to call upon you for a committment to the gradual freeing of your slaves, will you then sign?"

"Mr. Seixas," he said irritably, "I will not do it whatever language you concoct, because however much I would like to free my slaves, many of them are aged and need my care. If I free them, will you have them sitting on street corners, asking for coins from passers-by? Will you have them become public nuisances, criminals, and then public wards?"

"That is no reasonable excuse, sir," I said.

"If it is not," he replied, "will you, sir, on behalf of

your Abolitionist Party, contribute $30,000 to provide for the wants of my slaves after they have been emancipated? I shall let them go upon receipt of your check."

This is a cagey politician, Judah. He will try to please us all, and in so doing will please none.

Much luck, and would that we could see each other again soon! Unfortunately my travels do not take me so far south as you are.

                    Affectionately,
                    David Seixas

                                        January 2, 1844

The Honorable J. Benjamin
11 Bourbon Street
New Orleans, La.

Enclosed, good sir, is the prospectus on the land about which you made inquiry.

May I compliment you on your discriminating choice of property. While all the land in Plaquemines Parish is good for rice and cane, this particular tract is noteworthy for its fine drainage and its richness in topsoil. There is what amounts to a fine mill on the property, as well as an intact sugar house with kettles. It is too bad you did not have time to let me show all the buildings to you.

I am in receipt of your deposit, and will keep same until another appointment can be arranged. I am at your disposal, for I know you are a busy man. I would, however, urge you to contact me within the early part of the year, as the gentleman on the adjoining property has expressed interest in expanding his fences.

                    Sincerely,
                    Moon Lucerne
                    Parish Clerk
                    Plaquemines, Louisiana

May 4, 1844

Mr. Benjamin
2 Exchange Place
N.O. Louisiana

Dear Sir,

First, my compliments to you on your selection to the constitutional convention.

Herein are your instructions, your seat designation, the location of your quarters, and some information about Jackson, a town you may not be familiar with, but nevertheless an appropriate choice for a convention to reform the law for the whole state.

You did yeoman's work in speaking engagements and in fulfilling writing assignments, and we are also grateful for the use of your offices, centrally located in New Orleans, which made our stay there most delightful.

> Sincerely,
> Joseph Walker
> Whig Executive Committee
> Chairman

June 12, 1844

Dear J.P.

Your two weeks' visit to us should have lasted four, or six, or eight!

Even Momma broke into laughter with your rendition of the G.P. Stephens ghost story. We are grateful for the Stephens and the whole trunkful of books and periodicals which will keep us in touch a little more with the happenings in the world.

I should tell you what Momma is too proud to tell you herself: She reads daily, and with avid interest, each and every political article in the *Delta*. What a wonderful idea it was to have the paper sent here. It is like having you here when you are not, for there are so many stories in which your name appears. If your name appears, Momma will read the article two and sometimes three times. She reads your quoted speeches too, and I would not be surprised if she could recite sections. If she dozes off to sleep, I remove the paper lightly, so as not to wake her, and then it's my turn to read. It is a point of some contention between us who gets the *Delta* first.

How brilliant was your defense of New Orleans at the convention! How could they even consider not representing the city in proportion of its population? You made your point with honesty and originality.

I do not like the reporter who, in describing you, wrote, 'And then the little representative from New Orleans rose.' What matters a man's height at a constitutional convention? And how is this to be interpreted except as insult? My ire is up about this, just as it would be if I heard over the clothes line some nasty gossip. Put gossip into print and that is called reportage! Well, I am only a woman.

Becky

Editor's Note:
Several weeks later, in debate surrounding the basis of computation of population, Benjamin addressed the Assembly again, and detached sections of his speech:

February 5, 1844

I ask you, sirs, if the Federal basis of representation, as adopted in the report, is not a clear departure from the very principle and essence of democratic government? For what does it propose? It proposes taking a part of the representation from the electors, to whom it alone belongs, and conferring it upon the slaves. And those who raise

205

their voices against so flagrant a proposition are, it is insinuated, favoring the views of the Abolitionists! Why, sirs, it is the party who makes the accusation who is upholding the doctrine of the Abolitionists; they are for giving the slaves political consequence—the very thing for which the Abolitionists have been contending for years.

I, gentlemen, am a lawyer. I am for regarding slaves as they are regarded by the law—property. Is it not so?

Slaves are, by our laws, nothing but property. But, says the delegate from Lafourche Parish, we should allow them to form a part of the basis of representation because they are productive labor, and labor should be represented. If this argument hold good, then it might, with equal propriety, be urged that we should allow representation to horses and oxen, which are attached to the glebe, and which are equally productive of labor.

Editor's Note:

At the bottom of the legal paper on which this speech is written, two items are attached. First is the deed to Belchasse Plantation in the Parish of Plaquemines, dated February 2, 1844. Under the deed is a small notation in Benjamin's sure, clear hand:

"If I am to talk publicly of slavery, and if I am to defend it, as I believe is my responsibility, does it not behoove me to be an owner of human chattel in my own right? Otherwise I am subject to attack that I know not whereof I speak.

"I also confess to a fascination as to what it will be like to be the master of the lives of men, women, and children. Accordingly, I have given my consent to Mr. Lucerne of the Parish Clerk's Office to include in the purchase price of Belchasse seventeen of the twenty-five slaves who had belonged to the prior master. Of the eight other slaves, two were freed, three died, and three others have their whereabouts unknown, presumed run off."

January 18, 1846

Dearest J.P.:

Belchasse gets more and more beautiful every day. It was so right of you to insist mother move in here. There is so much to do to keep the house clean and to manage the slaves; she is constantly busy and has little time to dote on the troubles of her life.

I have had three more oaks planted in the front, next to the five which are already thriving there. It is perfect light for such trees. The rooms all need a fresh coat of paint, or perhaps it is that my taste differs from the previous occupants. But the paint will be the only thing I shall change. As to the halls and parlors, how I love them! I spend hours peering at the pictures, the shepherds and the gondolas and the swings. In one of the books you sent us years ago, there were copies of paintings by that Frenchman, Fragonard. How these walls of Belchasse remind me of his charming gardens!

We will have the broiled chicken, with plenty of butter, just as you asked for. We shall expect Rilleux, Walker, Foucher, Aime, and Monsieur Mazareau. Will Mr. Stringer be joining us this weekend? Try to let me know, for if he is, I shall have to take his favorite madeira out from the cellar and let it light somewhat. How funny you are, Judah! You said that the madeira was only for special occasions. Do you realize we've drunk the madeira every weekend now for three months?

Becky

March 1, 1847

Dear Mr. Benjamin:

I will not mince words with you. You know how bored I was at Belchasse, and what did you do? You brought your entire family into my house to bore me even more! Have you no feeling for your own wife?

I will not have that woman, that mother of yours, look askance at me. I will not tolerate this in my own home. I will not let her move to the center of the table a dish which I have placed to the side. If you only spent more time at Belchasse you would have seen for yourself. But, no! What do you do? You come on the weekend with your special guests and expect me to entertain as if everything at Belchasse were peaceful.

I did my duty, Mr. Benjamin. I was your hostess, but I cannot be any longer. When you defended your mother last night, asked *me,* your wife, to be more understanding, I knew that there was no more to discuss. If they, your mother and your sister, want to run Belchasse, let them run it. They never appreciated me, and your mother never forgave me for being who I am.

She can have Belchasse to put her Sabbath candles on the mantle of the great hall. Let them burn the whole week long, for I will not be there to see them. Let them burn and take down the whole house with them!

I am going to Paris with Ninette. I plan to take permanent residence there. My daughter will learn her catechism, as I did; she will learn to be a lady in a civilized place. She has no father where she is now. She has only a busy, busy lawyer, reputed to be her father, who visits once a month with a gift. Better that Ninette should be fatherless in Paris than in Belchasse.

I cannot conceal my anger toward you. You have been a terrible toad of a husband to me. I could divorce you, but I am willing to come to a financial arrangement within this marriage.

I will write you with details of my needs, from France.

Colette

September 12, 1848

Dear Judah:

Thank you for sending me your new address. Polymnia

Street is an attractive block. I myself was once going to build on that site.

It is a terrible shame that Belchasse was flooded, for I remember it fondly for the long easy weekends we spent there. Perhaps there is a good side to disaster, however, for now you have to throw yourself back into work and, may I add, into politics. Walker has told me that you can have the seat in Congress if you want it. You are now acceptable to the plantation owners, to the merchants, and, it goes without saying, to the lawyers.

I think the seat is yours for the plucking, and I am upset that your financial reverses are postponing your political bid. I can advance you $30,000, but beyond that I cannot go. I think that if you gain the seat, as I am sure you will, for the Democrats have only an illiterate and a mule-skinner to run against you, then cases will come your way.

If you go to California for the land commission reports, as is rumored, you can still be nominated by the caucus *in absentia*. Do I have your permission? Washington is a hot, awful city, without a sidewalk, and with mud up to your thighs, but the power and the intrigue are there; and there it is, as you have said many times, that the fate of the Union will be decided, and soon.

Please consider, without haste, but, Judah, I have to have an answer within a fortnight. I cannot chase after you to the gold fields.

J. Slidell

Editorial from the *New Orleans Delta,* October 10, 1851

He is sagacious, possesses great tact, and would make a very brilliant and effective Senator. His appearance in that body would startle the gossips at Washington. His youthful figure and girlish face—his gentle, innocent, ingenuous expression and manner—his sweet and beautifully modulated voice, would render him decidedly the most unsenatorial figure in that body of gray heads and full-grown

209

men. But when he should arise in the Senate, and in the most modest and graceful manner proceed to pour forth a strain of the most fluent and beautifully expressed ideas, of the most subtle and ingenious arguments, casting a flood of light over the driest and most abstruse subjects, and carrying all minds and hearts with him by his resistless logic and insinuating elocution—then would the old Senators stretch their eyes and mouths with wonder, whispering to one another, 'That's a devilish smart fellow'—then would all the ladies declare, 'What a love of a man!' So beautiful, so wise, so gentle, yet so terrible in sarcasm—so soft-toned, yet so vigorous in logic! The *quid nuncs* and politicians would join in the general wonderment, and give their decided opinion that he was a psychological, physiological, and intellectual phenomenon. But, with all his genius, his universal talents and eloquence, Mr. Benjamin will hardly be elected to the Senate, because he is too valuable and necessary a man in this state. He is the acknowledged leader of several great enterprises, in which our state and city have a greater interest than in being ably represented in the United States Senate in Washington.

Editor's Note:

Benjamin's notation, appended to the above editorial, is dated the following day:

October 11, 1851

This reporter has positively driven me to the looking glass!

What does this mean that I am a "phenomena"?

And how is it that they describe me with all this cute boyishness of affect? I am a man full into my fortieth year. There are other young officials. There is Soulé and there is Slidell, not much older than I, but nowhere have I read pertaining to them such infantilisms.

While I am happy for this endorsement, I am also

irked. I shall grow a long, long beard. Or shall I go to the shoemaker and say to him, "Man, put on a double heel. I go to the U.S. Senate where a man is measured by how much of a heel he has, or is! Nay, put on a triple heel if I get appointed to committee, and a four-times heel if they offer me a cabinet post."

I believe I am still smarting from my visit to Paris. In the week I stayed in her chambers (for which I pay dear rent), Colette must have had half a dozen gentlemen callers, all of high fashion and high society. By the time of my departure, I felt as if my new fitted frock coat were but a rag about my shoulders. Everywhere I am respected, even by my detractors—everywhere but in the presence of my wife.

"I am the wife of a United States Senator-to-be," she said. "I must live in a style appropriate to the position. And Ninette must have the finest tutors and finishing."

"I could be much wealthier, my dear," I said, "if I left off public service for private practice."

"But I would not have prestige, Judah."

"And you prefer prestige to money, Colette? I find that hard to believe."

"I prefer both," she answered, the perfect coquette, "and you shall obtain both for me."

And out of her chambers I stalked for my boat home. Across the ocean I am still slave to her. I would divorce her if it were not for Ninette, and if it were not for the Catholic Church, both of whom I would have to combat in addition to my constituents.

I must find the writer of this editorial. I will ask Stringer to write the paper a letter objecting to his style.

January 8, 1852

Dear Judah,

Well, sir, you have the Senate seat. I wish the campaign had not been so personal and cruel as it became, but then again New Orleans is where the Bowie knife came from, and our politics cut more here than in other places.

I dare say it is not over yet, which is the point of this letter. Soulé and the Democrats are making plans to unseat you. You will have to respond to your naturalization, on which technical points they will try to oust you when you take the seat in March. I think they are sure to fail, and I personally feel Soulé has no desire to do this, but he is obliged to represent the worst in his party. If the judge has any sense, and if you control your temper, the matter will die, as the petition is signed by less than a majority of the members in the legislature.

I know how touchy you can get around matters such as this, and you know the law better than I. If in fact the Virgin Islands or St. Thomas was your place of birth, then of course you will have to have some naturalization process, idiotic as it may seem, as this country practically owns those islands and, in the not-too-distant future, will in fact incorporate them.

Do not, under any circumstances, lose your composure. You are well approved in the right places. If the attempt should succeed (and I repeat that it will not), then President Pierce, who appreciates your work in California, will offer you a seat on the Supreme Court. So you can see you are holding good cards; I wanted to convey this to you ahead of other sources. And one last point, about this naturalization business: You know as well as I that they are going to call you foreigner and parvenu. Let them. Your general policy of not responding to calumny is especially necessary in this confrontation.

Incidentally, I saw your wife in Paris this summer. She gets more beautiful with each passing year. You should not leave her alone so long and so often. The Frogs are a romantic and hungry lot.

Your friend,
Slidell

May 4, 1856

Mr. Benjamin,
Honorable Sir:

May I compliment you on your recent address before the Senate on the subject of the Kansas Bill. Your analysis of the federal compact I find astute; and, I will not linger on points your eloquence illuminated, except to say that the sovereignty of the states, in my estimation, is not as entirely unqualified as you make out. For even as the poet says,

> Great were the thoughts, and strong the minds,
> Of those who framed in high debate
> The immortal league of love that binds
> Our fair, broad empire state to state

The federation *is* immortal, and the right of secession, I must put forth to you, is not one of the Constitutional guarantees. Let the Kansans make up their own constitution and name their own state free or slave, subject only to their own domestic institutions. That is the issue. Not whether a state already in the Union can, on the issue of slavery or any other issue for that matter, withdraw from the Union. This is not the right of secession, but rebellion; and it has no other name.

Your humble colleague,
Stephen Douglas

April 4, 1857

Mr. J.P. Benjamin
of Louisiana:

The legislators, magistrates, and property owners of my state, assembled, have given me the honor of inviting you to address a joint session of our government houses. The object of your speech, if you please, to be an analysis of the real motives of the Northerners and the Abolitionists.

I quote from you in the *Congressional Globe* of one month ago: "They do not act consistently with their professions of desire to ameliorate the condition of the slave. Their real object seems rather to obtain such political power as shall put these parties in possession of sufficient representation, in both branches of Congress, to change the Federal Constitution, and to deprive the South of that representation which is already inadequate to protect her rights. When that shall have been done—when she is reduced to a feeble minority, utterly incompetent to move, and bound subserviently to the will of the North, then will the last act of the drama be played; and then will the sentiments which they hide now, but which they entertain in their heart of hearts, be developed to the country, and ruin and desolation spread over fifteen of the states of this Union."

You are most cordially invited to stay in my home, during your sojourn in Tallahassee, and to be my most honored guest.

Yours,
Senator David Yulee, Fla.

November 1, 1857
Charleston, South Carolina

Mr. J.P. Benjamin
United States Senate Bldg.
Washington, D.C.

Dear Sir:

As you may know there is much talk of negro revolts inspired hereabouts by abolitionists and northern emissaries. I am writing to offer you my assistance in ferreting out these instigators from our midst. I am an actress by profession and have much opportunity to hear the conversation of visitors to the cities where I tour. My information may be of some assistance to the Cause. My father says there is going to be a civil war. I hope he is mistaken; but, perhaps, the foiling of northern plots by exposing them will head off the conflict.

You may ask why I write to you. It is because we had the opportunity to meet once or twice at the home of the Venuevels, while you were a resident of this city. Perhaps you do not remember, but we talked of these subjects and were much in sympathy. I read recently your talk to the Senate, the newspaper report of which I have cut out and carry with me in my purse: "The people of the South appeal first and foremost to the guarantees of the Constitution, and when those guarantees shall fail, and not till then, will the injured, outraged South throw her sword into the scale of her rights, and appeal to the God of battles to do her justice. I say her sword, because I am not one of those who believes in the possibility of a peaceful disruption of the Union. It cannot come until every angry passion shall have been roused; it cannot come until brotherly feeling shall have been converted into deadly hate; and then, sir, with feelings embittered by the consciousness of injustice, or passions high wrought and inflamed, dreadful will be the internecine war that must ensue."

Junius Booth could not have delivered a better speech, Mr. Senator. I shall be in Baltimore in the next month doing a new play entitled *Our American Cousin*. Perhaps you could come to the theatre, or let me know if I may come to see you at the Capitol, at your convenience.

Most patriotically yours,
Ada Isaacs

December 3, 1857
Paris, France

Mr. Benjamin,

Ninette will be enrolling in the Convent of the Sacred

215

Heart School in Amiens at the first of the year. As this is the best of the Jesuit institutions, the fees are quite high, and there is no way I can pay them with the allowance I currently receive from you. Would you prefer my having the school send the bill to you, or will you send me funds to set up in trust for Ninette until her education is complete? I think the latter the only real alternative. Ninety thousand francs ought to cover the tuition, room and board, and her other needs for the four years of the school. I await your answer.

Colette

Editor's Note:
Following is either a copy or the original of a letter Benjamin wrote to President Buchanan. As there is no record of its having been received by the President, in all likelihood Benjamin never mailed it; but, after writing it, inserted it into one of his diary ledgers. Perhaps, after the vigorous defenses Mr. Benjamin had already put forth for slavery, this letter was deemed by him too tame and apologetic:

June 1, 1858

The Honorable James Buchanan
President of the United States

Sir:

Mr. President, the thirteen colonies, which, on the 4th of July, 1776, asserted their independence, were British colonies, governed by British laws. Our ancestors in their emigration to this country brought with them the common law of England as their birthright.

If I can show that the nation thus exercising sovereign power over these thirteen colonies did establish slavery in them; did maintain, control, and protect the institution; did originate and carry on the slave-trade; did support and foster that trade: that it forbade the colonies permission either to emancipate or export their slaves; that it prohibited them from inaugurating any legislation in diminution or discouragement of the institution—nay, sir, more, if I can show that at the date of our Revolution African slavery existed in England as it did on this continent; if I can show that slaves were sold upon the slave mart, in the Exchange and at other public places of resort in the city of London as they were on this continent; then, I shall not hazard too much in the assertion that slavery was the common law of the thirteen states at the time they burst the bonds that united them to the tyrannous mother country.

> Yours,
> Senator J.P. Benjamin,
> Louisiana

July 18, 1858

Mr. Benjamin,

I would like to apologize to you formally for my harshness on the floor this morning. I have of late been suffering from an irritability whose source I do not know; and this weather, fit more for hell than a Hall of Congress, brought about my snappishness. Whether we allot one hundred dollars per cannon or one hundred twenty-five is a question not of sufficient weight to cause rancor among those of us who will soon, I fear, be thrown together in an alliance against the North.

After the appropriations committee meeting tomorrow at noon, will you not honor me by being my guest for a glass of port?

> Humbly yours,
> Senator Jefferson Davis

October 20, 1859
Charleston, S.C.

Dear Judah,

I am an old man now, and last time we had correspondence—was it as much as twenty years ago?—I felt more strength in my legs than I do now.

Forgive me the familiarity with which I address you, for although you are now one of our most splendid Senators and, in my estimation, the greatest legal defender of our states' rights, you are nevertheless to me still the brilliant boy who passed so many pleasant hours with me in my study.

Brown's recent insurrection at Harper's Ferry, which, thank God, was put down, has brought into the open the need for us to prepare to defend ourselves. Although it says "Nation shall not lift up sword against nation," we are confronted now with the issue of self-defense, and we have an obligation to protect our hearths, our traditions, and our families.

I had occasion to watch the 16th South Carolina Regiment on the green this afternoon. There were eight weak companies parading for inspection. A more ridiculous farce could not possibly have been enacted. Andrew Jackson's ragtag army of 1812, in which I was proud to have served, was, by comparison, Hessian and professional!

If six hundred citizens, drawn up in two ranks, without arms or equipment, ununiformed, and ignorant of the first principles of a soldier's duty can be called a regiment, then this was a regiment.

I will forego more elaborate description, only stating that what is a farce now, enjoyed by idle juveniles, may be at no distant day a tragedy over which the State will mourn.

I want to offer, Judah, all my resources and my ships for the defense of the South. I do not say South Carolina, but the South. I am a merchant of some means, but I am older, and in all likelihood I will not live to see the resolution of this conflict. What I have done, therefore, is prepare papers authorizing the liquidation of my assets, to be placed in trust, and then given to a central Confederate Government of Southern States for the purposes of its military protection. You, Judah Benjamin, I am naming executor of that trust, and I ask you to use it for the defense of a United South, when the day and the need arise. As you know, the fire-eaters here call for secession now and defense of South Carolina soil only. They say their regiments will not serve to protect Virginia or Tennessee or Louisiana. You use my resources to fight this self-defeating course in the establishment of a Central Confederate Government.

Would that I could see you again before I die. But I feel time is pushing me along, and we will, I think, have no opportunity for a peaceful hour with books, and brandy, and cigars. I have full confidence in you. Farewell,

Moses Lopez

August 11, 1860
New York

Dear Judah, my love,

It is true what you write that too much time passes and too quickly. But how can we see each other more, for you have your work and I have mine, which I expect you to value no less than I do yours. I am becoming quite well known now, but it seems more so in the North than at home. I think these Yankee audiences fancy a Portia with a Southern drawl. Our *Julius Caesar* is now into its sixth week, an unheard-of run for Shakespeare. The play brings applause every night, and I daresay the bloodshed of it all, highlighted in our production, is bringing out the mood of nastiness and all the bellicosity of this city.

As to your invitation to see you in September, I cannot accept. Our play runs right through the end of this month, and then there are the Jewish holidays. The last performance, in fact, is on Rosh Hashanah, and on that day I do not work, and never have, and never will. The manager knows this by now and no longer importunes me. I cannot get to see you, then, before the next session. Will you not yourself, at this lady's request, go to a Jewish house of worship this one time during the year? It will do you no harm to negotiate Jehovah's assistance for you, for us, and for the South for the coming year.

I embrace you,
Ada

February 2, 1861
Paris, France

Dear Mr. Benjamin,

All Paris is in a furor with news of war from America. The *Figaro* carries your speeches, and I must confess you are striking quite a gallant pose, at least in print. The Emperor's court, or so I hear at the beautician's, is amused at the squabbling of the American children. That's the expression they use—*les enfants Americans*. I believe they are worried about the cotton getting here, since there is much talk of blockade.

This brings me to the point: Prices are soaring again, and my allowance forces me to walk about either hungry or unfashionable. I cannot tolerate either state. You must increase 550 francs quarterly. I cannot accept your refusal, as per your letter of January 2. I shall never forget how, in spite of my strong objections, you had 200 silver dollars melted down to forge the plantation bell at Belchasse. I expect the funds on the next boat.

Colette

Editor's Note:
Scrawled on the bottom of this letter, in large angry capitals, in Benjamin's script, are the words, *"Bitch, bitch, bitch."*

Editor's Note:

The following speech, Benjamin's farewell address to his colleagues in Washington, was clipped from the *Washington Star,* and placed in an envelope and stamped. The envelope was addressed to Benjamin's father, Phillip. This would not be strange, but for the fact that Benjamin's father had died two years earlier and was buried in the Jewish cemetery at Savannah. I know of no explanation for this except that the envelope could have been addressed prior to the date and never sent. It then became a convenient place to put the speech, which Benjamin must have inserted in the ledgers of his diary. This would be an adequate explanation except for two facts: No other speech, clipping, diary entry, or letter is placed in an envelope in all of the Benjamin Diaries. And, second, the stamp on the envelope was issued only three months before the date of Benjamin's senate speech.

February 5, 1861

And now, Senators, within a few weeks we part to meet as Senators in one common council chamber of the nation no more forever. We desire, we beseech you, let this parting be in peace. I conjure you to indulge in no vain delusion that duty or conscience, interest or honor, imposes upon you the necessity of invading our states or shedding the blood of our people. You have no possible justification for it. I trust it is in no craven spirit, and with no sacrifice of the honor or dignity of my own state, that I make this last appeal, but from higher and holier motives.

If, however, it shall prove vain; if you are resolved to pervert the government framed by the fathers for the protection of our rights into an instrument for subjugating and enslaving us, then, appealing to the Supreme Judge of the universe for the rectitude of our intentions, we must meet the issue that you force upon us as best becomes freemen defending all that is dear to man.

221

What may be the fate of this horrible contest, no man can tell, none pretend to foresee; but this much I will say: the fortunes of war may be adverse to our arms; you may carry desolation into our peaceful land, and with torch and fire you may set our cities in flames; you may even emulate the atrocities of those who, in the war of Revolution, hounded on the bloodthirsty savage to attack upon the defenseless frontier; you may, under the protection of your advancing armies, give shelter to the furious fanatics who desire, and profess to desire, nothing more than to add all the horrors of a servile insurrection to the calamities of civil war; you may do all this—and more, too, if more there be—but you never can subjugate us; you never can convert the free sons of the soil into vassals, paying tribute to your power; and you never, never can degrade them to the level of an inferior and servile race. Never! Never!

February 24, 1861
Montgomery, Alabama

Mr. Benjamin,

You are hereby appointed Attorney-General in the provisional government of the Confederate States of America. May God bless us in our great endeavor.

Jefferson Davis
President

April 15, 1861
Charleston, S.C.

Dearest Judah,

I arrived here the afternoon before it happened.
The whole town was astir, nobody could talk of any-

222

thing else, nobody had slept for days. Life ascended to the rooftops, where the women went wild, and the men uttered imprecations on the Yankee fort. At midnight it became known that Colonel Anderson, commanding at Sumter, had received a final ultimatum, that if he did not surrender by four, he would be fired upon. The hours passed slowly. Boats maneuvered in the harbor and there was rumor the fort was to be invaded. My father came upstairs to where we watched from our balcony and said that Anderson would not fire a shot.

How right he was! At exactly four our cannon fire began and lit up the sky. Volley after volley, and with each one death and destruction! We could hear nothing but shells for an hour; for two hours, the sky was lit up, and the old fort belched fire from three places where the wall was breached.

I remembered suddenly the afternoon my father took me to picnic on the grounds of the fort. How green was the lawn, how lovely was the day!

Now the street below our balcony is filled with rushing men, and I can see the shadows of their rifles rising to their shoulders, as they march to the harbor.

At six when the sun came up I threw myself on the bed and began to cry.

The Yankees and Lincoln have brought this on. They shall have to pay for it. I will be in Montgomery to meet you at the end of the month, as you wish. I will have with me then the two copies you requested of all Yankee troop movements I have noted. Until then,

> My kisses,
> Ada

IV

FOURTH DIARY

SEPTEMBER 17, 1865—JULY 22, 1867

PART IV

September 17, 1865
Southhampton, England
Blue Goose Inn

I have just caught a glance of myself in the looking glass. I am browned as a walnut. My face is lined like a sea captain's. My hair is thicker and lighter, my beard twice the length it has ever been. I confess that if I were not a believer in science I might have evidence that this countenance staring back at me from the mirror is not Judah Phillip Benjamin.

Ada enters the room as I lift up the scissors from the bureau.

"Oh no! Don't you dare cut a strand of that beard without asking me."

"But the train leaves in one hour for London. I've an appointment at the *Telegraph*, Ada, and I cannot present myself as a journalist if I look like an old salt."

"Don't you know that long beards are more becoming in London than in Richmond? You look like Admiral Nelson. All the better. Aren't they going to ask you to write about the escape?"

"Hardly," I said, clipping away, to Ada's charming displeasure. "They are more interested in articles about international law. But, frankly, they don't want me offending the Federals. The situation is still all too raw. With President Davis in jail, and Lincoln dead, and the Yankees in a vengeful lynching mood, all the *Telegraph* needs is an article about how Benjamin eluded Union gunboats . . . here," I said, putting the last touches on a goatee, "how does that look?"

"Positively continental," said she. "I will not kiss you until it grows back."

"As if you will have any choice." I embraced her. "I will get lodgings for us in London, and then send for you. As of now we have fifty dollars and a hunk of cheese between us."

"We have been on open boats, underneath the tropical sun, without sufficient food and water for twenty-three days, Judah. Do you really think that another two weeks or even another two months of deprivation will make any difference to us? You and I, my dear, are survivors."

"We'll make a new life here, Ada. That's a certainty. But society does not have to know how we will live."

"Your meaning, please, sir?"

"I mean simply that I will secure separate quarters for us, rooms for you and rooms for me. We will not live together publicly."

"This again!"

"I have a wife and child and reputation. I know what you think about these matters, but I cannot plan a new career if I am subject to doubt about my personal life."

"Will you divorce Colette?"

"Impossible. Ninette is my chief concern. I've not seen Ninette in years. I must go to Paris as soon as I'm established, to look after her."

"All I know, dear, is that I am fifty-four now, and you are forty-two, and what difference does age make? I feel today that I have the energy of three seventeen-year-olds combined. And if you do not let me go presently, I will miss the train."

At the door she said to me, "Judah Benjamin, I think you will make me settle for sweet adultery for the rest of my life."

November 1, 1865

Much to my surprise and delight, one hundred bales of cotton, which I had bought, escaped Federal vigilance and arrived in London today. I have converted it immediately and now have ten thousand dollars. I can establish myself, as well as Ada, and send some to my family. Colette will have to wait. I am sure she has other sources of funds for the moment. In any event she and I have a score to settle before she receives one more franc. I am therefore no longer a beggar and can accept some of the opportunities

228

which are coming my way.

Adolph De Leon, the younger brother of Thomas, who served as agent for me in France, turns out to be one of the managing editors at the *Telegraph*, and he has insisted on my joining him for dinner.

"They all know you by reputation, Benjamin," he said to me when I met him in the editorial office of the paper, "and will probably do their best to give you the shortest route to the practice of law here."

"There are no short cuts to the practice of law, De Leon," I told him. "But I am grateful for your concern and theirs. No, I will enroll as a student in Lincoln's Inn and read law there."

"As you wish, Benjamin. But I know you. At least I know what Thomas has told me about you, and you will not long remain among a hundred and fifty chattering adolescents. You will find your way, and they will pluck you out. Mark my word, you will be counsel to the Queen within a year."

After this agreeable conversation I went to the post office and found, much to my worry, that my letter to Colette has again gone unanswered. This is the third I have sent. It is not returned "addressee unknown"; it merely goes unanswered. I wish I had the funds and the situation to cross the channel, but this must wait. I have asked the postal clerk to kindly look up the address of the Convent of the Sacred Heart in Amiens. I will write to Ninette directly and perhaps get more satisfaction than I do from Colette.

At the Kings Arms, where Ada and I have begun to meet for meals, I find her in an ecstatic mood. She is wearing a new hat, with a sash that must wrap twelve times above the brim before it descends in back to the neck. I thought it a little conservative for my actress's taste.

"I have been to Whitehall," she said.

"And here I thought you were at agents' offices in the West End."

"Oh, the theatre here is not like America, Judah. I do not think they will have much use for me. But let me tell

229

you where I have been. My father's cousin is Claude Montifiore, a merchant in Whitehall. He recognized me immediately and served me tea, taking time out from the middle of his day. He has offered me a position!"

"In the business?" I inquired.

"No, silly," she said, "in the Society."

"What Society, Ada? In your excitement you seem to have put the end of your story before the beginning." We ordered port, and the candle on our table was lit.

"Montifiore has another major interest besides the business. It's more than an avocation. He calls it a serious avocation. It's a society, of which he's president, and in which are numbered as members business people, lawyers, professors at the university, students, religious leaders, housewives. . . ."

"Ada, what does this Society do, if you please?"

"It's a Society for the Reclamation of Palestine from the Turks."

"Zionists?"

"Exactly, Judah. That was the word Claude used. I had never heard it before. Well, he has invited us, you and I, to dinner next Wednesday, and to stay afterwards for the monthly meeting, which will be at his home. I, of course, accepted."

"I'm afraid you'll have to decline, for me. Although you, of course, can do as you please."

"And why would you not want to come, Judah, at least to see what it is like?"

"I have a pretty clear idea of what the Society is like. To be honest, however, I feel I cannot accept any social engagements until I have improved my situation here."

"And one evening out will upset your concentration?"

"It's my way, Ada. Do I coerce you to listen to the debates in Chancery Court?"

"I suspect, Judah," she said triumphantly, "that you do not wish to be seen in such a gathering, and *that* is your reason for not attending, not the demands of your work."

"Let us not argue the point. I will admit that I do not approve of this Zionist program, or at least what I have read of it. We are in England now, and English we will

230

become. It is unseemly for Jews to call attention to themselves as Jews. It is a religion, Ada, not a nation-race with a homeland of its own. Go if you must, but I have other concerns. I am losing track of my family."

"And I, Judah, am losing track of you. It's time you stopped running away from your own self."

At this juncture our food was delivered. We finished our meal in silence.

February 4, 1866

I have spent these past months in such intense study that I have not seen Ada or anyone else with regularity. Just yesterday, I sat down absorbed in my work from ten in the morning until two hours past midnight. For a half-hour at sunset I took time for some light food. I find that when I am so deeply absorbed in writing, I can tolerate only light food.

I have sent most of my money to Rebecca, who is caring for Penina and Joseph, who, thank God, have survived the surrender unharmed and are making ends meet in Savannah.

My rooms can only be described as bachelor's quarters. There is an old man who serves as a concierge of the kind we had in New Orleans. He has been exceedingly nice to me, and has developed the habit, which I imagine he does with everybody, of calling me "Your Honor."

"Your Honor," he said to me this morning as I left my rooms, "a special courier brought this last night, but I didn't want to disturb your sleep. It has the biggest seal I have ever seen, sir."

I opened the letter the old man gave me.

By influence of Lords Justices and Pages of the Benchers Society, Mr. Judah Phillip Benjamin, the Secretary of the Confederacy, is hereby dispensed from the regular three years of unprofitable dining and called to the bar of Lincoln's Inn in Trinity term, 1866. . .

There was also a smaller envelope which he handed me. As much as I was elated by this news of my acceptance at the English bar, so was I disturbed by the note from France. It was from a nun at the Convent of the Sacred Heart, postmarked many months ago, and somehow arrived here via Southampton. The nun wrote that Ninette left the convent, after completing two years of study. That was in 1864, long after which I continued to send Colette money for our daughter's alleged education. The nun furthermore wrote that an unidentified man one day arrived at the convent to escort Ninette from the premises. There was no address left for her belongings, and they are still at the convent unclaimed after this considerable period of time.

March 8, 1866

This whole last month, which I have been spending on circuit at Manchester and Liverpool, has been a time of much anxiety for me. While it is a pleasure to be involved in my studies and in my labors, I must also get to France. When I got home I was pleased to find Mr. Adolph De Leon on the steps of my rooming house.

"I just this moment left a note with your man, Mr. Benjamin."

"And I just this hour arrived at Wellington Station. What is your news?"

"My brother has cabled me that President Davis is recently released from his captivity. I thought you would like to know."

"Thank God for that, Mr. De Leon. He is a noble man, and I had fears that his delicate health might be permanently injured by the incarceration."

"My brother had opportunity to speak to him and his wife."

"Yes?" I said. "Did they have a message for me, sir?"

"As you can read in the note, Mr. Davis told Thomas to tell you that you had performed a noble service for the Cause, and that your new English citizenship could be construed by no reasonable man in a bad light. He said he was going to commence a book on the rise and the fall of the Confederacy, and in that book your innumerable contributions would be justly noted."

"And Mrs. Davis? Was there special news from her, De Leon?"

"She said, sir, you should take care to bathe your eyes in cold water, and that you should watch your weight!"

This report made me smile broadly and break out into a little laugh, which De Leon himself found amusing. "And you, sir," he asked, "when will you write your memoirs about the American Civil War? I am authorized to pay you handsomely for serialization in the *Telegraph,* at your own pace and convenience, of course."

"I have no intention of writing any memoirs, Mr. De Leon. Memoirs are for people whose lives are over, and, as you know, mine is just beginning here. I have no time for this enterprise of summations, although I do not begrudge others their doing it."

"So you have no opinions on the events of the war in which you played so prominent a part?"

"I did not say that. I am getting along tolerably well now at this new bar, and my future is brightening. In this bar, sir, I have work that could keep two Benjamins up twenty-four hours a day every day of the week. When I am on my back, when my legs will no longer carry me to the office, and when my eyes only reflect on the curtain of darkness before me, then I will think about what has been. Now I have to get to work."

"Oh, by the way, Mr. Benjamin," De Leon said from the bottom of the stairs, "your friend Miss Isaacs is doing a capital job raising money for Montifiore. You know, I don't usually give to organizations like that Society of his, but I talked to her at a salon at the Montifiore home, and before I knew what had happened I had pledged her fifty pounds. Would you mind telling her I am good for the pledge, but that I shall have to remit it next month?"

My first impulse was to tell Mr. De Leon I would not get involved in this business, and that he should talk to Ada himself. But he is a friend, and I therefore told him I would be happy to do the favor.

When I got upstairs, I had only energy to jot these notes. I placed my pen down, fell on my bed, and slept. When I awoke, Big Ben was tolling. It was well past midnight. I threw cold water on my face, and found myself smiling at the thought of Varinia's advice. Then I worked on the Franconia brief until morning.

March 9, 1866

"Your honor, sir. Your honor," came the whispering from the hall.

I had dozed off at my desk apparently and was some minutes in orienting myself to acknowledge the old man. "Pardon for waking you, sir," he said, "but Miss Ada asked me to tell you she'd like to have a word with you as soon as possible, sir."

"Tell her, will you, that I'll be there within the hour?"

I brewed some strong tea and drank half a cup before I made my way around the corner to Ada's chambers. When I entered I found her dressed in a travelling suit, her belongings packed and standing ready by the door.

"Well," I said, "why so dramatic?"

"I'm going to be leaving London for several months, Judah. I wanted to tell you."

"A play?"

"No. I know you wish it were a play, but you know very well why I'm going. I'm to tour with the Montifiores in the north and east of England."

"More fund-raising?"

"Yes, Judah, more fund-raising."

"And a little proselytizing thrown in?"

"I don't understand you at all, Judah. Is this what is causing the trouble between us? You know I have not been with you in two months!"

"And now, when I am returned from the circuit, and we

234

can be together, you call me here to say that *you* will be away for two months! And when you return maybe I will be on my way to the train station!"

Ada sat down on her suitcase. "Close the door," she said. Her dark hair was neatly parted and pulled back. There was a determination in her eyes. "For a brilliant man, Judah Benjamin," you are acting like a complete fool. For a man who has always lived his life his own way," she said, "you begrudge me my own life's choices now as you have never done. And you are arrogantly aloof from me only because I have joined Montifiore's Society. Deny it, Judah, if it is not true."

I felt sad in the face of this interrogation, but at the same time felt a burden lifted from me. "I don't deny it, Ada."

"Are you so confirmed in your beliefs on the subject that you will not attend even one meeting?"

"I will attend one, I suppose. But only if you promise not to offer me as a specimen of assimilationism."

"You don't understand, Judah. Claude and Mrs. Montifiore are rich as the Rothschilds, and cultured and elegant as you, sir. This Zionism is quite a fashionable new doctrine, and I can see you fitting into it quite well."

"One meeting, only one meeting, I promised. I did not say I will subscribe and contribute."

She took her bag and asked me to escort her to Wellngton Station. In the carriage to the station she lectured ne about race, culture, religion, and a hundred other subects which only she could squeeze into a single performance. "Can't you cancel this trip for a week or so?" I isked.

"Impossible," she said.

"How about cancelling it for three days then? You could lecture me some more in my bedroom. You know ow susceptible I am there, and how much easier to convince."

"A fine thing to say! Oh, there are the Montifiores," he said excitedly, and I turned and saw a couple wrapped up in very expensive fur coats. "Would you like to meet hem, Judah?"

"When you get back, my dear." I put her suitcase on the train, straightened her collar and kissed her. "Write me, will you? You know I'm missing you terribly already." She stepped up onto the train, which suddenly lurched and began to move.

"I forgive you for everything, Judah. Do you forgive me?" she asked as I walked faster and faster beside her to keep up with the moving train.

"Yes, I forgive you for everything."

"Here, then!" she shouted to be heard above the shrilling engine. "Read this. It's Disraeli's latest speech," and she handed me the morning paper. "He said a positively wonderful thing. Look there, I've underlined it."

The train sped on and I reached the end of the long platform. "I love you, Judah," she shouted, and then she leaned back inside her car.

On the carriage ride back I pondered what Ada had underlined in this speech of the other day in Parliament. "It is true," Disraeli wrote, "that I am a Jew, and when my ancestors were receiving their Ten Commandments from the immediate hand of the deity, amidst the thundering and lightnings of Mount Sinai, the ancestors of the distinguished gentleman who is opposed to me were herding swine in the forest of Scandinavia."

I suppose I could have made the same speech in Confederate Congress! And yet this Disraeli is a convert, is he not? Does one first have to be baptized before one can be proud of his religion? Rubbish, I thought to myself. How exceedingly safe it is to be an enthusiastic convert. Look at Rothschild! He accepts Christianity and then buys vineyards in Palestine.

I shall not accept Christianity, but, on the other hand, neither will I shout from the rooftops that I am a Jew.

Such were my thoughts, at least, when I rounded the corner and turned up the steps of my building. The perennial old man was there, staring at me with a sly look. "Sir," he said, "you'll pardon me for being so personal, but that daughter of yours, Miss Ava, is a feisty lass. She must'a had some mother!"

"She must have," I said as I walked by him. "Daughter

236

indeed!"

Paris.

I do not know what came over me. Perhaps it was Ada's absence from London, but I have worked almost day and night, sleeping at my desk for the most part, for the entire past month, and I am near to finishing a small book, which I have named *Treatise on Sale under English Law*. Unplanned and unexpected, I felt urged to write, and the words came out in one draft. It simply sets forth the basic principles of a rather complicated branch of the law, which has heretofore not been done. A legal printer, whom De Leon put me on to, has accepted the book and is going to press with it immediately. I am as pleased now as when I wrote my book in '32. I feel sure it will increase my reputation, and perhaps put an end to these pecuniary problems which trouble me night and day.

Thus, on the strength of this expectation, I telegraphed Erlanger that I was coming to Paris. He was most gracious in inviting me to stay in his home. My room looks out over Notre Dame, and I am not twenty minutes' walk from Colette.

Erlanger and I met for lunch at Maxime's.

"So why on earth, Benjamin, did you not let her know you were going to come?"

"Perhaps I like surprises, Baron."

He smiled and lit a long thin cigar of poor quality.

"One does not call on a woman this way, Benjamin, even upon one's wife, if she lives abroad. There is privacy, there is. . ."

"Baron," I said, "you know first hand what my wife did to me in the last few years. Since I will not prosecute her, and I will not divorce her, permit me at least to take delight in barging in on her. If I were a reporter, perhaps I could make headlines. Who knows what high government official's shoes I may find in her parlor."

"Poor Benjamin," sighed the Baron, "permit me to buy

you another pernod to prepare you for your greetings."

I had seen Erlanger six months previously in London, where he had been on business. It was the first time we had met, and instantly we had enjoyed each other's company. He is a man of medium height, with a short full moustache, a barrel chest and large shoulders which convey the feeling of continuous lifting of large heavy objects, even as he sits across the table quietly talking. The Baron is a widower, his wife having been drowned when her pleasure boat overturned in the Seine. There was much scandal that the Baroness was out boating with her lover, and the French press, which can be savage indeed, made much to-do about the cuckolding of the financial wizard.

When the waiter came with our drinks, we toasted love and friendship and success, but not necessarily in that order.

"I must not be late," he said, rising. "Please stay with me as long as you please, Benjamin. My house is very large and you are always a guest of honor."

I stayed seated at the table for several minutes after the Baron left, and I watched him walk, his short, solid form gradually becoming a rectangle of black disappearing in the crowded intersection at the far end of the boulevard. Erlanger had offered me a number of plums in Paris, but how could I live here now? I took great pleasure in speaking French once again, and the lovely manners of this culture are as seductive to me now as they were in New Orleans. One day perhaps I shall move here and build a house as the Baron has done. But there is much business to be taken care of first with Colette, who would not allow me the peace I am working towards.

It is midday and Colette is usually indoors, as she has always complained of the effect of bright sun on her skin.

I buy some marigolds from an old woman on the *Place de la Republique,* whose stern face strangely reminds me of my own mother's. Some orphan boy working the streets seems to spot me for the visitor that I am, and he asks me for money. I walk a block, two blocks, with the dirty-faced boy in the red shirt following me, and I strangely do not indicate to him either that I will give him some *cen-*

times or that I will not. So he tags along, he in his torn breeches, and I in new tweeds.

I turn the corner of the block where Colette lives, when the boy finally pulls at my coat. As my hand moves to push him away, I look across the street and see the windows of the house completely boarded up, all three floors sealed at the windows and stairway lattices by wooden planks.

I rush over to the gendarme who stands in front of the building. He gives me one word answers.

"Explosion," he says. "Closed. Building is closed."

"But tell me, man, when did it happen? I am related to the residents of this building."

"Two months ago, monsieur. The Socialists."

"Who?"

"Socialists," he repeated. "Building closed. Police investigation. I can tell you no more."

"Where is the prefect?" I demanded.

The *gendarme* pointed his stick. "Was anyone hurt? Was Madame Benjamin. . ." I asked. But he wordlessly pointed his stick; he was either mute or under orders not to speak.

"I show you where police station is," said the urchin boy. "For five centimes, I show you."

I let the boy lead me several blocks away to the prefecture of police. I ascended the steps.

"Eh, monsieur, eh, the money!" the boy demanded.

I had no change, I realized. Only notes, and the smallest was a five franc. I gave the paper to the boy, who smiled through the crisscross of smudges on his chin and cheeks.

Then the boy started laughing. *"Eh, les fleurs, les fleurs."* And of course it was the marigolds for Colette which I still had in my hand. I must have looked ridiculous walking into the station with flowers.

"Here, take these, too," I said to him. "My wife has no vase to put them in. Sell them to someone if you want." Then I want in and asked to speak to the captain.

After twenty minutes of waiting in one of the most uncomfortable straight-backed chairs, the captain consented to see me and to hear my questions. He was a tall, thin

239

man, with ramrod posture, and big forlorn eyes, entirely out of context in his military bearing; the eyes seemed to have been placed upon his face as an afterthought.

"You must learn, Monsieur Benjamin, not to listen to what the *gendarme* on the street says. He is the very soil where rumor first grows in Paris."

"So there was no explosion, captain?"

"No—of course there was, *monsieur*. But we do not know if it was done by the Socialists. Perhaps a bomb factory of the anti-monarchists."

"And my wife. Was my wife injured?"

The captain looked through the file on his desk and then said, "No, Monsieur Benjamin, there was no woman killed or injured in the explosion. No woman was treated at the hospital."

"Then where is my wife, captain?"

"I do not know, sir. Would you like us to look?"

It occurred to me that since there was an accident at her house, Colette may be staying with acquaintances. I decided it would be more discreet not to involve officials yet. I thanked the captain, who saluted me, and then I left.

I called on Mrs. Slidell, who told me she had not seen Colette since the end of the War.

Then I called on June Belmont, who said that she at one time saw a great deal of Colette, but since a certain man had appeared on the scene, Colette entirely changed her circle of friends. "When was that?" I asked. "Oh, at least ten months ago, Mr. Benjamin," was the reply. "And who was it?" June Belmont said she never even learned his name.

I returned to the Baron's and found a letter waiting for me, which the servant presented me, along with my wine. The letter was from De Leon, who had been kind enough to look after my London affairs in my absence. There were two pressing matters, he wrote. First the galleys of my book need immediately correction. If the printer cannot have them within four days, the project must be scratched. De Leon wrote that there was no way the printer could be made to be more reasonable. The second matter was the MacRae case. It was coming to court a week earlier than I had planned. A calendar change, wrote De Leon. RETURN IMMEDIATELY, he wrote on the bottom of the letter, in large print.

Here I had just purchased a ticket to Amiens to pick up Ninette's belongings! I had come to find my daughter, and I end up losing track not only of my daughter, but of my wife as well! I drank the full glass of wine and called for another. Erlanger was not expected back until late in the evening. I sat down, wrote an explicit note for him, and placed it on his desk in the library.

> Be a friend now to me, Erlanger, as you were a friend in the past. I shall return as soon as possible to locate my family. In the meantime, here is the name of the captain of police to whom I spoke, but I would prefer to be discreet as long as possible. I will be in touch with you. In deep gratitude, I am,

> Judah Benjamin

I found a carriage bound for Calais, and was on my way back to London before dark. The channel waves heaved, the boat listed, and the lantern was doused by the spraying water. The crew of the boat urged everyone to get below, yet I found myself standing on the deck, my hands clenched tight on the aft rail. The boat bucked like a horse gone wild, and there was even a conference in the captain's cabin about turning back. But they decided to make for Dover, in hopes that the weather ahead would be better than that which was behind us. It mattered not to me, however, as I felt the storm was intended particularly for me, and I gave it my face, letting the water wash over me and punish me at will. Had they asked me, like Jonah, to step into the boat we had in tow, in order to placate the God of Storms, I think I would not have refused.

April 17, 1866

Erlanger has just written me what I most feared. The house had been abandoned by Colette for six months. There was no forwarding address that he could obtain either from the police or from postal authorities. The investigation of the explosion centered on some anti-monarchist groups which had moved illegally into the house. There was no connection suspected between Colette and these political elements, yet her whereabouts, which are of interest to the Paris police, have not been determined.

Erlanger apologized for being the writer of bad news. I immediately wrote him my thanks and told him I would handle the situation from now on. I have a bad feeling ebout what seems to be developing, and I do not like to have others involved. Yet he offers continued assistance: "Let me be your eyes and ears in Paris, Monsieur Benjamin. It will be a pleasure to notify you if anything productive comes to the surface. In the meantime I am honored to await your instructions."

May 10, 1866

I have written again to the police, to Mrs. Slidell, Mrs. Belmont, and to the Convent of the Sacred Heart. From all except the sisters I get the same response: Colette had not kept company with any suspicious characters; there was no police record on her. I had her officially listed as missing, as I did Ninette. I supplied verbal descriptions, and facsimile portraits were drawn and distributed to prefectures throughout France. Colonel Levoy, formerly of the Confederate Intelligence, who had once worked with me, was in Europe last month, and he did me the service of reviewing the police work done so far on my behalf. He pronounced the French police sound, and indicated no leads had been left unexplored. And still no trace of daughter, no trace of wife.

"They could not have vanished into thin air, Judah," Ada said from across the table where we were dining. "Mark my word, your Colette, wherever she is now, is thinking of you and planning an appearance. Of Ninette I cannot tell. She is a relatively young girl still and with her it is tragic. Colette deserves disaster and bad luck, if you ask me."

"She is still my wife, you know."

"Wife is just a word, my dear Queen's Counsel," for we were having a special dinner to celebrate my latest promotion at the bar, "and although I don't bear the title, never will, and never want it, I am, pardon the expression, your real wife."

"Is it possible, Ada, for a woman to wander about a country for months, without identity, without support, without being recognized?"

"How do you know, Judah, that she is travelling alone? Maybe she is with Ninette, maybe she is with a man, maybe all three are together. Maybe she is not even alive, as if she deserves to be after nearly ruining you in Richmond!"

"You have the penchant this evening, Ada, for expressing yourself in the gloomiest terms possible."

"On the contrary," said she, "I am being realistic. Colette turned against you very early in your marriage. She is your enemy and always was. And you barely got a chance to know your daughter. These people are your family in name only."

"They are my family because my blood flows in them, Ada. I must find them."

"You will," she said, with a reassuring smile. "In the meantime, let our lives go on. You have hired a private detective, you have put ads in newspapers in Paris, Amiens, Calais, the entire country. You have even asked Erlanger to talk to the Minister of the Interior for you. What more can you do? Do you want to go over there and knock on doors yourself?"

"The thought has crossed my mind."

"Your work suffers, Judah. You yourself said that if it were not for your book, cases would not come your way of late. You know your clients can tell when their barrister is preoccupied. But enough of advice, sir! I have some news: Ninette's trunks have arrived from Amiens. I sent the old

243

man to pick them up. He'll bring them to you this afternoon. Perhaps there will be some new clue."

But, alas, there was not. After our meal I went directly to my chamber. (Ada went off to see Montifiore about some new international committee on which, she said, she had entered my name, whether I liked it or not!)

Ninette's clothes were in one trunk, and her shoes, books, comb and mirror were in a second small bag. In this I also found a pouch with sea shells, stones and pebbles of different colors and striations, and leaves. Who is my daughter, I wondered? I had not seen her since she was nine years old, and what I know of her I know only from her mother, who never let her write to me. Maybe Ada is right about Colette; if the earth opened up and swallowed her, it would not be an undeserved fate. But Ninette is innocent, and I owe her much love.

I sat down and immediately wrote Erlanger to offer a thousand-pound reward for information leading to the whereabouts of my daughter.

June 10, 1866

Nothing from the police.

August 18, 1866

Erlanger writes that the Minister has closed the case; he sends his regrets.

September 18, 1866

I have smoked eight cigars today. I pace my office as I smoke. This is a new habit. Erlanger has invited me to visit. But I cannot get away. If I could, I would not want to go to France now. I would be dizzy from staring into the faces of the women on the street. And if there were two, who seemed like mother and daughter, I would not hesitate to go up to them on the sidewalk.

October 12, 1866

Between work and worry I get little relief. Ada is about the continent again for her committee which now calls itself the *Alliance,* for the defense of Jewish rights throughout Europe. All well and good! In the state I am in, it is better that she be away from me.

Editor's Note:
Here follows a long letter, tucked into the diary, which Benjamin wrote to his sister in Savannah.

Dearest Becky,

I long beyond measure to see you all once more, but I am plainly to be disappointed this year. The simple truth is that I cannot afford the visit. You may have deduced this by the substantially smaller amounts I have been able to send you. I had anticipated the growth of my reputation at the bar here and from the reassurances of those in the profession who ought to know, it will still take time.

But the growth of business is very slow here, unlike in America. Here the competition is severe, so severe that the attorneys give their briefs, whenever they possibly can, to barristers who are connected or related in some way with them or their families; and in an old country like England these family ties are so ramified that there is hardly an attorney who has not in some way a barrister whom it is in his interest to engage. This accounts for some of the difficulty under which I must labor. I cannot get along with less than 1400 pounds, say about seven thousand a year, including my professional expenses at the Temple for rent, clerk hire, robing room, wigs, gowns, etc., which are endless.

I had hoped strongly that by this year I should be able

to make ends meet, but my receipts have not increased. If I had not written my book I should be nowhere in the race. I think from the present aspect of things I shall nearly succeed this year, and if so, my subsequent career will become more rapidly prosperous, if I preserve my health, which is excellent—quite as good as ever.

November 15, 1866

"How do you feel, sir?" the voice floated down towards where I lay. "That's right. Open your eyes slowly. You must feel very tired."

At the foot of the bed stood a short, youthful boy. Next to him I began to make out my Ada, her sweet dark face beaming at me. "This is Nathan de Mendes, Judah. He is a cousin of your mother's. He is also a doctor."

"A doctor?" I tried to rise from the bed, but felt my arms quiver under my own weight.

"You have had a nervous collapse, Mr. Benjamin," said this boy. "It is my honor to assist you back to health."

December 3, 1866

"Dr. Mendes," I said, "I must be up and about."

"Two more weeks, Mr. Benjamin, and then I will allow you to sit at your desk. For now your armchair will be quite enough for you."

Mendes has a wide full face, which looks even larger because of his bushy sideburns and beard. His eyes are a placid blue, which is a fine calming color for a doctor's eyes. And indeed he is a good practictioner of his art. He emanates an utter devotion to my care. Though he is but thirty years old, I find myself listening to his counsel. Or perhaps it is the Mendes blood in him, the blood of my mother, which commands me. In any event, I will stay in my armchair and put off work for the two weeks more he advises, although I feel good enough to start.

"And who is handling my briefs, Mendes?"

"I believe Miss Isaacs," was his answer. "She is contacting your clients, most of whom are waiting for your recovery, rather than change counsel. Quite a compliment, I would say."

"Mendes," I said to him as he was about to leave, "tell me, from a medical point of view, what is it that can possess a man's wife and daughter to vanish from France and never to contact him?"

"I don't know, sir. But I do know that your preoccupation with this has caused your collapse. You must exercise control. Miss Isaacs has told me the story, and my medical advice to you is to practice patience. Perhaps one day they will turn up. And then again they may not. You make yourself sick over this and if a man desires to make himself sick, there is nothing a doctor can do to stop him."

"Are you married, Mendes, and have you children?"

"No on both counts, uncle. But does one have to experience a thing in order to render an opinion about it? You must rest completely and then concentrate on your life here in London. That is what your body is telling you, and you must listen to the dictates of your body. I have left some tablets for you to take, and a pamphlet you may be interested in reading."

Before he left, I looked at the pamphlet on the night table: *A Proposal for the Establishment of the Alliance Israelite Universelle.*

"You, too?"

"Me, too. It will be good medicine for you; read it." And then he left me to my armchair. I dozed and then read.

"No member of the Jewish race can renounce the incontestable right of his people to its ancestral land without thereby denying his past and his ancestors. Such an act is especially unseemly at a time when political conditions in Europe will not only not obstruct the restoration of a Jewish State but will rather facilitate its realization. What European power would today oppose the plan that the Jews, united through a Congress, should buy back their ancient fatherland? Who would object if the Jews flung a handful

247

of gold to Turkey and said to her: 'Give back my home and use this money to consolidate the other parts of your tottering empire?''

I dozed again. I was awakened by Ada when she came in with my dinner. "So Nathan actually left you the proposal! What did you think?" she asked as she put some broth before me.

"I think I am a perfectly happy man as an English lawyer in England, and I have no need of and no feeling for a strip of desert beside the Mediterranean. I furthermore feel you and Mendes are collaborating to foist this Alliance of yours upon me at a weak moment. If I had an ounce more strength I would be preparing cases instead of reading pamphlets. I believe I've had my fill of pamphlets, platforms, positions, and politics."

"A fine, objective, clear legal mind at work," she taunted me. "Here, have some soup."

"I prefer a cigar."

"Prefer all you want. You'll not get one from me. You have a letter, Judah, from Mrs. Jefferson Davis. Shall I open it and read for you, or do you prefer to read in private?"

"No need for privacy. Read, if you please."

"Dear Mr. Benjamin," she writes, "Mr. Davis and I heard that you had become ill. We wanted to wish you a quick return of your good health and vigor. Mr. Davis, thank God, is regaining strength after his long ordeal. So I have faith that the body and mind renew themselves even after the most enduring trials. We are still wracked here with humiliations forced upon us. The amnesty bill has again been rejected and there is talk of reparations. A part of me is envious of you, now in another country, freed from this strife. Yet I know a part of you also must yearn to be here, to lend your voice and your talents to the Cause. Good health to you again, sir. May we one day hope to see you again?

"Incidentally, your friend Mr. Yulee, survived the hostilities unharmed. In Washington, where I chanced to talk to him, he told me had been briefly in the same Yankee prison as that Lieutenant Colonel Jones, your clerk's brother. The officer said he had seen his brother only a month before, that he was wounded badly but alive and waiting outside the surgeon's tent. Whether Jones survived or not the officer wouldn't say when he realized Mr. Yulee was ferreting information from him. Mr. Yuiee said he was going to return to his chicken farming in Florida. He said to tell you he wished you the best, as I do—Mrs. Jefferson Davis."

"I killed him," I shouted. "I killed him. I know I did."

"Judah, calm yourself."

"I know I killed him. The bullet hit here, in the chest."

"Don't shout so," she said, "you'll relapse. Lean forward, here." And she gave me the pills Mendes had left. Soon, thank God, I began to sleep again.

March 2, 1867

I continue to feel better. Almost complete recovery. I was deeply scared by a temporary failing of the eyes, such as happened to me years ago.

So, with the advice of Mendes, whom I have grown to trust like a younger brother, I now work but four days a week. My practice improves, and there is talk of my appointment as Queen's Counsel being extended for all England, so my London business will as a result prosper.

On Friday of every week I am at work on my garden.

"It does not require close use of the eyes," was Mendes' advice, "and it also affords a little exercise for a man used to the sitting position."

"You know, Mendes," I said to him as he watched me in my shirtsleeves, "I once wanted a plantation very much. I wanted to raise sugar and crops. And you know what I did? I went out and worked and bought Belchasse, a soil-ich river-front plantation, with seventeen slaves. I lost the plantation. I never, on the other hand, had even an inkling of a desire for a garden. And here it is! See what I have grown." I showed him the lettuces and tomatoes and the black-eyed peas I had planted. The peas were already beginning to sprout, their curling green tendrils pushing through the soil.

"You've planted a Confederate garden, uncle," Mendes said.

"Confederate, indeed! I would call it Southern," I corrected him. "The peas were always my favorite. Black-eyed peas and deep fried chicken. My sister Rebecca can cook that dish with a talent that comes only once in a generation. Each and every time the food is exquisite. You should know about this, Mendes, and write her for the recipe. It should be part of your book of remedies; it will cure any ailment."

Mendes has a way of standing, a position where his body leans against a piano or a chair, or in this case, the balustrade that runs beside the border of the garden. So he leans, and then he folds his hands across his belly, in a relaxed but somehow stiff posture, as if he were posing for one of Daguerre's portraits.

"I'll wager you it does not cure homesickness, uncle," he said.

"Because a man plants black-eyed peas, he doesn't necessarily want to eat them in South Carolina or Georgia, Mendes. I miss my family. I do not miss the recriminations, the misadministrations, and the carpetbagging that presently prevail in the South."

"Do you think you will ever return?"

"That is what Ada is constantly asking me. If I am allowed to return, and if the conditions are suitable, I would like to visit, but it will be in years to come."

"As an English citizen?"

"Of course as an English citizen. How else?"

"So how many citizenships will you have had in your lifetime?"

"I thought I was supposed to relax on this day in the garden, Mendes! Why this interrogation? But I figured for him anyway. With my birth as a British citizen, my naturalization, the CSA, and now, the English, it made four.

"And which one is it that you hold dear, uncle?"

"I value the one I presently hold, regardless of what it may be."

"Montifiore says the Jew is always a guest in a host cul-

re; he is always passing through. I know of no one
hom that more aptly describes than you."

"A brilliant cross-examination, Mendes. You should
ave been a lawyer as well as a doctor. But I repeat again
 you what I told Ada: there are no laws now, no bars to
y full equality in England. Now go on your way, meet
me nice girl and get married. Dispense with assaulting
ur poor uncle with these theories under the hot sun. Let
e tend my garden. Does no one else do anything in this
untry but listen to Montifiore?"

Nathan Mendes uncrossed his legs, picked up his brown
strument bag and stepped carefully over the garden fur-
ws. "May I harp at you with just one more piece of this
eory, sir?"

"If it be the last."

"I would just have you think, uncle, if to be accepted is
e same thing as to belong. Montifiore says they are dif-
rent, and he says the Jews must recognize this and seek
eir own territory."

"Legally, to be accepted is to belong—or so it seems to
e."

"It seems to me that in the province of the spirit and the
art, they are two separate things."

"You should have known my father, Nathan. You
uld have liked his talk of spirit, too. I listened, and as
r as I could make out then, and now, this spirit you
eak of is intangible. What is real is not land or citizen-
ip, or for that matter, even love. Everything changes and
in constant motion and the only lasting truth is the truth
change. The Jews do not need to emulate the nations of
e world and acquire land and fight wars and make
rders and patrol those borders. Let all the nations of the
rld follow the example of the Jews and realize that the
ound under their feet is not so permanent and unchan-
able as they would like to think. And if there is such a
ing as this spirit you speak of, a Jewish spirit or an En-
sh spirit, it is not planted in the ground and does not
ot there like these peas. Where it is, I don't know. Then
ain, I am a simple lawyer; I am not a theologian."

"All right, uncle, I'll keep my promise and not argue

251

with you any further. Bend slowly, and please keep you
hat on."

"Yes, yes, Mendes, good day." And that is how I sper
my Friday, a day of philosophy among the peas. Even i
England there seems to be such chaos, such ferment! All
want is security and tranquility and knowledge of m
daughter's whereabouts.

I believe I gave the lettuce too much water today.
make a note to skip two days watering, lest I kill it wit
too much care.

May 1, 186

Today I received a patent of precedence from the offic
of the Queen. My business is secured now; this places m
above Queen's counsels and sergeants at law. I am muc
pleased. I have the patent sitting in front of me on m
desk.

It is on parchment, and to it is annexed the great sea
which is an enormous lump of wax, and the whole thin
sits in a red morocco box highly ornamented. As nothin
of this kind ever seems to get done under a monarch
without an endless series of charges, it cost me $400 t
pay for stamps, fees, presents to servitors, etc.

July 12, 186

I presented myself today in full regalia—for the fir
time. I had to wear a full-bottomed wig, with wings fallin
down on my shoulders, and knee breeches and black si
stockings and shoes with buckles, and in this ridiculo
array to present myself in front of the next levee of H
Majesty, to return thanks for her gracious kindness. Wh
with the heat and the chafing, it was all I could do to kee
myself from stripping off the garments right in front of tl
Queen.

When I returned to my office I found some papers fro
Fletcher and a note asking me to kindly check them for

252

client of his. Accompanying the note was a five-guinea piece. I decided that I should put the papers aside. As of this day, my rates have gone up.

July 22, 1867

Fletcher has come by to ask what I think of the papers.

"I have not looked at them yet, sir," I said.

"But I enclosed five guineas," he replied.

"Of course, you did. That was my fee for taking the papers in. It will be twenty more to read them."

He hesitated a moment and then put the coins on the table.

Later in the evening, Ada, and I went shopping, bought two delicious steaks, cooked them to perfection and ate them with black-eyed peas. The steaks were from Fletcher. The peas were from my garden.

Editor's Note:

Here occurs the largest gap in all the Diaries—some fifteen years without an entry. Varinia Davis visited England twice during this period, but Benjamin makes no mention of it. All the cabinet ministers of the Confederacy eventually return to American soil—all except Benjamin. Although their returns are highly publicized in England and Europe, Benjamin makes no mention of it.

In her one public interview about her trip abroad, Mrs. Davis simply noted, as regards to Benjamin, that the silver was missing from the timbre of his voice.

The fifth and last diary begins in the early 1880's in Paris.

V

FIFTH DIARY
JUNE 2, 1882—JUNE 19, 1883

PART V

June 2, 1882, Paris

Ada has again induced me to accompany her to the international conference. The Society has grown so large now—she says there are members in ten countries—and she is become such a celebrity in her own right, that she needs constant escort. It isn't seemly, Montifiore told me, that she not be escorted. So the elegant man, the elder statesman of the Confederacy and the notable English attorney, Mr. Judah P. Benjamin, is her courteous public companion.

I must say that with the cane Nathan has prescribed, which I now use, I certainly look the part of a famous lady's escort. Into hotels and out of hotels, the crowds gather around us and ask Ada questions: How go the negotiations with the Sultan? Do you think the Czar will answer your letter, Miss Isaacs? Does Whitehall express any disposition to discuss the sale of Uganda to the Zionists? What of the objection of the orthodox rabbis?

Ada answers all questions with charm. Every cause needs a leader, and in every leader there must be a bit of the actor. Or in the case of my lady, an actress.

My role in the drama? Montifiore gave me specific instructions for this trip. He pulled nervously on his ascot as we spoke in the lobby of the Hotel Napoleon.

Montifiore has a badly pocked face, and a nose that rises from it and then veers a little to one side, as if it were broken. It is a fascinating face, a face that should belong to a laborer, or a poor man, one who could not afford medical care. And yet it belongs to Claude Montifiore, heir of one of the great Anglo-Jewish fortunes, a man I have grown close to indeed, even as our political views have grown farther apart. I have noticed that here with Montifiore and Nathan, and especially with Ada, I seem to love most those people whose opinions in politics I disagree with most. Perhaps it is friction that fuels my affection.

257

I had not seen Montifiore for a month, during which hectic period I had announced my retirement from the English bar and moved, with Ada, to a property Erlanger purchased for me on Avenue Huysman. This is easier for Ada whose work on the committee is now centered in Paris.

In any event, Montifiore's wonderful face stares at me, from above a twenty-guinea silk ascot, from below one of the most expensive top hats on the continent; it is a face wrapped in wealth, and animated by a passionate love for this Zionist program.

"How is the gentleman of leisure?" he asks me.

"Still no Zionist, my dear Cluade, but the happy escort of Miss Isaacs."

"And the house?"

"Lovely. I am happy to be in France, Claude. Here no one knows me. I can take my walks and read my books, and edit Miss Isaacs' speeches."

"I trust not for content, but for grammar and precision," Montifiore says, making his point with a gesture of the pearl-handled walking stick in his right hand.

"Ah, you are a Zionist in spite of yourself, Benjamin. Every Jew is."

"No debate today, my friend. The early summer weather is too nice. I shall take a walk and return to the lobby by three to meet you and Ada. We can take lunch at Maxime's."

"But I thought you were going to prepare one of your famous salads. Ada promised."

"Apparently she forgot to tell you that we do not yet have a garden."

"First things first."

"When the salmon radishes come up, in two or three weeks, rest assured you will have a salad of them, from the very first of the crop. Go to your business now, Claude," I said, as I saw him nod hello to a man I had been introduced to the other day but whose name I had already forgotten. There was the sound of the vote being taken in the hall of the hotel and some shouts for order. "Tell Ada that if she raps the gavel any harder, she will surely break the lectern in two."

I left the hotel and went out into the clear sunshine. Down the Boulevard St. Germaine I walked and then along the Seine to the Pont Neuf, where I stood and took my hat off on the landing above the embankment.

The indolent Parisian sun began to warm me. I went down the steps, took off my coat, and sat on a bench by the blue-gray water. The small yachts passing began to unfurl their spinnakers in the wind, and an occasional boatload of travellers floated by on which I could make out American accents. I opened and closed my eyes and I must have begun to doze, as an old man will, for the sights of the boats and the brief waves of American speech that rolled towards me became like a mixed melody of sensations. I began to think of the harbor in Charleston where I had spent so much time as a boy. Pictures of the riverfront at Belchasse on the Mississippi floated up on my imagination, to such a degree that I began to hear with clarity the Creole patois:

> *Danse Calinda, bou-djoumb!*
> *Danse Calinda, bou-djoumb!*

And my feet began to stir and to tap the cobblestones with the remembered rhythms of masques, of courtyards blanched in moonlight, and dancers, stopped for a respite from their whirling, sipping absinthe beneath the mournful willows.

> *Bou-djoumb, djoumb!*
> *Eh, monsieur, hou-djoumb!*

And I remembered all my walks through the winding streets of the Creole quarters, and the clacking on cobblestones of the drays; and on the roofs of the houses the sunset sky the color of light red wine!

At moments between waking and sleeping, a man's life seems short; the people and the places seem to race by like the view of trees from the window of a rushing train. I opened my eyes and saw a group of old women, beggars in rags, walking along the water's edge a few feet from me. I dozed and listened again: *boud-djoumb, petite, bouddjoumb.*

The beggar women, three of them, all hunched over and

259

hooded in coarse cloaks, chased the pigeons away and bent down for the discarded crumbs of bread on the landing. A *gendarme* walked by them and they held out their hands pathetically for food or money. He laughingly pushed one of them as he walked by. An old woman staggered and fell not ten yards from me, and began to shriek. She was hurt. The other two bent down over her, muttering sounds I could not make out, and then lifted her and carried her towards me.

As they neared, I saw they were going to put her down to rest on the bench. I took my coat, got up and stood to the side as these three approached, all hysterical, their mouths toothless, their faces begrimed.

As they placed their injured comrade down, she began to moan, and then I realized I had not been hearing an imagined patois, but that it had come from the horrible lips of this woman.

I moved closer and heard her cry:

Danse Calinda, djoumb, djoumb
Pov piti Lolotte a mouin, a mouin,

When the other two women saw me, they left their friend and shuffled towards me, their hands held out in front of them supplicatingly for money: *"L'argent, l'argent, eh, monsieur?"*

I walked between them over to the bench. The injured woman had curled herself up under her cloak like a baby. I stood above her and hesitated to do what I knew I had to. *"Pov piti,"* she moaned, *"piti djoumb,"* and then she was shaken by a kind of paroxysm, for her legs shot straight out, kicking several times and then returned to the infant-like ball in which she was curled.

Her back was toward me, her head covered so that only strands of filthy gray hair were visible. I put my hand on her shoulder, but she resisted and curled up more. I walked around to the other side of the bench, knelt down and beheld beneath this mask of suffering and disease what was unmistakeably the face of my wife.

"Colette, my God! Colette!" I called her name six times, a dozen times, but her face did not respond. Nothing, not even the eyes, responded. The features contracted in pain, and then expanded, the eyes opening wide, the mouth open too, but only spurts of soundless breath came out. No words but *"bou-djoumb, djoumb!"*

"This is Judah. This is Judah," I sounded the syllables for her. She then moved her head in a bobbing fashion from side to side like a bird. *"Jooda, Jooda,"* she said as if she were learning her first words. *"Jooda, bou-djoub! Pov piti, Jooda, pov piti Lolotte a mouin."*

August 1, 1882

Colette is lying upstairs on the third floor of the house. Even as I sit in the parlor, I hear her moan between the banging of the workmen's hammers on my unfinished roof.

"Ada," I scream, "tell those laborers to finish at another time. Enough of the racket."

September 4, 1882

Colette now lies on the second floor north wing in a guest bedroom.

"Ironic, isn't it!" I say to Ada and Mendes, who dine with me tonight. I have lost thirty pounds and have not eaten a proper meal in weeks. "My wife lies upstairs, insane, in the guest bedroom of my house."

Ada puts down her fork and looks at me sternly from across the table. "Don't lash at yourself, Judah."

"And why should I not? Am I not responsible for this?"

"You *are*," she says to me, "absolutely sure this is Colette?"

"For the twelfth time, Ada, this *is* my wife. If by nothing else, I know it is her by the birthmark on her knee."

Some minutes we sat in silence except for the sounds of our silverware cutting and scraping, and the muffled stream of noises which had become by now the only conversation Colette was capable of.

"Is there no way, Nathan, that she can be helped?"

"Uncle, listen to me. Her fracture is set. It is healing slowly, but well enough for an old woman. As to her mental state, I can tell you it is of long standing. This is no acute episode. She may be helped, but only time can tell. As of this moment she is victim of a psychosis, and I would tell you candidly that the outlook is grim. These states are almost beyond our ability to control."

"You are a doctor. What can your profession do?"

"If we arrest it now, we can consider it a success. That is all I can tell you."

"The best sanitarium in France is in Neuilly, ten kilometers from Paris. With your permission," Ada said, "Nathan and I will have her moved there after the High Holidays."

"Why after the High Holidays?" I screamed. "May God damn your High Holidays. Do it now. Get her out of my house now! Get her out tonight, this minute. I cannot stand her moaning any more. Get her out," I yelled. I left the dining room and walked coatless out to the street.

When I returned home it was dark, and I could not have told where I had been. I stood in the foyer and listened for Colette. But the silence of the house was unbroken. When I went upstairs to her room, I found an open door and an empty bed. The window was open and the white curtains were blowing slightly in the breeze. The room had in it the sweet, yellow, sickly smell of old daisies.

They have taken her to Neuilly.

November 15, 1882

I have been visiting at the sanitarium with considerable regularity. Colette's condition is not improved. She hardly recognizes anyone, no matter how long she knows them. Even the nuns and the other patients in this place are new to her every day, as if in sleep the experience of the preceding day is wiped clean.

Ada and Mendes and Montifiore have all tried to induce me to leave her. They want me to go with them to this city and to that one. They say it will do me good to get my mind off Colette. But I know better. I have a plan. I always have a plan.

Well and good—let us say, then, that Colette is beyond help. But what of Ninette? The earth has not opened up and swallowed her. Perhaps I can get some clue from Colette.

I spend my time at the sanitarium either by Colette's bed or with her in the garden of the institution. There is a white wicker swing in the courtyard and she likes me to give her rides on it. She cannot say "faster" or "higher," but, like a child who cannot speak, she expresses her delight with yells and none-too-feminine grunts, which, I have now learned, mean that she is afraid and wants me to stop the swing and go away. On certain days, however, she lets me sit beside her after we have finished with the swinging, and in the garden I try to talk to her.

"Where is Ninette? Ni-nette? Where is your daughter, Ni-nette?"

"Ninette, poupette, lo-lo lo-lo lolette, Ninette," says she, sometimes staying seated, and other times jumping up to dance and sway about as she repeats these sounds. Yet my theory is that perhaps in the middle of one of these reveries she will say something that will give me a clue.

I try to repeat familiar words to her, and today I have had some kind of breakthrough. I repeated my name to her several times, and she responded, if that is what it was, with "Joooda, jooda, jooones. Joooda, jooda, jooones. Jooda, jooola, jooona, jooetee." And then she pointed her finger at me and smiling her toothless smile she said, "Jooda Jones. Tu es Jooda Jones."

Judah Jones indeed! I thought. I tried to elicit more from her, but nothing was forthcoming. She flew at me and began to beat her fists on my chest. My glasses were knocked off, and one of her long nails scratched my face so that I began to bleed. The nuns came running, along with a nurse.

"I would not advise you to visit again," the nurse said. 'Monsieur Benjamin, Madame is in need of complete rest for the next several weeks."

"If she has a lucid period," I begged the nurse, "please notify me."

"Of course, monsieur," she said, "but I would not expect it."

January 2, 1883

The other day I brought some cakes and some presents to Colette. She, of course, does not realize it is the new year. She has become silent and speaks only with her eyes, which still convey an occasional flicker of emotion. Before he returned to London to take a special course at the University, Mendes prescribed a new medicine which has calmed her somewhat. The nuns are able to confine her less and give her more attention. For this I am glad. But her silence seems to put an end to my last hope of a connection with Ninette.

As a result I spend my time with Colette trying to re-teach her the alphabet and the numbers, one through ten. The months have purified me of my hate for her, and I only want her to have more from her remaining years than this antiseptic confinement.

My method is to say a number (I start with numbers because they seem somehow much more basic to human nature, and much easier to teach than something as complicated, as sophisticated as the alphabet). I then repeat the number over and over again and make it into a kind of sing-song until Colette joins me and we are chanting make-believe ditties, all composed of one number. I do one number each visit, and then, when I have reached ten, I will try to help her repeat the numbers in order and to give her some idea of how three stones are two less than five.

This morning, however, something unforeseen happened.

I had been teaching her the number "seven," when all of a sudden she began to make up her nonsense rhymes, which she had not done for months. *"Sept, sept, babette, mete, ninette, sept, ninette, mete, sept, sept."*

I listened as carefully as I could, but without expecting to hear anything but the sounds she had uttered at the beginning. I was therefore surprised, not so much because I heard Ninette's name mentioned—she had done it before in other rhymes, it probably being the name she associated with me, as I had tormented her so much with that name in the beginning—but what I seemed to hear was something different. There was a word which was not a good rhyme. What was "mete"? Or was it "meta"? But none of these made any sense, even in Colette's confused terms. I listened more carefully and thought I might be making out the name of the town, Metz, in Alsace.

I repeated the name, and Colette started up again animatedly saying it, "Meta, meta, meta."

Perhaps it is something, perhaps nothing at all.

I took Colette by the hand and led her to her room. Once there, I could see how tired she had become. She could not have weighed more than eighty pounds. I helped her onto the bed and under her sheets for an early nap.

January 5, 1883

It is two o'clock in the morning. I am wracked by visions all night and unable to sleep. I have just awoken with a shuddering from a dream of my childhood. For it is clearly Charleston and the house in which I grew up.

My mother speaks first, "Yehuda," she says, "didn't you know that your father is that rare bird, that *rara avis*, an unsuccessful Jew?"

I run to my father to ask him if this is true, but he is holding a book in front of his face, a book of Spinoza's philosophy. The book suddenly looms so large that I must climb over it. I must scale it as if it were a cliff. So up I go, crawling along the precipice of the spine, higher and higher up the face of the book. When I am near the top such that in two more pulls I will be able to see over and behold my father's eyes, there is a sudden shaking, a wind blows across my back, and it is all I can do to hold on, to keep from falling off into the pit, falling hundreds of feet

265

to my death on the living room floor below.

My father is getting up from his chair; he is closing the book, putting it on the table, and leaving the house.

Then I walk back into the bedroom where mother is opening a chest of linens she has just received from her relatives, the Mendeses of London. The sheets are of polished cotton and especially beautiful. She holds them up to the light, one after the other, then throws them all back into the trunk.

"I will send all these back to my family. I will not forever be the recipient of gifts."

Now I see mother's face close up, as close as I could have seen my father's, had not the book been in obstruction. She is now making up the bedroom. Pain moves insensibly across her face as she arranges the sheets.

January 6, 1883

It is with special pleasure this morning that I ring early for the servant and take breakfast with my newspaper in bed. I have decided that I will rest for the remainder of the month and then journey to Metz. It cannot hurt. Except for my eyes, which perennially bother me, I feel quite good, I think, for a man who has already passed his three score and ten.

January 19, 1883

I have just read Mr. Davis' *Rise and Fall of the Confederate Government*. It is not a bad book; but, like all books which seek to capture events, as if events were butterflies that could be netted, Mr. Davis' volume has many defects. He dwells on our successes, and foregoes mention of some of our failures. A terrible source of trouble glossed over in this volume was the disorganization, inefficiency, and incurable jealousy of the states of the general Government. Each state had its own way of appointing officers. Until disaster forced the Congress to pass conscription laws, all we could do was get laws passed calling for certain quotas of troops from the states. There was such state loyalty throughout the war that we could not even get power to consolidate regiments. If a company was reduced to five men, or a regiment to fifty, we could not remedy this, for God forbid that five Mississippians be commanded by a colonel from Georgia! From this distance of time it is still appalling to consider the severe restrictions imposed on Mr. Davis by the jealousy of the Congress and the States.

When I look back on it all, I am lost in amazement that the struggle could have been so prolonged. One of the main sources of strength and encouragement to the President was the genius, ability, constancy, fidelity, and firmness of General Lee. And this in spite of the Executive's not-always-concealed jealousy of that noble Virginian.

No, the whole history of this Confederacy will never be published. Much of it is in me alone, and there it will stay when I die.

Whenever it is that I begin to feel death's hand about me, I have decided to let it be known that all my papers and correspondence will be burned. I do not want the hounds of publishers sniffing about me. At least not right away. This mania for books and print distorts who we are and what we did. Time needs to pass for the passions and events of which a man was part to fall into perspective.

If fifty years after my death, these diaries and papers are unearthed, the better my life will be understood. The year after I am gone, they will praise me for being a great jurist, a great patriot, a great Jew, a great this, or a great that. And none of it will be true. I am only a man.

Better a hundred years should pass. Still better a hundred and fifty. Then will my diaries and papers be understood by all who read them. And there will be no need for an editor. For there are gaps in one's life, much as there are silences in a conversation, and these empty spaces have their meaning, too. After all, what is a hundred years but a blink in the eye of eternity?

Our conversation is almost inaudible, so great is the thundering and churning of the locomotives at the *Gard du Nord*. Montifiore is standing next to me. He leans on his pearl-handled cane, and his white gloves rest on the bulbous top of the stick as if they were meant to be this way, a statue for all time. The new black fedora is tipped jauntily to the side, and you would hardly think this epitome of fashion is journeying to Metz to cover some trial for his Society for Zion.

"Dear Sir," I said to him, politely as possible, "you know I am perfectly capable of traveling alone, and have done so many times throughout the course of my life."

The conductors scurried about the train entrances, and Montifiore gestures with his white gloves, the perfect essence of command. Our trunks are summarily put upon the freight wagon and taken down the platform to be loaded.

"Where in the world did you get the idea, Benjamin, that I am come along to hold your hand? My plans were made long before you decided to go to Metz. It is merely a felicitous coincidence. It is just too bad Ada is too busy to make the trip with us. She has always wanted to see one of these monstrosities of justice performed to the hilt."

We boarded the train and took comfortable seats in the parlor car. Drinks were brought, and I gave Montifiore one of my havanas. We moved out of the station, and then with slowly gathering momentum began to leave the environs of Paris. The train entered the lush countryside and began to consume the green miles like a sleek black worm on a leaf. We headed north and then veered northeast towards Metz.

"Are you familiar with the case, Benjamin?" Montifiore asked, pushing a pamphlet written in both German and French onto my lap. The title was: *"Concerning the Use of Christian Blood by Jewish Sects for Religious Purposes."*

"So who is the author of this pamphlet, this Lutosanski? Is he a material witness?"

"Material?" guffawed Montifiore. "They do not have a real witness in sight."

"So what is there to cover? The case will be dropped for lack of evidence."

Montifiore looked at me askance, as if he was waiting for this. And then he pounced. "Judah, is such a trial ever settled on the weight of evidence? This anti-Semite publishes a pamphlet. All of Metz reads it. They talk of nothing but how the Jews must have Christian blood once a year for Passover. The killing has taken place before Passover. There are trumped-up witnesses. There is a jury chosen, who do not dare go home without a conviction or their neighbors will jeer them and their monks will refuse them absolution. The trial becomes a circus."

Montifiore gestured with his cane when he spoke. Up and down, to left and right, the handle of the cane moved as he made his points.

"You should drop by, Judah, and you shall see what the Revolution has unleashed, you shall see what the enlightened peasants of France are capable of."

"I'm afraid I've private affairs to pursue in Metz."

He tapped his cane twice on the floor of the car. "This trial is the business of every Jew in the west. It is your business too, Benjamin."

"The answer to the next question is no, my friend. I am sure the accused has adequate counsel. After all, if Ada arranged it through the Society, it must be the best. Who is it?"

"Oh, rabbis, doctors, a whole committee headed by a lawyer whose name I forget. It couldn't hurt, Judah, to lend your name to the list of notables protesting the proceedings."

"You have enough notables without me. What do they know of a Confederate Secretary of State, anyway, in Alsace?"

"You're as impossible as Ada says you are, Benjamin. Are you retired from being a Jew, from being a human being?"

"No, sir," I answered, "I am just retired. Retired from strife and argument."

269

"Impossible," he cried. "The whole world is outraged by this trial. And here you are, a man with an illustrious legal career behind you, in the same city as the trial is taking place in, and you will not even make an appearance, not even a statement to the press. It is all political, Benjamin. All political. It is a stage so they can attack the Jews and get the rightist sentiment on their side before the local elections. It's an old story, but it goes on and on and on, and you know why, Benjamin?" Here Montifiore's big face flushed, and the pocked craters of his cheeks each seemed to fill with a little shadow of crimson. "Because too many good men like yourself keep silent. Too many good men think there are others who will do the refuting. Too many lawyers think another lawyer will take care of the case. Too many—"

"Claude," I said, "put down your cane before you strike me with it."

"I'll lower the cane," he said, "but not my indignation. Ada and I have been patient with you too long about this."

"I have a wife who has gone mad, Claude, and a missing daughter I have not seen in twenty years. Aren't these matters important to a man? Should I not attend to them? If I don't attend to them, there will be no committee of lawyers and doctors and experts to help me. I am my own committee. Will you not permit me to take care of my business?"

"Yes, but will you not at least attend one day of the trial? It concludes during our stay."

"I can make no promises, Claude. I may be detained. I may have to follow leads that take me out of Metz."

"You waste your time on a wild chase, Benjamin. We've been over that a thousand times. An obscure mumbling is hardly a lead, hardly. . ."

"Montifiore, I'll hear no more of this."

Thus we argued, smoked, and drank our brandy all the way across the French countryside, past the fields speckled with brown farmhouses and barns, past the dumbly grazing bovines who pay less attention to our roaring train than they do to the titmouse that alights upon their back, past the broken fences and the bursting silos until we see far to the right, through our window, the glinting string of water which is the Moselle River.

"We shall be in Metz in another hour, Benjamin," Montifiore said. "May I have back that Lutosanski trash? I must begin my article."

"Just transcribe your speech to me these last few hours running, and you shall have a gem of an article," I said. "With it you could not fail to convince any man."

"Any?" he said, with undisguised irritation. "Any except you, Benjamin."

"Yes, my friend, perhaps with the exception of me."

February 10, 1883
Metz

"Well, then," I said to the police corporal at the desk in front of me, "perhaps you may have some record of my daughter under the name Mazareau. Ninette Mazareau."

The corporal went to the one tall file cabinet in the provincial prefecture, and, turning his long narrow back to me, proceeded to look through the papers. During his search, two flies alighted on the corporal's neck, rimmed with scraggly hair. But he seemed undisturbed by them and went on with his search through the papers. As he shifted from foot to foot, the corporal reminded me of a long thin reed moved slowly by the wind.

Returning to the desk, he shook his head. No, there was nothing under Mazareau.

"Nothing at all?" I persisted. "How far back do these files of yours go, monsieur corporal?"

He shook his head again, the circles of the eyes moving lusterlessly like marbles that have missed their mark and lost their momentum. Surely, I thought, there is someone else I can deal with in Metz besides a deaf-mute corporal of police!

I spent the remainder of the day between my hotel and the local convent, where I interrogated the sisters about Ninette. Here too there was no information, no recollec-

271

tion, even from the hoary old superior I talked to, a woman whose age I daresay was fifteen years greater than mine, and who would have memory of Ninette Mazareau or Ninette Benjamin if she was at all known in this town.

I even betook myself to the graveyard beyond the Moselle River, found the caretaker and inquired of him. The name was unfamiliar, but he did not mind my examining the grounds. So up and down the rows of crosses I walked, reading the stones, squinting at the ones already eroded by rain and the elements, some part of me indeed hoping to see the grave of my daughter. Not that I wished her dead, but I only wished some peace from this not knowing of so many long years.

Under the sunset drizzle I walked and then started. I looked carefully at a newly hewn stone: *NINETTE ——* *————*. I approached closer and knelt down on the ground. *NINETTE MARQUETTE* read the stone, baptized December 2, 1882, died January 11, 1883.

February 15, 1883

With all his running around, Montifiore is rarely in the hotel, where I have been spending the last two days. After searching out two more convents, and asking shopkeepers whose white hair recommended them to me as long time residents, whose memories might have in them the key to Colette's "meta, meta" mumbling, I am fatigued and essentially just where I was when the train pulled into this town. Perhaps Ada and Claude are right, that I only clutch at straws now, and that I have forgotten my own legal training; that is, that there is a point in every case where the lawyer may simply not be able to do any more for the client and should change his line of argument or withdraw.

I spend the remainder of the afternoon writing a rider to my will, allotting a portion of my estate to my daughter, if, upon my death, she appears and properly proves her identity. What more can I do now?

Out of my window I can see the old medieval wall of

Metz, where some of the townswomen now hang their laundry.

February 16, 1883

"You should have heard the testimony this morning," Claude is gesturing to me over dinner. The white napkin is stuck in his neck and moves with all the bobbing, animated gestures of his head. "I have never heard such drivel in my entire life. The judge actually took over the cross-examination from the prosecutor, actually took sides with the prosecutor. Listen to this, Benjamin." Claude took out his notes, held them in his left hand and read, while he held the fork in his right and brandished it above the untouched food. "This poor Jewish laborer, Henri Levay, works in the rock quarry at the north of the town. He is away visiting his brother who is, of all things, a lieutenant in the garrison at Moselle. He is away two weeks. During these two weeks Francois Tartan's boy disappears, is presumed kidnapped. There is a ransom demand of ten thousand francs in a note left in Tartan's pew in the church, and then nothing. No instructions even as to where the father can deliver the money. The father wants to pay, mind you, to get his boy back. Days pass without sight of the boy, or further instructions from the kidnapper. Then one day—mind you, Levay is still in Moselle, by his brother's testimony—a woman walks by, the daughter of a Mason, and sees two shoes sticking out from under the stones. She descends into the deserted quarry and finds the little Tartan boy, with his throat cut. And no one around, no one in sight. Five days later when Levay returns he is arrested. On what grounds, Judah? On the grounds that some woman testified that she saw Levay at the quarry when the boy disappeared, and that on a previous occasion Levay had been noticed nosing about the church. Do they listen to the testimony in written form of the esteemed brother, a lieutenant in the French army? It is inadmissable. The court does not even know about it. I found out through connections. The officer in Moselle is confined to

273

quarters, Judah. It is a complete travesty. They are blaming it on this poor Levay, and the judge, believe me, has his orders."

Montifiore got up, stood on the chair and imitated the judge. "Why, the man winked in recognition at the prosecutor, Judah! They both have orders from the same source. How high it goes, I can't be sure yet. But it is way up there.

"Poor Levay is so beaten now, he is answering questions which have no meaning for him. He looks like he hasn't slept in a week. Still he denies everything. Listen to this:

"'When did you see the boy last?' asked the judge.

"'I have been away, not in many weeks, sir.'

"'How frequently do Jews need Christian blood?'

"'Jews need no Christian blood, neither of adults nor of children.'

"'On this point we have experts familiar with Jewish secret books. Tell me, Levay, where have you hidden the vial of the dead child's blood?'

"'I have nothing to do with this, your honor. Jews need no Christian blood.'

"'There is scientific testimony from Dr. Lutosanski and from former rabbis, which you have heard, to the contrary. What say you to this, Levay?'

"And on and on it went, Benjamin. 'Scientific' testimony indeed! It was all we could do to restrain ourselves from screaming out the truth. But they have police lining the back of the courtroom, and that is exactly what they want—more Jews misbehaving."

Over brandy I asked the logical question. "So who is the killer of the boy, if it is not Levay?"

"Who knows? We are working on it, but it is in Paris where the leverage is being applied; it will be some time before we know. The lawyers are going against the testimony of this Boisneac woman in the meantime. She is a mass of trembling nerves and is obviously full of lies and circumstantial testimony. But she sticks to it tenaciously, says she has heard for many years that Jews love and in fact need to drink Christian blood at least once a year to keep from dying. I tell you this poor creature actually believes this stuff, a testimony perhaps to the thoroughness of her teachers."

"Well, my friend," said I, feeling the weariness of my eyes, "I have made arrangements to leave on the ten o'clock train tomorrow. I have had enough of Metz."

"But, Benjamin, you have not even been to the trial."

"You'll recall, Claude, that I made no promises. I am fatigued to the breaking point. I need to rest."

"If you must, then you must. Please take my article to Ada in Paris, if you will, Judah. You will be quicker than the post."

"With pleasure, my friend," I said. "I shall even edit it to make sure no English grammar has crept into your French."

"Just do not edit out my fire."

"Impossible," I answered. "There is so much of it."

February 17, 1883

"Whoa, Benjamin, whoa!"

I looked up and above the ceiling of bobbing hats and heads at the train station I saw the flashing ebony cane of Claude Montifiore. I checked my pocket watch, always accurate, and saw the train was to leave in less than a minute; in fifty seconds to be precise. What could my friend want of me?

Slicing his way through the crowd, his fedora askew, he finally stood in front of me, erupting, and out of breath.

"They telegraphed me this morning, Judah. We have the name of the culprit, the one the Ministry is holding."

My train began to move. I had to shout to be heard, as I began to board. "Bravo, Claude. Soon you will stop the trial in its tracks. Goodbye, then, and good luck. I shall see you in Paris."

"My God, man, do you think I would have raced out here unshaven and unbreakfasted to tell you only this?" The train lurched forward with a little more speed. "You know the killer, Judah. He is an American fugitive, one

275

Beauchamp Jones."

It was incredible. I almost did not hear Claude shouting my name. I leaped off the step of the car onto what remained of the platform. I brushed Montifiore's shoulder, then my legs gave out from me like two broken sticks, and I fell to the wooden platform. The train raced by, the trunks floated above me like amorphous black clouds, the whole station whirled before my eyes like the kaleidoscopic toy of a child.

When I awoke, I saw Montifiore wringing out a cloth in cold water. We were in the stationmaster's office, and I was lying on the sofa which smelled deeply of horse leather. Claude applied the cloth to my forehead and spoke softly. "Dear Judah! We shall never let you travel alone again. You have had a severe fall."

I tried moving my limbs, then my fingers, and then slowly turned my neck. Everything seemed to be in working order. "I do not think I broke anything."

"God only knows how you didn't. But you have bruised everything, Judah. The doctor. . ."

But I did not want to hear any more talk of myself. I moved slowly up into a sitting position. There were only two words on my tongue, and I kept repeating them in disbelief. "Beauchamp Jones! Are you sure? Are you positive, Claude?"

He took out his notes and read to me the telegram which was tucked in between the sheets of paper. The description was precisely my man Jones, aged fifteen or twenty years since I had seen him last. Since I had killed him! No, it was impossible. I had shot straight and I had seen him fall, had seen the circle of blood on his white shirt as he lay on the ground at the top of the hill.

"According to what we can make out, Judah, this Jones has changed his name to Boisneac, settled in the area several years ago, let it be known that he was a respectable Mason, and so forth. This daughter of his, Nell Boisneac, is a lesser-known commodity. What we know for certain, however, is that she is no daughter, but wife, or more probably, paramour."

"Is the court in session today?"

"Of course, but—"

"I want to go to the courtroom, Claude."

"Impossible. You cannot walk. The doctor is returning with his wagon in half an hour."

"I must go, Claude."

"You may risk a seizure if you strain yourself now. The doctor said you are not to move under your own power."

I struggled to my feet. "If you will not help me, Claude, I will go myself."

"Judah, sit down. You can go tomorrow or the day after. This circus of justice is hardly over. I will get some men to carry you."

I felt the blood pulsing through my temples and a wave of nausea pass over me, as if someone had his thumb on my stomach pressing as hard as he could. Yet I put one foot down, and then the other, and I stood at the desk by the office door. I opened the door and the cool air cleared my head.

"For God's sake, Judah," said Montifiore, throwing down the compress on the table. He pulled his jacket off the chair and draped it over my shoulders. "At least lean on me."

"I must go to the courtroom, Claude. I must."

"Just lean, Judah, lean," he said as we made our way to the street. "Come, man," I heard Montifiore's voice calling to the carriage driver, "give me a hand, there, under his arms, heave, lift onto the seat. There. . ." The door closed. I opened my eyes to the darkness. I blinked until the darkness began to dissipate. I felt Claude's arm next to me and soon could discern his dismayed smile. "You fainted on me, Judah. You're a complete fool."

"I have to go, Claude."

"I know," he said. Then he leaned his head out the carriage window and yelled up, "To the courthouse, driver."

I have no recollection of the carriage ride except the soft pressure of Montifiore's hand upon my shoulder. Then there was the sensation of being lifted once again, and the cacophony of shouting voices. When I opened my eyes, I was in the back row of seats in a small courtroom. The flag of France draped the wall in back of the judge's bench, and to his left and right were elevated rows of straight-backed chairs. Montifiore pointed out to me the goateed Professor Lutosanski, whose pamphlet had fueled the trial with its easy catch phrases and incendiary pseudo-history. Then there was the old Rabbi Mazpeh, with his white beard down to his belt. He sat in the front row, almost placid, his hands were on his lap; he might have been praying. Then the jury came in, peasants and shopkeepers in their Sunday suits, looking awkward and uncomfortable, as if the tailored restraints were being broken by arms, legs, and muscular backs that wanted to be free. It was a jury that wanted its obligation completed, and swiftly.

"I must move closer, Claude," I said.

"Let us do it now, because when the judge enters, we all must remain quiet as schoolchildren. Hold on to my arm. Govrinski is the chief lawyer. He'll make room for us behind him. He's a good man. There—careful, Judah." He sat me down in back of the lawyer. His collar was high, his hair short-cropped. When he turned around, to acknowledge Montifiore's introduction, I beheld a face with a steep, furrowed forehead, small intense eyes, and a sensitive mouth. One lawyer recognizes another quickly. I had seen his face in a photograph in one of the international journals. He had sent me a telegram at the banquet upon my retirement from the bar in London. So our meeting was altogether pleasant; I felt the situation was in good hands with this Govrinski.

"He is of Russian parentage," explained Montifiore, "but a French citizen. Strong supporter of the Society. Eloquent, quick. But the format of the trial has him bottled up." Then the noise of the courtroom quieted. "Here enters the general," said Claude. "I mean, the judge."

However, I was interested in only one face. "Where is she, Claude?" But he was not listening; he was whispering the telegraphed information to Govrinski.

The robed prosecutor stood up and called in his witness: "Madame Nell Boisneac, to the stand." A side door opened, and out stepped a woman. She was small-boned and not very tall. My eyes ascended the green velvet of her dress, buttoned to the neck. The face was petite, except for the large, dark brown eyes. I leaned forward and strained to look at the small drawn mouth that was repeating the oath.

Minutes went by, and then she was answering the prosecutor's leading questions.

"Yes, I had seen the Jew Levay accost the boy several times. Once I had seen him give the boy a stick of candy, but the boy was frightened; he gave the candy back and ran away."

"At approximately this time," the prosecutor went on (while the girl's eyes never left his) "did you notice anyting else in the deportment of Monsieur Levay or the other Jews working in the quarry to arouse your suspicion?"

"Once, as I returned from the baker's, I saw Levay and two others, who were also Jews, sharpening knives upon a stone."

"Was there anything unusual in this?" interrupted the prosecutor.

"Objection," shouted Govrinski. "Counsel is leading the witness on."

The gavel banged down. "Overruled," said the judge.

"We're damned if we object," whispered Govrinski to me, "and we're damned if we let this claptrap go unchallenged."

"Silence!" demanded the judge from his perch. "Examination of the witness will continue."

"I repeat," said the prosecutor, "was there anything unusual in your observation of the Jew Levay and two of his associates sharpening knives by the quarry?"

"Yes, sir," she answered. "There was a prayer book of the Jews opened upon the stone."

"Is that all?"

"No, sir."

"What else was there, Madame Boisneac, which seemed out of the ordinary?"

"Next to the prayer book was a large vial. The vial for the blood, your honor."

The courtroom erupted with curses and deprecations. "Swine! Christ-killers!"

"Objection!" shouted Govrinski, until his voice was hoarse. But he was not heard, and the judge made no effort to bring the room to order. Two rows in front of us sat Levay, his arms folded across his chest, his head slightly bowed. Towering Rabbi Mazpeh, who sat next to him, was whispering to Levay and running his hand over the top of the boy's head.

In the confusion of the courtroom, as photographers stepped up almost in front of the judge's bench, I stood, and, supporting myself on the backs of chairs, made my way to the witness stand. I felt a surge of strength, enough strength at least to do this. I lost track of time. Explosions of light arose from the photographers' flash pans as they crowded around Levay.

In three more steps I was beside the chair of the girl. I stood there, staring, until she noticed me and slowly turned.

"Ninette?" Her eyes were unblinking, almost glassy. "Ninette Benjamin?"

"Non, monsieur."

"Ninette Mazareau?"

I looked carefully at this girl until my stare forced her to regard me once again. *"C'st votre père, Ninette."*

"No, monsieur," she repeated. "My father is dead, many years ago." When she said this, her mouth moved free, untightened for a moment, and I beheld the face of my daughter, the face I had last kissed twenty years ago.

"No," she said standing, her face flushed. "Monsieur le prosecuteur," she shrilled, "please help me. This Jew is bothering me. Monsieur le prosecuteur, these Jews will not leave me alone!"

March 2, 1883, Paris

"No," I said to Ada, who sat beside my bed, "She was completely unreachable. Before I left, I tried to talk to her half a dozen times. I brought her gifts; she threw them on the floor. I showed her letters; she refused to look at them, and ordered me from her house. I think she cannot accept me, or she will go insane like her mother. Jones ran off with her, and changed their name after he tired of Colette. Is it any wonder Colette went mad!"

"It was Jones, along with Colette, maybe even inspired by Colette, who poisoned her against me. Since her father was a Jew, it had to be atoned for; thus, the convent. And since the father was alive and reminding her, and the rest of them, that he was a Jew with every breath he took, the father had to be eliminated. They told Ninette I had been killed in the War." Here I coughed over my words. My breathing has been labored for a week, but I felt better this morning. I could at least feel the air as it entered my lungs."

"Will they bring her up on a murder charge, also?"

"She wasn't there when he hacked the little boy to pieces. Thank God for that! After he killed the boy, he got cold feet. He told Ninette exactly what to say, and to go to the priest five days after he ran off to Calais; they were to meet there."

"Oh watch them turn on each other now, with the guillotine facing them! What a terrible thing to happen to your daughter!"

It was strange indeed, I thought, to hear her refer to the girl in Metz as my daughter. For although I knew she was the child I had sired, I found myself accepting the estrangement the girl so tenaciously believed in. Her father had died in the war, she said. And, furthermore he could not be me because he, her father, had converted to Holy Mother Church before he died. And I , she said, was clearly a Jew.

"Judah," Ada said, with her back to me, as she stared out over the garden, "all the vegetables are coming up beautifully. Soon you will be able to go out to do some light work."

"How are the peas?"

"The peas are less than a week from picking, my dear."

There was a long silence. I heard the wagons on the boulevard, where I had not been able to walk for a week. I looked at the soft line of Ada's neck, her sturdy back, her still slender waist, and I reached my hand out to grasp her there, for to my hazy eyes she seemed near enough to touch, though she was not. Yet I held my arm there, without saying a word; my fingers outstretched towards her, for as long as I could.

Ada turned around and could see me strain in the bed. "You can move them a little more today than yesterday, I think, Judah. Your left leg will improve a little slower than the right, according to Nathan."

"Nathan isn't fooling me, and you aren't either, my dear. It is my body. And believe me, I know that the paralysis is spreading. No need to act with me, my actress."

Ada bit her lip until it grew pale. Then she cried.

"I love you, Ada, with all my heart. But do not say your goodbyes. I am not dying just yet. Come dry your eyes and read me this letter from Claude. It feels heavy enough; perhaps the business in Metz is finally over."

"Rest for now, Judah, I'll read it to you this evening."

March 5, 1883

Claude has written that the trial is completed.

My note to old Erlanger was enough for him to put pressure on the Minister of Justice. Even the French Minister is not so anti-Semitic that he wants a deposition lodged against him by the American ambassador to the effect that the French Government is harboring an American fugitive. The result: Jones is tried in France, for the more serious crime. He is this very minute on a prison ship en route to the penal colony of Guyana, where he will spend the rest of his life.

At the trial Ninette began to babble incoherencies; she drew her hair into her mouth and chewed it. She dug her fingers into her own breasts. And under Govrinski's questioning, she finally collapsed. My daughter, poor creature! She was unable to return to the courtroom, and her sentence, twenty years in prison, was read to her in the hospital.

Montifiore, God bless him, prevailed on the Minister in Paris, and the sentence is commuted to five years. Claude writes that even upon hearing this Ninette was stoic. She reads her Bible and clutches her cross in her hand. "The anti-Semites of Metz," he writes, "all walk about now with their long tails between their legs."

Later this afternoon, much to my pleasure, Nathan came by with a primer on Hebrew grammar, a volume on Jewish law, and a book Ada and Montifiore have been trying to get me to read for years, the program and platform of *The Society for the Reclamation of Palestine*.

March 5, 1883, evening

I am setting up two accounts at the Banc du Rothschild in Metz. One account will be a trust in the name of Nell Boisneac, neé Ninette Benjamin. She will be able to draw upon it for the rest of her life. The second is a trust for the other children in the Tartan family. It will be anonymous. Govrinski will supervise the funds on my behalf. I know he, as well as Claude and Ada, will object to the Tartan fund. But Ninette was an accomplice, and Ninette is my own flesh and blood.

Now, as I write these notes, I see the three volumes lying upon my dull lap, beside my legs which no longer stir, which need to be lifted onto a chair if I am to move from this bed of mine. I hear the servant mopping the hallway outside my door, and up from the garden float the notes of Ada's whistled song. I may be mistaken, but I think it is something from her *Mazeppa,* of so many years ago.

April 4, 1883

Nathan, who reads good Hebrew, has been tutoring me

twice a week for a month. He says I am making considerable progress with the ancient Hebrew alphabet. I told him I felt like a schoolboy.

"Nonsense," he answered, "you have a gift for languages. You should have studied this long ago, Judah."

"I did, my young friend. I simply forgot."

April 5, 1883

After Ada shaved me this morning, I asked that the mirror be left on the bed table. I looked at myself for a long time, as I have not done in many many years. I remembered standing in front of the mirror in my mother's house trying hour after hour to straighten my wavy Jewish hair. And at the mirror of Moses Lopez's, at the tall mirror in the grand hall of his house, how I stood there one afternoon, while he tended to the business which had interrupted our lesson, and I tried to imagine what style of coat I could choose to best disguise my stocky build.

Now I look at my face, deeply wrinkled, and my hair, grown pure white. How a lifetime is passed between two glances at a mirror.

I stare at my own smile. I spent my life training that smile to take into the world. How I whipped myself mercilessly to succeed. How I did not allow myself a moment to remember from whom I sprang into the world, and from what grand tradition. It has taken me all this time finally to find a terrible reflection in my own lost daughter's glassy eyes.

How many other mirrors I looked into without ever seeing myself!

I am a man of seventy-two years. After sixty years of estrangement, I am returning finally to my people.

May 4, 1883

Feel too weak to write: Penina has written that Becky died a week ago in Savannah.

May 5, 1883

Nathan, Erlanger, Claude, and six other men gathered around my bed this morning to help me recite the memorial prayers.

June 2, 1883

Too tired today to be carried to the garden.

June 19, 1883

Because of a change in Nathan's lectures at the medical college at the Sorbonne, our lessons are switched to Mondays and Wednesdays.

I think I have now mastered all the letters of the Hebrew alphabet. These large, dark, solid figures are a source of fascination and solace to me. I especially like the next to last letter in the alphabet, the *shin*. It means tooth, and the letter is shaped like an old molar, like one of mine. But with its stem and three prongs it also looks like a trident, like old Poseidon's trident rising out of the sea.

I must remember to ask Nathan about this when he arrives.

LEISURE NON-FICTION

**WITHOUT A MAN
OF HER OWN**   LB282DK $1.50
Linda DuBreuil

A lusty look at learning to love again after the divorce, written by a woman who did just that. Not only does the author tell her own story, but also those of several other women who have had the experience of waking up in unfamiliar places as they sought the cure for the empty-bed blues.

STREET HUSTLER   LB301DK $1.50
Norman Rubington

This is the brutal, sordid inside story of the street prostitution in New York. There is no glamor here, no mixing with movie stars or wealthy businessmen. These girls are used, cheated, pushed around by their pimps and the police. Often they are beaten and killed. This is what the dirty life of a street hustler is really like.

SUSIE'S GIRLS   LB314DK $1.50
Susanna Sheldon

She went from an ordinary housewife to become one of the highest paid hookers in the business. Susanna Sheldon was a thirty-six year old divorcee, a former Broadway chorus girl, ex-Jewish American Princess who changed her lifestyle—proving that it's never too late.

THE KEPT MEN   LB341DK $1.50
Linda DuBreuil

There are independent women who don't need some movement or law to guarantee their rights—they take what they want when they want it. Instead of being kept by a husband, *they keep their own men*. This is the true story of women who live beyond the wildest dreams of Women's Lib.

LEISURE NON-FICTION

JIMMY CONNORS   LB330DK $1.50
Jim Burke

This is the amazing story of James Scott Connors—
known to his millions of fans as Jimmy—the No. 1
tennis player in the world. Still only 23, Jimmy Connors' aggressive style and flamboyant personality
have made him world famous. This is the story of his
loves, his life, his incredible career.

HOLLYWOOD CONFIDENTIAL LB331DK $1.50
David Hanna

This astounding book contains all the secrets, gossip
and inside stories that you have always wanted to
know about the biggest of the Hollywood stars—written by a man who was there!

HOUSEWIFE HUSTLERS   LB334DK $1.50
Linda DuBreuil

Women's Lib and the sexual revolution have pro-
duced a unique kind of hustler—the housewife who
wants to supplement the family income and show her
independence at the same time. Many are turning to
prostitution—often with their husband's consent—
making money and relieving the boredom of married
life.

THE TWO CAROLINES   LB339DK $1.50
Gloria Martinis

This is the true story of the most famous teenagers in
the world: Caroline Kennedy and Princess Caroline
Grimaldi. This is the honest, frank story of their
lives and loves, tragedies and successes and the tremendous future that lies ahead for both.

LEISURE BOOKS
P.O. Box 2301
Norwalk, Conn. 06852

Name _____

Address _____

City _____

State _____ Zip _____

Please send check, cash or money order. No stamps. No
C.O.D.

Book Number_____Price _____

Book Number_____Price _____

Book Number_____Price _____

Book Number_____ Price _____

Book Number_____Price _____

Book Number_____Price _____

Add 25¢ per book to help cover cost of postage and handling.
Buy 4 or more books and we will cover all costs. Allow 4 weeks
for delivery.